A Place with Promise

Also by Edward Swift

PRINCIPIA MARTINDALE

SPLENDORA

A PLACE WITH PROMISE

Edward Swift

Doubleday

NEW YORK

1987

Library of Congress Cataloguing in Publication Data
Swift, Edward, 1943–
    A place with a promise.
    I. Title.
PS3569.W483P53   1987   813'.54   87-6677
ISBN 0-385-24287-5

A Note

During the War Between the States outlaws and pacifists from all over the South sought refuge in East Texas. They disappeared into what the Indians called the Big Woods and what later became known as the Big Thicket. After the war some of them emerged, changed their names and started life all over again in the small communities and towns that were springing up. Others had become accustomed to the solitude of the Thicket and remained there—almost entirely isolated from the rest of the world.

Those early settlers were a hearty breed, sturdy, imaginative. Their character still lingers in the names given to the people and places. Many of the names in this book are common to East Texas. In no way are they meant to represent actual places, or people living or dead. Overstreet, Treadway, Faircloth, Izella and Navasota: These names were chosen for their beauty, and for the Spirit of the Place contained within them.

A PLACE WITH PROMISE

PROLOGUE

Isaac

In 1863, shortly after the Battle of Sabine Pass, a woman by the name of Roberta Hightower set a trap, not for the man she loved but for the man she wanted. Roberta was an only child. When she was three, her mother died of diphtheria, and her father never remarried. He operated a ferry that crossed the Sabine River four times a day, and Roberta helped him collect the fare. From the age of five, she never felt secure without a coin in her hand.

Earl Singleton was a regular passenger. He crossed into Texas several times a week to tend his beehives. "The honey is sweeter on the other side of the river," he told Roberta. But she didn't believe him. Earl was a man of many occupations. He fished the Sabine and sold his catch. He split shingles and repaired roofs. He was an expert chimney maker. And when he needed to be, he was an able blacksmith. He could repair almost anything.

Earl Singleton was a man who had very little spare time. That was only one of his two attributes, according to Roberta. The other one was his ability to make money. What she detested was his inability to hold on to it. When she collected his fare for crossing the river, she shortchanged him every chance she got. Sometimes he caught her, but most of the time he was oblivious to her trap.

"I've saved a lot of your money," she confessed after many crossings, "and there's only one way you'll get it back."

They were married shortly thereafter, but Earl never regained his money.

In two years they had a son, Isaac, named for Roberta's father. At the age of five Isaac was already working. His first job was pulling weeds in a neighbor's garden, and Roberta saw to it that he was paid for his time.

By then Roberta's thriftiness was completely out of control. She wouldn't allow Earl to spend a cent more than necessary, and kept most of their savings in fruit jars buried along the bayous. She knew exactly where every jar was hidden. She kept the record in her head, but she never divulged the hiding places, not even to her husband. She kept him guessing, and kept him digging too. Only once did he find a jar of pennies. "That's the last one he'll ever find," Roberta said to herself. Shortly thereafter, her husband was dead.

He was digging for money on the banks of the Sabine when his heart played out. A few days later he was found floating faceup. Everyone said that Roberta Hightower had poisoned him, or aggravated him to death. "There's not a bit of truth to that," she said, "but I did consider it lots of times."

Then she dug up all her money, just to make sure it was still there, and buried it in different places. No one ever saw her mourn her husband's death, and the only time she ever wore black was on dark nights when she buried her savings.

She raised Isaac to fish for a living and to pick up odd jobs here and there. She tried to instill in him her own brand of thriftiness, but it didn't take. Every night she went through his pockets and buried over half of what she found.

As a young man Isaac was anxious to marry and move away, but his mother was determined to keep him at home until she found a woman who was worthy of him. Isaac placed his future in his mother's hands and never stopped to consider that it might be her intention to die before giving him away. He was thirty, she was somewhere in her fifties, and the snake that killed her was as long as her arm. Her dying words were, "Boy, the right woman don't exist."

"She does too," Isaac argued. But his mother was already dead.

He had never touched a corpse before and didn't intend to start now. He used a spoon to close her eyes. But they didn't stay closed, and he refused to use nickles to weight them down. Rocks, he thought, would do just fine. He chose two heavy ones.

She had died shortly after midnight. Isaac sat with her body until dawn, and while waiting for the sun, his mother's last words kept rolling through his mind. He wondered if she had placed a deathbed curse on his future happiness, so before he buried her, he consulted Navasota Blackburn, who lived with the ivory-billed woodpeckers on the high banks of the Sabine.

Navasota was old, but no one had ever come close to guessing how old. No one knew for sure if she was Indian or Mexican, black or white. Just to look at her, there was no telling. She wore men's overalls with long-sleeved shirts starched stiff, beaded moccasins or logging boots and a black shoestring tied in a bow knot around her neck. Her brown hair was cut in a straight line from earlobe to earlobe, and she had a mustache that was the envy of every twelve-year-old boy on the Sabine. As well as not being able to guess her age—her face was a web of wrinkles, yet her hands were as smooth as a young girl's—no one was dead certain that Navasota was a woman. People referred to her in the feminine for convenience sake, but when pressed to tell exactly how they felt, almost everybody who lived along that stretch of the Sabine would say, "Navasota's Navasota." Or they would say, "Nobody knows where she came from or what she's all about." And to their children they would say, "Navasota ain't supposed to be laughed at neither."

Because she wasn't like anyone else, most of the river people believed she could solve problems by predicting the future before it turned into the present. A few words from Navasota could right all wrong. And for that reason, Isaac consulted her upon the death of his mother.

Navasota told him there was no need to hold a service and that the best way to break his mother's spell, if there really was one, was to wrap her in a feed sack and bury her facedown with a snake's skin wrapped around her neck. Together they dug the grave, and after the moccasin's skin was properly tied, and the body was covered with earth, Navasota pressed an empty bottle, neck first, into the ground. "To trap the restless spirit when it tries to escape," she said. Then she planted a stinging nettle over Roberta's head and told Isaac to find a new place to live, a place where he could feel comfortable with himself. She also told him to change his last name and plant two flowering trees in his new front yard. She did not give him a new name. She left that up to him. But she did give him two small trees that had come off a boat in New Orleans. "They call them mimosas," she said. "They say they'll grow anywhere, even in sand."

In a few days Isaac moved into a one-room house in Camp Ruby, a river community with a small, steam-operated sawmill as its major reason for being. He planted the two trees in his front yard, and took the name Overstreet. It was fairly common. He felt comfortable with it, and right away he expected his life to change. But it didn't. He fished for his living and was success-ful at it, but he wasn't satisfied. He wanted a wife, but no one in Camp Ruby interested him, and he was beginning to wonder if there was anyone anywhere in the world who would. Navasota made him a charm of oak bark and fish scales to wear around his neck. That didn't work either. No one special came along.

"I can help you believe," said Navasota. "But I cannot *make* you believe."

Finally, he stopped asking for charms and magic words, but he didn't give up hope. He had always wanted to have a way with women, but he had never known how or where to start. He didn't know what to say to a woman he loved or might love, and was hoping that one day he would meet someone who would not expect him to say very much at all.

PART ONE

Camp Ruby

Whenen Isaac Overstreet turned forty, Camp Ruby was a sawmill community of no more than thirty unpainted houses. The "camp," as everyone called it, was located along a high, sandy ridge that sloped into the Texas side of the Sabine River. The Louisiana side wasn't much different. In both states the land was laced with waterways: winding creeks, muddy rivers and slow-moving bayous named after the people who lived along them. There were eight months of heat, twelve months of heavy humidity and a lifetime of mold. The air of Camp Ruby was permeated year around with the damp smell of rotting wood and the blistering scent of fresh sawdust. Sand found its way into every household. There was no way to keep it out.

The houses in Camp Ruby were a cluster of thrown-together dwellings and some of them were on the brink of sliding into the river. Isaac's house was one of them. But most of the others were spaced far away from the sloping riverbank and, due to the lack of level ground, were so close together that side doors opened onto backyards and backyards faced front porches, windows stared into doors and doors opened onto porches that did not belong to them.

Isaac's house was the smallest. He had one room with three windows, a tin roof and no porch to sit on. The house was balanced on hickory blocks, two feet off the ground, and chickens, Rhode Island Reds, were penned underneath it. There were no back windows, and no front steps, other than a rock placed on the ground in front of the only entrance. Inside there was almost no furniture: an ironstead bed, a straightbacked chair and a woodburning stove.

The house was off to itself, separated from the others by the spreading mimosa trees and a three-legged water tower constructed of heartwood and covered with vines. The water tower was no longer in use. The tank had rotted away and so had its windmill. The entire structure was considered unsafe, but no one would take the time to tear it down. "One day nature will take its course," Isaac said. "I just hope nobody's standing under it when it falls."

The water tower and the mimosas formed a barrier around Isaac's house, and he was glad of it. He hated people crowding in around him and discouraged company by keeping his door closed and his windows half covered with cardboard.

He was a lean man with heavy eyelids, a square jaw and a serious streak running all the way through him. His lips were thin, he rarely showed his teeth when he smiled and his stare was straightforward, steady and intense.

Six days a week he fished on the Sabine, selling his catch to anyone who came along, but what he wanted to do was work at the sawmill. Once Lester Jenkins, the foreman, had hired him part-time, but Isaac had lasted only a few days. He didn't do a bit of work, just walked around as if he didn't have a worry in the world. But he did. On dry ground he worried constantly, but on the river the water lulled him into forgetting his troubles.

He was known as an easygoing man who drank too much and believed he had to share his whisky with the river or the fish wouldn't bite. He was a good fisherman. Some people said he was the best on the Sabine, but, since moving to Camp Ruby, he had never done anything else successfully. Hard labor just wasn't part of his everyday life, and no one expected him to change. The least amount of extraneous movement seemed to sap him of all his strength, and therefore, he spent most of his time resting. When he did stir about he took slow, almost feeble steps, gave the impression that he was continually lost in his thoughts and, during the week, it was nearly impossible to persuade him to utter more than a few words a day.

Only on Sunday afternoons would he come out of himself long enough to talk a blue streak. He would sit on the steps of LeRoy Redd's commissary or inside around the fire, and tell the loggers about all the Saturday night women he had met and loved. To hear him tell it, he was quite a lady's man.

But the loggers knew better. They knew, although they did not let on, that Isaac spent his Saturday nights alone, drinking in his fishing boat while floating aimlessly downriver or while hidden in the shadows of a pier. He knew his way around the backwoods. He knew the locations of the stills, and the public houses, but he rarely went to those places. He didn't feel comfortable there.

On a Sunday night before his fortieth birthday, he told the loggers that he had a sweetheart in every river town between Camp Ruby and the Gulf of Mexico. He wanted everybody to know that he could turn his boat loose, and it would travel all by itself from one beautiful woman to the next.

"The girls get prettier the closer you get to salt water," he said. "And I can testify to the fact that they get wilder too. It's mighty hard work trying to please them all in one night."

"Maybe you better take me with you next time," said Sam Bostic, a distant cousin, nicknamed Bunyon because of his feet.

"Can't take you," Isaac answered. "Don't want to be stirring up trouble with your wife. You can't do all I do and still be married. Besides," he added hesitantly, "I might not be stepping out anytime soon. A man needs to rest his bones ever once in a while."

The next Saturday night Isaac stayed home, but no one realized it until Sunday morning at dawn when he started tearing down an abandoned house. The noise of his hammer brought everyone out of their beds.

"Come see Isaac Overstreet working up a sweat," Lester Jenkins told his wife, Martha Lane, who was stepping out of bed and into her skirt. "I believe something might be the matter."

Isaac had already ripped down one wall of the house. Now he was pulling nails and straightening them on a brick.

"This has to mean something," said Lottie Faircloth, the only schoolteacher in the camp.

"Yes, it does mean something, but what?" asked Mary Twitchell. Mary sawed logs for a living and up until then she thought she knew everything.

Before long everyone was watching Isaac.

"It's work just watching somebody work," said Izzie Burrow. Izzie graded lumber at the sawmill and collected deposit bottles on the side. By midmorning he felt lightheaded, breathless and his joints ached.

Pretty soon everyone was tired except Lottie Faircloth. She went around saying that it was such a peculiar Sunday, so peculiar that it didn't seem like Sunday at all and that something was bound to happen. Izella Wiggins, fifty-five and four times a grandmother, thought it felt almost like a holiday until the river became suddenly calm and not a current could be seen crisscrossing the surface. The water level dropped noticeably, too. She swore it did, but no one believed her.

LeRoy Redd, not a small man by any means (he was just under three hundred pounds), seemed to be the one most affected by Isaac's doings. Redd was suddenly seized with loss of appetite— the first time he could ever remember that happening. He put down his sausage sandwich and jar of heavy cream and moved his cash register out to the front porch so he could ring up sales and watch Isaac work at the same time. Redd never closed his store, not even for Thanksgiving, Christmas or New Year's day, but suddenly he found himself considering it. Watching Isaac work had made him sleepy. All he wanted to do was lie down somewhere, just anywhere would do.

Toward noon, some of the men who worked at the mill offered to give Isaac a hand.

"I'm not one bit tired," he said, without stopping to look up. "This is something I've got to do all by myself or it won't turn out right."

Puzzled by his answer, the loggers left him to his work. Mary Twitchell, however, wasn't one to give up so easily. "Just what in the hell do you think you're doing, Isaac?" She put her face right up in his.

Isaac backed off and didn't answer her right away. Mary stood there twisting a hairnet safety-pinned to her dress. It was her way of soothing her nerves.

Realizing that she wasn't going to leave without an answer, Isaac spoke up. "I'm aiming to add a few rooms on to my house."

"You don't know the first thing about carpentry," said Mary, her fingers rapidly working the hairnet.

Isaac replied, "That's all right, isn't it?" and went back to work.

He was well aware that he didn't know anything about carpentry, but that didn't stop him. As he tore down the house, he painstakingly studied the way it was constructed. After every nail had been removed, he carried the lumber, a board or two at a time, to the other side of the camp and stacked it near his house. Next he sat down under a mimosa and drew floor plans on the back of an envelope. That night he got up several times to study his "blueprint," and the next morning at dawn he was ready to lay the foundation.

For fourteen days and most of fourteen nights he labored, while his neighbors looked on. When he slept they slept. When he worked they watched him until they were exhausted almost beyond endurance. The loggers were so distracted by Isaac's sudden change of pace that they made one mistake after another. Boards were sawed too long, or too short, or too wide or too narrow, and finally Lester Jenkins decided it was best to shut down the mill until things got better. Redd had a similar problem. He lost track of what he was doing and sliced all his lunch meat at once. He got mixed up on his prices (something that never happened) and complained that his cash register was always out of balance because he had lost the ability to count.

"If Isaac don't stop this foolishness soon, nobody's going to get any rest," said Izzie Burrow. He hadn't picked up a deposit bottle in over a week.

But Isaac was too caught up in what he was doing to stop. On the river side of his house he had already added a sleeping porch with five windows, all of them crooked, and a floor that was level only in places. On the water tower side he had added a kitchen, a dining room and a small storage space with a window. Then he built a porch that started in the front and ended at his new back door.

Finally, he walked around the camp gathering up all the used tin, shingles, and scraps of tar paper he could find. He spent a day flattening out cans and oil drums, and then he went to work fitting it all together. When he had finished, he said, "That makes as good a roof as any." Then for the first time, he sat down on his porch.

While he was sitting there his neighbors decided to inspect his *new* house. They also placed bets on how long they thought it would hold together. Isaac, they agreed, might be the best fisherman on the river, but a carpenter he was not. "I think I could bring this house down with one shot," said Boyce Faircloth, Lottie's husband. He was proud of his muscles and thick mustache as well as of his collection of guns.

But Isaac paid no mind to his neighbors' comments. He liked his house, even though it was unpainted and unleveled, and the seams showed, and the windows slanted and nails stuck out on all sides. He realized that some of the boards didn't meet, or they overlapped where they weren't supposed to, but these flaws didn't bother him because he had done his best and believed the house would bring him everything he wanted.

That afternoon, while his neighbors were trying to rest, Isaac gathered up all his possessions, including a woodburning stove, a straightbacked chair and an ironstead bed with the mattress he had been born on. He threw it all into the river. He threw his tin plates into the river, too, along with his coffeepot and cups and all his shoes, socks and underclothes. Then he went to the store and bought a new wardrobe: khaki pants with creases already in them, white shirts, a pair of lace-ups and a bow tie, the first one he had ever owned.

After he was all dressed up, he decided to have a trim. LeRoy Redd wiped off his hands and jacked up the barber's chair. While cutting Isaac's hair, he occasionally made trips to the cash register to ring up sales. When his customer was relaxed, he started his interrogation.

"What do you need more rooms for, Isaac?"

"Just do."

"Expecting company?"

"Maybe."

"Mind saying who?"

Isaac paused. "I'm expecting me a wife."

His answer gave Redd the shakes. He felt his heart speed up and his fingers lose control of the scissors. He stopped cutting. "You found her, have you?" he asked.

"Not yet, I haven't, but I will now that I've set things in motion. It don't pay to go out looking sometimes. You got to set things up so what you want will come to you. That's the best way I know to put it."

The idea had come to him on the river. He had been fishing all day, and his catch had been good. Toward evening when the water was still, he pulled in his line and allowed his boat to drift. His mind drifted also, and when he was far away in his thoughts something told him that the only way to attract a wife was to make his house into a showplace. Then a woman would surely come along and settle down with him.

But, after he finished his house, nothing happened. His neighbors returned to their daily routines and so did he. Then, after weeks of anticipation, he was fishing from his rowboat on the Louisiana side of the Sabine when he looked up and saw Elizabeth Treadway for the first time. The river was sandy at that point. She was standing in the shallow water on the opposite shore, whistling a single note which she seemed to be able to sustain forever. The skirt of her white dress disappeared into the water, and her auburn hair fell to her shoulders and caught the sun. It was evening. Three white cranes she had hatched from stolen eggs stood beside her as still as could be. The river had gone from lavender to purple to match the sky, and the surface of the water was as smooth as a piece of cellophane stretched over a bowl.

For a few minutes Isaac watched her picking flowers from an overhanging limb. He couldn't believe his eyes. He looked away and looked back again, and she was still there.

He watched the night creeping around her, and when it was almost dark, the cranes wobbled like old men up the steep bank.

But Elizabeth Treadway, staring toward the opposite shore, hardly moved at all. Isaac wondered if she was really looking at him. Surely not, he told himself. Yet he couldn't take his eyes off her, and when it was too dark to see, he remained in the same place for a long time and wondered if she was still there. Every so often he would catch a glimpse of her shining through the night and would hear her one note skimming the surface of the river. Finally, he convinced himself it was only the wind and his imagination. He drifted home in the dark.

The next morning he was on the river again and so was she. Standing in the same place under the overhanging limb, the three water birds at her side, she appeared to be transfixed. "Was she there all night?" Isaac wondered.

As he passed by, she didn't make a sound and didn't move except to turn her head to follow him. He watched her until he could see her only in his mind, and for the rest of the day he wondered who she was, where she had come from and if she would be there when he returned. Toward midafternoon, he began to doubt that he had actually seen her. He decided that he had not. His mind had been playing tricks on him again. Everyone had predicted he would become a crazy bachelor, and, in spite of his new house, he was convinced that it was happening. With a troubled heart, he started home.

Near Sabinetown, Elizabeth Treadway was waiting for him. Her feet were in the water. Her skirt was slightly damp. And her three pet cranes were watching from the high bank. When she saw the boat she whistled for it. The vibrato in her one sustained note was like a ringing in Isaac's ears, and for the longest time he refused to look toward the shore. When he did, she lifted a hand in a motion that could have been a wave. She meant it to be a wave, but she was unaccustomed to being that familiar with strangers, and what was meant to be one thing ended up being another. She ran her fingers through her hair, not realizing she was being seductive.

Isaac didn't pass her by. He turned his boat in her direction, and when she saw him coming, she stopped whistling, dropped her arms to her side and began wading along the shore. The cranes, flapping their clipped wings, came running down the steep banks and followed her through the shallow water. Suddenly they stopped at the same time and stared at the boat coming their way as if in stern judgment of what was about to happen.

Isaac rested his oars across his legs, and the boat drifted toward her. From up close he realized that she was much older than he had thought, and not exactly what he would call beautiful. Her complexion was pale. Her eyes were marked with dark circles. Her mouth drooped slightly.

She's desperate to get out of here, he thought. And he was right, but she wasn't desperate enough to run off with the first man who came along. Dozens of fishermen had already stopped to ask her name, but she had not given it. She had not liked their looks, but when she saw Isaac, she said to her cranes, "Wonder where he's been all this time." Ignoring the past and disregarding the future, she waded out to meet his boat. As it drifted by, she lifted herself into it, hardly making a ripple on the water.

On the high banks, her two married sisters shouted for her to come back, but she dismissed them with a wave. "Don't go to any trouble on my account, Sisters," she said. Her voice was slightly above a whisper. Then she turned to Isaac. "I've already made up my mind," she told him, "so we better get going right now."

Afraid they were being left behind, the three cranes made sounds like squeaking doors and followed her into the boat. "I can't leave without them," she said, caressing the nervous birds. "I'm all they have."

Without saying a word, for he didn't know what to say, Isaac rowed his boat to the middle of the river and released it to the strongest current. Elizabeth Treadway leaned back and angled her long legs into the water while the cranes settled in her lap and arms. They blended into the folds of her white dress, cradled themselves close to her body and rested their long necks on her arms and legs. Each bird had a special place on her. For a moment the communion was such that Isaac could only see one being, neither human nor fowl. It was as though the birds were resting within her.

"We feel right comfortable in this boat of yours," she said.

"Don't we look it? And one other thing, before I forget. We don't care where you take us as long as you never bring us back."

"That suits me." Isaac wanted to say more, but he didn't know what else to say.

She studied his face. It was lean. She liked that. And his cheekbones were high. "You've got some Indian in you somewhere," she informed him. "That's all right. I'll marry you anyway. But I'll not give you more than two children. Three's a bad number. I was one of three, and four's two too many."

"Were you the middle one?" he asked, looking back to see if her two sisters were still there. They were.

"No, sir," she answered. "Fortunately, I was not the second born. Can't you see. Middle ones are never any count."

As they drifted with the current she turned her back on him, rested her long arms on the prow of the boat and leaned forward like an ornament of petrified wood. With two cranes nesting in her lap and the other standing at her side, she stared straight ahead, as if looking into her future. After a spell of silence, she told Isaac that she had been waiting for him a very long time. He didn't answer. "There were days," she said, "when I almost gave up hope." Still he didn't say a word, and somehow she didn't expect him to. Her pets, however, began losing faith. They picked their feathers and dropped them into the river where they floated like a trail of bread crumbs on the surface. She caressed all three birds at once. "We don't have to worry about finding our way back," she assured them. "Wherever we end up, we'll like it just fine."

* * *

Elizabeth Treadway was born in Sabinetown, a prosperous community of frame houses and gravel roads leading either to the river or the mineral baths, the community's major source of income. Jessman Treadway, her father, operated a three-story boardinghouse near the spa. He had built the twenty-five-room establishment one year after a great hurricane had caused the Sabine River to overflow its banks and the sky to rain fish.

After the hurricane, hot mud began bubbling out of a lake

created by the overflow. The mud contained healing properties, and people from all walks of life came to bathe in the warm, red sludge that smelled of sulphur and oil. At night fire could sometimes be seen floating over the lake, casting shadows across the river and the rooftops of Sabinetown, a place hardly anyone had heard of until then.

Over the years the boardinghouse absorbed all of Jessman Treadway's energy. People wondered how he would ever find time to have a family, but he did. In the space of three years, his wife Zeda, the daughter of a Methodist minister, presented him with daughters: Lettye, Elizabeth and LaMerl.

Elizabeth, the middle child, was called "Bessie-the-Best" by her mother and "My Dependable One" by her father. Jessman insisted that she learn every facet of the family business, and she did so without any trouble at all. By the age of fifteen she had made herself totally indispensable. Her family refused to make a decision without consulting her first. She felt trapped for life.

"My Dependable One, you've found your place," her father said. "And that place is right here."

But Elizabeth didn't want to be right there. She was anxious to marry and leave the family business behind, but she realized that her chances of finding a husband her family would accept were slim. "Someone will come along," she assured herself.

At first she dreamed of a large wedding, but as the years passed, the ceremony lost its importance as did the dress, the veil and, because of her mother, the cake.

During a long period of Zeda Treadway's life, wedding cakes were her specialty. She had baked some of the most talked-about wedding cakes Sabinetown had ever seen until she decided there would never be another marriage in her family.

Zeda had somehow worked it into her mind that a good marriage depended entirely on a beautiful and extravagant cake. When her three daughters were infants she started baking for any bride who had money to spend. It was a profitable way of practicing for her own daughters' weddings.

Zeda's early creations were simple and elegant. When Lettye, her first daughter, married at the age of nineteen, the local ladies described the cake as a "dream of white roses." But not long after that Zeda allowed her passion for decorating to run wild. At times she would instruct Elizabeth to bake as many as two dozen cakes. After they cooled, Zeda would piece them together with icing or toothpicks or long broomstraws sterilized in boiling water. Then with little or no mental preparation she would begin decorating according to whim. Elizabeth was never allowed to decorate. "That's for me to do," Zeda always said, "but Bessie-the-Best is the best mixer-upper in the world. She's liable to grow up to bake some very pretty pastries. I believe fancy meringues will be her specialty, if not her downfall, just as hard candy flowers are mine."

Zeda's decorations became ever more elaborate. When LaMerl married, everyone said that Zeda had baked the "cake of her life."

"The cake to end all cakes, I hope," was the way Jessman put it.

The creation was called a nightmare, and even Zeda's family agreed that she had gone too far. Elizabeth and three assistants had spent two days baking four dozen pound cakes, which Zeda Treadway, standing on a stepladder, had pieced together with simple syrup. The cake was over four feet tall and leaning dangerously when she ran out of layers. "I guess it's time to stop and go on to the next part," she said, descending the ladder to admire her good work. Then, without much forethought, she covered the cake with waves of white icing and sugar violets individually made. She used candied orange peels and slices of strawberries to add color to the sides, and on the top she created a tower of red roses. The icing turned gray in the summer heat, and the violets melted and dripped and made LaMerl cry.

The cake was too big to be carried through the kitchen door so the wedding guests had to line up to view it ten or twelve at a time. Finally, it was sliced down to a manageable size and taken piece by piece into the parlor, but Zeda was unable to put it back together again.

"This is the last wedding cake I'll ever bake," she said, giving herself to a bout of breathlessness. "Bessie-the-Best has no business getting married. She doesn't want to and she doesn't need to. That's the way I look at it."

" 'My Dependable One' is too set in her ways," her father said.

" 'Bessie-the-Best' has always been set in her ways," Zeda told him. "There's nothing anybody can do about it."

After Zeda Treadway gave up her passion for baking, she took up gardening with the same fervor and expected Elizabeth to do likewise. This time the seed of Zeda's desire was a yellow daylily. It was blooming near a neighbor's doorstep, and Zeda had to have it. Something came over her when she saw the flower, something so intense and all consuming that she snatched the lily from the ground and planted it in her own backyard. In a year's time she had acquired other lilies the same way. "They're so special," she told the boarders, "because as their name implies, they only last a day."

People were streaming in and out of Sabinetown during that time, and Zeda met many gardeners who shared her enthusiasm. "It just about stimulates me to death to find out that there are other people in the world just like me," she told her husband. "I never knew that before."

"Don't get yourself too stimulated," Jessman warned. But it was too late, and he knew it.

The daylily obsession was unending. When the backyard was overgrown, Zeda planted the front yard, and then the side yards, and before many years had passed, there was hardly any space left over. Then she became stingy and wouldn't part with a single lily.

After there was no more room in the yard, she resorted to planting in galvanized tubs placed on the front porch, in the breezeway, on the roof of the boardinghouse and all along the edge of the street. Finally, she pursuaded her neighbors to allow her to plant a portion of their yards as well.

As the years passed, she became deeply involved with transplanting for artistic reasons. One year she would attempt to separate all the colors, and the next year she would mix them up again, or try her hand at growing geometric patterns.

With Elizabeth working at her mother's side, daylilies were dug up and moved from one place to the next, even during blooming season. And, like Zeda's famous wedding cakes, each year's garden had to be more spectacular than the last. To keep track of where everything was planted she kept elaborate charts, notebooks and rough sketches.

"Knowing all this is going to come in handy one day," she told her only dependable daughter. "Even if somehow or other you do manage to find yourself a husband, which is not too likely at this point, you'll need something else to occupy your time."

* * *

Elizabeth Treadway was almost thirty-five years old when she got into Isaac's boat. "You have not made a mistake by stopping for me," she assured him, as Camp Ruby came into view. She knew, without having to be told, that they were going there. After studying the high, sloping riverbanks, and a few houses scattered along the rim, her eyes settled on the water tower, then Redd's commissary and finally, the sawmill located on a low, flat plane near the river. The saws were singing across the water, and the air was redolent with pine and cedar. Some of the workers were loading lumber into a flat-bottom boat. Others were guiding the logs into the mill. Mary Twitchell, driving a team of oxen, was coming out of the woods with another load of timber. Her husband, Peg Leg, the victim of a near-fatal logging mishap, was hobbling along beside her.

"This is our new home," Elizabeth said to her pets. The cranes stood on her lap and straightened their necks. They opened their beaks but made no sound. A few feet from the landing, the birds leaped into the water and flapped their way to dry ground. "Pets!" Elizabeth stood in the boat without losing her balance. "There might be mean dogs about. You better let me carry you until we get ourselves settled." A breeze swept her voice through the sawmill and up the slope to the houses. Suddenly everything and everyone came to a standstill.

"I don't believe I've ever heard that voice before," said Lester Jenkins. "Wonder who it belongs to." At his command the saws stopped buzzing. A heavy silence fell over that stretch of the river. Children stopped crying. Lottie Faircloth dismissed her classes for no reason at all. And the stray dogs sniffed the air to find out who was arriving.

Mary Twitchell came to a dead halt, but the oxen she was leading kept up their steady pace toward the mill. "Peg Leg," she said, squinting toward the river. "Come here and tell me if this ain't a woman Isaac's got in his boat."

"It's a woman all right," said Peg Leg. "Wonder how far he had to go to find her."

While Isaac docked the boat, Elizabeth gathered all three birds into her arms and stood with them on sand as fine as cake flour. "We're home," Isaac told her. She looked up and liked what she saw. There were no potted plants, no shrubs, no grass and no flower beds to be tended.

"I expect you'll want to plant some pretty flowers the first thing," said Isaac.

"No, sir, I most assuredly will not want to plant some pretty flowers the first thing," Elizabeth answered politely. "I hope you will not mind my saying this," she added, smoothing the feathers that framed her face, "but due to all I've lived through, I will not be spending my time baking pretty party cakes, either. I believe I've baked my last pastry, and I've planted my last flowering plant. That's just the way I am."

Again, her eyes scanned the community for a flower or a blade of grass that looked as though it might spread. But there was nothing except sand, mimosa trees, a few clumps of dried-up grass burrs and chain vines wilting on the hot ground.

For a moment her thoughts returned to Sabinetown. She wondered if her mother had stopped gardening long enough to realize that her dependable daughter wasn't at home that afternoon. She wondered who was going to make the beds, sweep out the rooms and help her father balance the books. She wondered who would remember to place fresh drinking water on the table in the breezeway, and wipe off the wicker chairs on the front porch. Who would feed the goldfish, the two housecats and the parrot that had never been friendly to a soul? She wondered if she was already missed, and if her family would take her back, if it came to that. While standing in the river, whistling and watching her feet turn white and wrinkle, none of these things had occurred to her.

Isaac smiled, took her by the hand and proudly led her up the riverbank. He carried a crane under one arm and so did she. The other bird marched before them like a self-appointed herald.

From the back window of her schoolroom, Lottie Faircloth spotted them coming. She told Gert McCormick who told Izella Wiggins who told Izzie Burrow who told Doc Broom that Isaac Overstreet was coming home with a strange woman and three river birds.

As she followed Isaac through the community, Elizabeth noticed that most of the houses were not level. The sand had shifted, leaving many of them resting at severe angles, or sitting flat on the ground. "Folks better be looking out where they build their houses," she said. "Something bad might happen if they don't. Sand is known to shift something awful. You'd think people would remember that."

"We do our best," said Isaac. He was trying to disregard his neighbors. Some were following them, others were leaning on porch posts or staring through bare windows.

"One of the good things about a place this high off the river is the breeze," said Elizabeth. "I bet the wind never stops blowing way up here."

"There's more good than that," Isaac assured her. He pointed to his house. "That's what I been working on all this time. It's brand new except for one room."

"I believe it would be hard for me to guess the new part from the old part," Elizabeth said, "but it appears to me this place has promise and lots of it, and that's what counts."

Isaac smiled.

From her back porch, where she was balling up her hair, Izella Wiggins could see his teeth flashing. "Isaac's face just now lit up like a match," she shouted to Lottie, who was three houses away. "We better go encourage the woman to stay before she walks into that empty house and decides to turn around."

"I believe I like her looks," said Doc Broom, whose wife had just died of pneumonia. "I wonder if she'll like mine." He was sitting on his front steps, a portable laboratory balanced on his knees. A black hairnet held his tangle of white hair close to his head. "Isaac's found himself a wife after all," Doc Broom announced to his neighbor Clarence Pritchard. "If he can find somebody, looks like you could too."

"I better go ask Isaac if she's got a sister," said Clarence. He oiled and combed his hair before he started out.

"I'm just dying to meet the woman and find out all about her," shouted Gert McCormick. Her husband, Bud, could hear her all the way to the sawmill. He and the other loggers were on their way to Isaac's house.

Elizabeth had not yet gone inside. She was staring at the front steps, wondering if they were safe. When they passed her inspection, she moved on to the porch and took heavy strides from one end of it to the other. The cranes followed her back and forth. It seemed to Isaac that the birds were imitating Elizabeth's walk. "Pets, I believe this porch is sturdy enough," she said.

Then, hanging on to a post, she allowed her eyes to drift from one part of the camp to another. Over to one side were five tar paper houses, each long and narrow like boxcars. They were standing end to end, connected by common porches and seemed to be moving slowly through the sand. "Looks like a train without tracks to run on," Elizabeth said. "Reminds me of the way I used to be just a little while ago."

Then Sunflower Baptist Church caught her attention. It was perched on a dangerous part of the slope, and some of the houseblocks had already rotted away. "I hope you don't mean for me to worship there," she said. "I'd be afraid for my life, I believe." Her eyes moved on. Stern and without a trace of emotion, they settled on the sawmill.

The Camp Ruby mill was affiliated with a larger sawmill located in the town of Splendora. It was barely breaking even, but Isaac saw it as a lucrative opportunity and promised Elizabeth that he would soon give up fishing and go to work there. But Elizabeth said it would take more than good management and hard work to make a success of anything built over shifting sand

—especially a sawmill. It seemed to her that everyone should know that.

Still, Isaac assured her that he knew what he was talking about and pointed to the sawmill and Redd's commissary as proof of a thriving community.

The commissary was centrally located. Redd had planned it that way. It was taller than the other houses and stronger, but like the rest it too was unpainted. Near it five small houses, built with scraps of lumber and cardboard, were clustered together. "One wind is all it would take to finish them off," Elizabeth said. In her estimation Camp Ruby looked lonely, but it didn't feel lonely. It did, however, need just about everything she could think of, including a road out. There were only logging trails. There wasn't even a ferry that crossed the river. There was nothing at all, except a handful of weatherbeaten houses, a store, a church and a sawmill on its last leg. But it was now her place. It was where she knew she was supposed to be. That's all that mattered. At that moment, she had no second thoughts about being there.

Isaac, standing on the other side of the porch, was filled with misgivings. Why is it that you can't be very sure of anything anymore, he wondered, not even when you're on the other side looking back? She won't stay here. She won't like it here. This place isn't for her.

"I know what you're thinking," Elizabeth said, "but you're wrong. I'm going to like it here just fine. Now, I believe I need to see inside this house you've built for us to live in."

Isaac held the door open, and the cranes, marching single file, followed Elizabeth inside. "You can decorate it any way you want to," Isaac said as though making a solemn vow. "That's what I made it for. That's why there's nothing in it. I don't know how to choose, but you do."

Elizabeth walked into the living room, her steps echoing throughout the empty house. "There's promise here," she said. "Some people might not be able to see it, but I can. Takes special eyes, I guess."

Once in the dining room, she kept expecting to find a chair, a bench, a table, just anything to let her know the house had been lived in. But there was nothing, not even a window shade or a curtain. "I have always been able to see something in nothing," she told Isaac. "And I can tell you for sure, promise is here. I see it. And, I feel it."

For a moment her heart wanted to sink, but she refused to allow it. She inspected the kitchen instead, and found nothing there, not a pan, not a stove, not a cupboard. "Just the kind of kitchen I always wanted," she said. "Kitchens always have too much in them to suit me, but this one's just right. Yards are a problem too. The smaller they are the better they are. That's my opinion."

On the sleeping porch, all screened in with rusty wire, she found no bed, only a pallet on the floor. "Something's got to be done about this," she said. Her pets were preening in a corner. "This room is crying for a proper bed. A body's got to look after himself better than you do."

"That's right," said Izella Wiggins, coming in without being invited. "Isaac's needed somebody to take care of him for a long time, and I see he's found somebody at last."

The two women introduced themselves, after which Izella went to the front door and invited the neighbors inside. "Come meet Isaac's lady friend," she shouted. "I don't know where he found her but she's right pretty, and we better help her get settled before she decides to leave him."

"He'll never find another one if she does," said Izzie.

"She might not either," Mary Twitchell said. "Ever thought of that?" She was trying to balance Peg Leg up the steps.

"You can send her over to my house when you get tired of her, Isaac," said Doc Broom. He was standing outside and glaring at Elizabeth through a window. She felt his eyes ripping her apart.

"Show some decency for once in your life, Broom," Lottie Faircloth demanded. "This is a very important day."

"You better send for Brother Clovis to pronounce you," said Peg Leg. Elizabeth was holding the door for him. "But don't expect me to go 'cause I need a flat surface to navigate."

Clarence Pritchard, soon to be Camp Ruby's most eligible bachelor, went for the preacher. He thought that would bring him good luck. While he was gone, Isaac made two rings from fence wire and changed his shirt. Elizabeth wound up her auburn hair at the nape of her neck, the style she would wear for the rest of her life. A few minutes later Brother Clovis Caldwell married them under the mimosas.

"I got something to say," Izella said the moment the wedding was over. "Elizabeth goes with Treadway, but Elizabeth don't go with Overstreet. It don't sound right to me. So I think you ought to go by Bessie. Bessie Overstreet's the best."

"I always end up being called Bessie," said Isaac's wife.

"That's because that's who you are," said Lottie Faircloth.

"Sometimes you don't have a choice in these things," said Mary Twitchell. "It's already decided for you."

"Not any of this matters right now." Izzie Burrow was exhausted. "I'm dying to sit down, and there's no sign of a chair, but back home I've got two that Bessie and Isaac can have. Now who's got a table to get rid of?"

Before long the house was filled with tables and chairs that no one needed anymore. An ironstead bed was brought in piece by piece and assembled on the sleeping porch. A woodburning stove was set up in the kitchen. Kerosene lamps were placed in every room. And when the sun went down, Elizabeth, now called Bessie, lit every lamp in the house and supervised the arranging of the furniture.

Most of the neighbors managed to part with something, even if it was nothing more than a cup towel or a pair of used sheets. LeRoy Redd surprised everyone by giving away six matching window curtains. No one had ever known him to be so freehearted. "I couldn't sell them anyway," he finally admitted.

As the house filled up with furniture, the echo that had been living there vanished, and Isaac heard his neighbors' voices as he had not heard them in a long time.

"What we need is some refreshments," said Lottie Faircloth, coming into the house with a pitcher of tea. "This is sassafras with a little bit of lemon. It ought to be real good."

"I've got a pineapple upside-down cake in my pantry," said Izella Wiggins. When she went back to get it, she found that her devil-of-a-daughter, Kay Linda, had already taken out a slice.

"Don't that beat all," said Izella, as she finished cutting the cake. She carefully moved the slices apart, and between the spaces she filled in with crushed pineapple from a can. On top of it all she sprinkled brown sugar and cookie crumbs. "Now nobody will ever know it's been eaten on," she said, running the cake back to the Overstreet house and presenting it to the bride.

"This is more than likely the first pineapple upside-down cake ever used for a wedding," Izella said, "but I guess you know I didn't have advance warning. I'd have baked something prettier if I'd known."

"It don't matter what kind of cake it is just as long as it's yours, Izella," said Isaac. "I believe you've got everybody beat when it comes to baking."

"I'm sure glad to hear that," said Bessie. "I've seen plenty of wedding cakes in my day, but this is the best one yet because I can hold it in one hand."

She thanked everyone for their generosity and excused herself to check on her pets. In the small back room, they were sleeping with their heads under their wings. She left them undisturbed, and for a little while she stood alone on the back porch and watched the river. That night it was as shiny as a new coin, and laced with more currents than she had ever seen. The moon was almost full, and the air was scented with hickory sawdust, pine resin and damp river smells that she was unable to distinguish. "I always liked the smell of a sawmill," she said, as her eyes settled on an empty place where the river deposited its silt. The ground wasn't sandy there. It was dark and rich, yet nothing grew on that spot except a few cattails. Bessie Overstreet studied them for a few moments. She listened to the wind rattling their stalks. Then she found herself wondering if daylilies would grow there too.

* * *

After Bessie had left home, her parents didn't know what to do with themselves anymore. They had relied on their second daughter so long that they had forgotten what needed to be done and when. Without Bessie around, nothing went right anymore. Oil lamps were left burning all night. Candles were allowed to drip onto the fine linen and eventually scorch the table. The goldfish were not fed, the daylilies were not watered and after a few days, dust began gathering along the window-sills.

Not long after that, the town was almost destroyed by fire. Some people said that flames floated up from the mud lake and fell upon the shingled rooftops. But Lettye and LaMerl were convinced that the fire didn't start that way at all. "Had Sister not run off so foolishly, and unexpectedly, and with a total stranger and without training anyone to take her place, this tragedy would never have happened," LaMerl said.

"The fire started in the boardinghouse." Lettye had no doubts about it.

Old Mr. Pop Meadows, who lived across the street and whose own house was miraculously spared, said that he believed the Treadway sisters were right. On the night of the tragedy he had been awakened by an uneasy feeling and a room filled with light. He put in his teeth and found his glasses. "It can't be morning yet," he said, going to the window. The boardinghouse was already in flames, and the fire was spreading rapidly. Jessman was nowhere to be seen and neither were the houseguests, but Zeda, wearing a cotton nightgown and robe, was in the backyard trying to save her lilies. While digging them up and carrying them into the street her gown caught fire.

From his bedroom window, Pop Meadows watched her run-ning toward his house. Her dress was covered with flames and so was her hair. Lilies were falling from her arms. She paused for a moment, seemed to try to say something and then turned and rushed into the boardinghouse, as if it were the only safe place to be. She never came out again, and neither did anyone else.

Bessie Overstreet received word of the fire on the day her parents and friends were buried. She arrived in Sabinetown shortly after the mass funeral. The graves had not yet been filled in. What was left of the town was draped in gray smoke. Black flags hung from the scorched and leafless trees and the streets were lined with mourners. Lettye and LaMerl lived on the out-skirts of town. Their houses were not damaged, but they refused to allow their sister to set foot on their property. They accused her of leaving their parents in a helpless state of affairs, and sent her away.

After dark Bessie returned to the still-smoking town to stand where the boardinghouse had been and think about what she had or had not caused. Without knowing what she was doing or why, she dug into the charred earth with her hands and brought up clumps of daylilies. "They'll come out again," she said, carrying the first armload to the river. Back and forth she went carrying the lilies to her boat. And when it was full, she got in and allowed the current to take her downstream to the clearing she had seen from her back porch. Three times in the dark she rowed to Sabinetown, filled her boat with her mother's lilies and transported them to the only place she felt they might grow. The next day she planted them in no particular order, and the following spring, they came up and bloomed.

In a few years the lilies took over. Like the mimosas, nothing could stop them. They multiplied. Bessie separated them. They multiplied again and again, and each year they required more space.

Navasota Blackburn taught Bessie the secrets of cross-pollination. Together, they transferred pollen from one lily to another. Cloth bags were tied over the flowers pollinated by hand and seedpods were saved. The seeds were planted, and their blooming season was eagerly anticipated. In time, lilies of many different colors and sizes were blooming everywhere. Bessie recorded her experiments with elaborate graphs and journals. Her goal was to develop a deep purple flower, so purple it was almost black. Navasota assured her it could be done. And that's all Bessie needed to hear. With her cranes at her side, she worked diligently to develop the color, and each year she came a little closer to the desired shade.

Everyone wanted to know how she could grow flowers where nothing much had ever taken root. "I just ask them to grow," was her answer. And she did. She addressed her lilies every time she watered them. She also gave them names: Lavender Lady, Red Sunset, Lemon Rose, Dark Beauty. Sometimes she would ask Isaac to help her with the naming. Sometimes she would ask

Lottie Faircloth or Izella Wiggins. She never ran out of names, but she could see the day coming when she would run out of energy and growing space. That's when she started selling her plants for profit. She would dig them up while they were blooming and arrange them in a boat that Isaac had given her. Then she would travel downstream, away from Sabinetown, making stops at each community and houseplace until her lilies were sold.

With the white cranes draped around her, and her boat filled with flowers, Bessie Overstreet became a familiar figure on both sides of the Sabine. She would whistle a long, sustained note to signal her arrival in the towns. Seemingly, the note would carry to every corner of every house, and people who had not shown their faces in days or who rarely appeared in public would be seen walking down to the river to meet the flower boat and listen to what Bessie had to say. She carried news with her. She carried advice, and letters and a radiance that everyone enjoyed. Housewives bought plants just to be able to say they had spoken to her for a few minutes, and that she had told them that the breeze was good upriver, or that the fish were spawning and not to disturb them in the shallow coves. Occasionally, she would bring a message from Navasota Blackburn. One spring Navasota saw seven shooting stars in one night and one of them fell into the river. Bessie carried the news to every landing. "What a good sign that is," she told everyone. "What a good year is ahead of us. Even the hard times will be made bearable."

PART TWO

The Ruby-Jewels

Somewhere between Camp Ruby and a little town called Hotel Dew, Bessie gave birth to Coleta, her first daughter. The three white cranes attended her. Like nervous midwives, who had forgotten what to do, the long-legged birds paced back and forth along the rim of the lily boat, stopping now and then to search for a resting place on Bessie's lap. "You'll soon be able to sit there again, all of you," she told them. She was lying on quilts. Daylilies balanced her weight on the other end of the boat. She had dropped her oar with the first pain and was now floating with the current. "Isaac will find us before we end up in a bad way," she said, as unconcerned as could be.

The Sabine had never frightened her, even in its most turbulent channels, and she was glad to be giving birth there rather than at home attended by Doc Broom. From the beginning he had shown an interest in Bessie that disturbed her. Several times he had taken his supper to his back porch and stared at the Overstreet house while he ate. He had said that it was his medical duty to keep an eye on all the pregnant women in Camp Ruby. But Bessie had said that it was his duty to look after his nine-year-old daughter, Elsa Mae. She was almost albino white, suffered one headache after another and, since the death of her mother, was anxious to have a child.

"Doc Broom loves to deliver babies more than anybody I ever

knew," Bessie had told her husband. "But we've got one he won't deliver. I promise you that."

"I just hope you pick a good place to have it," Isaac had said. Bessie assured him that she had already decided to have their first child in the lily boat. "Not that our bed isn't a comfortable place," she explained, "but the boat you built me is like a chair you've sat in all your life."

On the day Coleta was born, Isaac was fishing downstream near the shore. Since his marriage he had stopped drinking, except for a ceremonious cup of whisky shared with the river each morning. He had just completed this ritual when he saw his wife's boat drifting sideways down the river. The cranes flapped their wings and whistled for his attention, as Bessie lifted the child above her head. "It's a girl," she said, "so we can go ahead and name her after your daddy's mother. She didn't cause me one bit of trouble either." Isaac paddled over to meet them, and for a while the two boats, caught in the same current, traveled parallel only a few feet apart. "I'd like to know her now," he said, extending his arms to receive his daughter. While passing the child from boat to boat, Bessie lost her strength and dropped the baby into the river. Isaac fished her out with a net. "You'd think getting wet would upset her," he said.

"I believe she's too much like you for that." Bessie leaned back against the lilies while the cranes settled into her lap for the first time in months. Their necks fell limp over her shoulders.

Isaac wrapped his daughter in a dry seine and lay her at his feet. Then he paddled upstream, pulling the lily boat behind him.

On their way back, Bessie noticed a pain in her side, but she paid it no mind. That was just her way. Isaac, carrying their firstborn in a sling around his neck, was helping his wife out of the boat when she said she didn't believe she could go much farther. A few steps later, she sat down among the maroon daylilies and gave birth to another daughter.

"She's too little to live," Isaac said.

"She'll make it," Bessie told him. The baby was in her lap. The cranes, standing some distance away, were peering over a barrier of red lilies. "I guess we'll have to call this one Ruby."

Bessie spoke directly to her pets. They scrambled through the
lilies and stood close to their keeper, framing her with their
flapping wings. "Everybody will think we've named her after
this town," she said. "But we haven't. We've named her after
these Ruby Reds. It's a sight how they're blooming."

It didn't take long for the news to spread. Before Bessie had
the twins washed and dressed, all the neighbors were standing
at the front door. Lottie Faircloth was the first in line. She loved
babies better than anything, had an eighteen-month-old son
and couldn't wait to be a grandmother. That had almost become
her life's ambition.

"There's something mighty special about these twins of
yours," Lottie said. She couldn't take her eyes off them. "I felt
the same thing about my boy when he was born." She lingered
at the crib longer than anyone else, and was the first to notice
that the twins slept in the same position, turned at the same time
and seemed to share the same moods. They opened their eyes
together, kicked together and when they cried they sounded like
one baby, not two. "They take the cake for being the most
identical set of twins I have ever seen," exclaimed Lottie. "Let it
be known what I think, will you please?"

Before evening Lottie Faircloth brought her son, Peter, to see
the babies. "These little girls are going to be your playmates in
just a few years," she prophesied. "They're going to be famous
around here."

"Let's not make them any more famous than they need to
be," said Bessie. "They're still in the crib, you know."

After everyone went home, Bessie reminded Isaac that she
had promised him only two children.

"Well, I guess we're done now." He spoke as if his life were
over.

"I intend to count these twins as one," said Bessie. "I don't
know why I think that way, but I do."

Isaac moved his daughters' crib close to his side of the bed so
he could watch them throughout the night.

"I predict they'll take to the Sabine without a bit of trouble,"
he said the next morning. And he was right. Ruby and Coleta
grew up with their feet in the river. Bessie saw to it. During

warm weather she would dress them in identical smocks and sunbonnets and take them to the water's edge, where a small chair was anchored in the shallows. She would strap them into the chair and go about her business in the lily gardens while the twins amused themselves catching minnows in a teacup. They each held the cup with both hands and jabbered while they fished. Finally, they decided to break off the handle. It was so small they couldn't both use it, and therefore, it wasn't needed.

When they were tall enough to unlatch the screen door no one could keep them out of the river. After a few years of fishing with a teacup, while speaking what Gert McCormick said was an offshoot of the 'postolic language, they suddenly started using words everyone could understand. It happened on a Sunday morning. Brother Clovis Caldwell was preaching on the porch of Redd's store, and everyone was sitting or standing around him. "The faithful do not smoke, swear or show themselves off in revealing garments," was the theme of his sermon, and he had prepared it with Elsa Mae Broom in mind. At fourteen she was the mother of a son.

Brother Clovis was all wound up that day, and he preached until his throat was parched. When he stopped for a moment to take a sip of water, offered him by Izella Wiggins, the twins spoke up.

"River water is the only water fit to drink."

"River water is the only water fit to drink."

They delivered the same words, almost at the same time, causing what Izella said was a strange echoing in her ears.

"A minnow in your teacup

"A minnow in your teacup

"will quench your thirst faster than anything."

"will quench your thirst faster than anything."

According to the people who heard them for the first time, the Overstreet twins sounded as though they had rehearsed a script. And, in their own way, they had, for they had spent most of their lives sitting in the shallows practicing what they wanted to say and how they wanted to say it. Their two voices created a third.

It was as though the whole world came to a standstill when

they started talking in public. "They share the same mind!" shouted Lottie Faircloth.

"Well, they'll never be happy if they do," said Brother Caldwell.

"Oh yes they will," argued Lottie. "I've taught school for over ten years, so let it be known I speak the truth."

"The minnows appreciate us," Ruby said, staring into her sister's eyes as though their next words were written there.

"They like us because we never swallow them."

"They like us because we never swallow them."

"They're telling the truth, so help me," said Elsa Mae Broom, bouncing her baby boy. "I seen them both put three little fish in their mouths and spit them back in the river one at a time."

"I told you they were special." Lottie Faircloth was beside herself. "Let it be known that I'm always the first to see these things."

"Wonder if they could live without each other." Boyce Faircloth amused himself with the thought. "If something bad happened to one, wonder what the other one would do. That's what I'd like to know."

"Don't think such thoughts as that," Lottie scolded him, while taking Elsa Mae's child into her arms.

"Well, I have never in my entire put-together life heard of such as this," said Mary Twitchell, twisting her hairnet to shreds. "How do you know what you're supposed to say next?" she asked the twins.

"Practice makes perfect," they answered, but their timing was off.

"There's but one place on this earth they'll ever find peace of mind, and that's a sideshow." Clarence Pritchard was fond of carnivals.

"That's not true," said Isaac, stepping out of the crowd. "They're no different than the rest of us. They just happen to look alike and think alike, that's all. I knew they would talk when they got ready."

"That's more words than I've ever heard Isaac speak in his entire life," said Mary Twitchell.

"Marriage must agree with the man," said Peg Leg.

"Our girls have been talking to themselves for a long time now," said Bessie. A crane was in her arms, and two were at her feet. "I was the exact same way. Only there was just one of me."

* * *

Not long after the twins began talking in public, Bessie announced that she was carrying her third child, a daughter. "I dreamed we named her Zeda Earl," she told Isaac, "Zeda after my mother, Earl after your father."

"Zeda Earl is on her way," Isaac told the twins.

"Zeda Earl will soon be here," the twins told everyone they met. So did Isaac.

"I pray to God in heaven that Zeda Earl isn't a twin," said LeRoy Redd. "We've got enough confusion around here as it is."

One morning after a fitful sleep, Bessie announced to her family that Zeda Earl didn't want to be born. "She's not ready to meet us," she told her daughters. "Zeda Earl told me so last night in my dreams."

That afternoon Bessie miscarried. She was in bed on the sleeping porch, watching the clouds drift over the Sabine, and Isaac was with her. "The time wasn't right," Isaac told his daughters. "But Zeda Earl will come to us when she gets ready."

Bessie buried Zeda Earl in a fruit jar. She used two rocks to mark the grave, which she separated from the lilies with a fence of cypress knees driven into the earth.

"Somehow I can't help but be glad that baby wasn't born," said Mary Twitchell. "Bessie's got her hands full with the two she has. I fear for what the woman might bring into this world next."

Life went on as usual after that. Bessie returned to her lilies and Isaac to his fishing. Their daughters continued to entertain everyone by seeming to share the same mind, and within a year they became the most talked about twosome on either side of the river. They had valentine lips and fine auburn hair. Their eyes were blue, and their cheeks maintained a perpetual glow. "They're just beautiful," said Lottie Faircloth. "There's no other word to describe them either, so don't anyone try to think of one."

Although Coleta started out much larger than her sister, eventually their height and weight equalized, while their dispositions continued to show no outward signs of difference. The older they got the more identical they seemed to become. Only Isaac and Bessie could tell them apart. "They look alike," Bessie told Lottie Faircloth, "until you've been around them a long time, and then you start seeing the differences. Coleta is generally the leader. Ruby's voice is higher pitched. And their smiles aren't a bit alike. I can tell them apart the same way I tell the cranes apart: I just know without having to think about it."

Bessie took pride in showing her daughters off and insisted that they always be dressed alike from the bows in their hair down to their socks and shoes. She crocheted identical hats for them to wear in the sun and pinned corsages of real or paper flowers to their collars, cuffs or belts. They cried when given different flowers to wear, or when they were pinned in different places. If Ruby's corsage were pinned to her sleeve, Coleta's could not be pinned to her collar. If Coleta's hat had a ribbon, Ruby's had to have a ribbon of the exact same width and color and tied the very same way. Nothing could be different, not even the buttons on their winter coats which otherwise matched perfectly. They pitched fits until Bessie saw to it that each coat shared not only the same number of buttons, but the same color, size and shape as well. Everything had to be just the same or no one was happy.

Mary Twitchell decided to put them to a test. She gave Ruby a pair of blue gloves and Coleta a pair of yellow mittens just to see what would happen. The twins couldn't have been happier. They each wore a mitten and a glove at the same time, but said they preferred the gloves.

The Overstreet girls practiced doing everything together. They ate from the same plate, taking the same number of bites and chewing the same number of times. They took the same number of steps whether going to the store or just to the next room, and they went to bed, woke up and took naps with their arms wrapped around each other. They were handy around the house too. Bessie made sure of that. But it took four hands on the same broom to sweep the floor, four hands on the same plate to wash it clean, four hands to hang up a garment, four to raise a window or wipe off a table. When they didn't have anything to do they would sit down and face each other until they thought of something, or they would arrange and rearrange the same vase of flowers. Their favorite flower was the purple thistle, and Bessie was glad of it.

"Daylilies," she said, "can be very time consuming if you're not careful. It's best to like something that grows wild."

During the growing season she would take her daughters down the river to help her sell clumps of lilies. Soon the twins developed a sideline business of their own. They would instruct even the best of fishermen on the proper way to hold their rods, as well as the best colors to wear when fishing. Between towns and stopping-off places they polished their speeches: "If the sky is blue, wear blue that day," they would say. "That makes sense, doesn't it? If the sky is gray, wear gray. Never wear white. Never wear red. Never wear green unless you're fishing close to the shore."

Because Isaac was known as the best fisherman on the river, people were willing to listen to his daughters' advice and buy it —for the price of a lily. For a little more they would come up with magic words to make the fish bite. "You can't use the same word for too very long or else the fish will get wise to you, they sure will." They spoke as if singing a familiar song. "What you got to do is buy yourself a new word every time you see us coming, and don't forget it either."

One week their magic words would have animal themes, and the next week they would use places, or plants or names of their favorite things to eat. They could convince even the most experienced fishermen to sit in their boats and whisper dumpling, biscuit or rutabaga three times before wetting their hooks. Words such as pancake, flapjack and baking soda were considered two words, and for them the price was a penny more. Some people thought it was sheer nonsense, others swore that it worked. Many of the best fishermen wouldn't think of starting a week without a new word to charm the fish.

Back home the Overstreet twins weren't nearly so appreciated. LeRoy Redd thought they had the nastiest dispositions of
any pair of sisters he had ever known. They didn't much care for
him either and called him Tub o' Guts to prove it. They were
forever putting their hands on everything in his store and leaving fingerprints behind. He had to follow them around to keep
his merchandise straight. "All they study about is what they can
mess up, or rearrange or hide out of sight," he said. In an hour's
time they had completely reorganized his yard goods and
moved the school supplies to a place where no one would ever
think to look.

Redd was on to them constantly, and so was Izella. Because
she had a thin blade of flesh that extended from the tip of her
chin down to her cleavage, they named her Wattle Wiggins and
never gave her a moment's worth of rest. "All they want to do is
mock everybody in sight," she gobbled. "And I'm sick of it too."
She swore if they imitated her one more time she'd slap their
faces on both sides. Gert McCormick, nursing her baby in broad
daylight, said she failed to see what there was about Izella that
was worth imitating.

"Lots of things, according to them," said Izella, spitting her
snuff into a tin can without removing it from her apron pocket.

They started the rumors that Bud McCormick beat his wife
every Sunday afternoon at three o'clock, and that Izzie Burrow
picked up deposit bottles because he enjoyed sucking on them
in his spare time. They called him Easy Bottle.

They found out that Mary Twitchell had followed Peg Leg all
over East Texas until he broke down and married her. They
were convinced that she had chopped off his leg to slow him
down, and that she kept it under the bed. They called Mary, Ole
Twitch, because she had a nervous tic that kept her head bouncing from side to side, and her fingers twisting on a hairnet found
anywhere but on her head. They could mimic her perfectly, and
told everyone she was really a man. "Why would a woman want
to saw logs?" they'd ask. "It just doesn't make sense."

"When you're married to a man who only has one foot, you're
forced to help him out," said Mary. "It's as simple as that."

She had a few opinions about the Overstreet sisters herself.

She was standing in the post office part of the store when she told Lottie Faircloth that those twins were the most vicious eight-year-old girls she had ever seen. "They remind me of little mad dogs," she said. "They are just as dangerous too."

Lottie took up for them. "They may seem that way at first, but you have to keep in mind that they treat their parents like gold. I do wish I could say the same for Peter Lewis Faircloth, who came into this world after ten years of false alarms and two days of hard labor, but I can't. Not unless I lie. He's been a disappointment all the way, but I think he'll grow out of himself and learn to be more like Bessie and Isaac's two. Girls mature faster than boys, you know, and these twins certainly prove it."

"I don't want to hear anything good about them," said Mary, looking to escape.

"But you're going to," said Lottie, taking Mary Twitchell by the arm and holding her in place. "Those Overstreet girls are the smartest, most sensitive and most talkative students I've ever had the privilege to teach. Now you may already know what I'm about to tell you, but most people don't. The girls do not always talk at the same time, and when they do they don't always say the same thing at the same time. It just sounds like they do. One is just a little tiny, tiny bit behind the other and the other is just a little teensy bit ahead. And most of the time they have a pretty good idea of what they're going to say way before they say it, but sometimes they don't."

"Clarence Pritchard thinks they ought to be in a freak show," said Mary.

"Not anymore, he doesn't," said Lottie. "I set him straight on that account. I said, 'Clarence, they are geniuses, and geniuses are so close to being idiots until it's scary sometimes. Sometimes you just can't tell one from the other. Now try to keep that in mind.' And he said he would, and you know what? I believed him."

"They got pretty auburn hair," said Mary. "I have to say that much because I've tried to match the color and can't. But their eyes are just too blue and steady-staring. Makes you wonder what they're really looking at."

Elsa Mae Broom, now the mother of another son, put an

aspirin under her tongue and jumped into the conversation. "They have the pinkest lips I've ever looked at," she said, adjusting the wet rag tied around her aching head. "I been wondering if they'll ever need to paint them."

Elsa Mae wouldn't think of going anywhere without her lipstick, but she didn't mind who saw her in pin curls or in almost any state of undress. She was a constant source of entertainment for the Overstreet sisters, and she enjoyed knowing that she amused them. One of their favorite pastimes—and Elsa Mae was well aware of it—was spying on her when she lured her boyfriends under the logging bridge that crossed Woods Creek. They called her Sticky Pants and went around imitating every whining, moaning, gasping sound she made. But Elsa Mae didn't care. She was proud of her reputation.

"I don't know how those two Overstreet girls can come up with so many gossiping lies," said Doc Broom in defense of his daughter. The twins called him Bloomers because every summer he wore his underwear out to the front porch to cool off. They were certain that he had poisoned his wife, Alice, by feeding her homemade medicines. "But, of course, that was way before our time," Ruby said. "So we can't be too sure now, can we?" added Coleta.

Clarence Pritchard said, "They are conniving, and there's no other way of putting it. Who would have thought Bessie and Isaac could have created such as that." Clarence would forever be angry for what they had done to him when he had both arms broken in a logging accident. He was wearing two plaster casts at the time, couldn't bathe, dress or scratch himself, and everybody was talking about how awful it must be for a young man like Clarence, a bachelor at that, not to be able to do a thing for himself. The Overstreet sisters picked ticks and fleas off stray dogs and put them in Clarence's bed. The next morning they went around owning up to what they had done and talking about it like it had made history. That irked Izella.

But Lottie Faircloth, who at times had more patience than anyone had ever heard of, told Izella that the Overstreet sisters were completely normal whether they acted like it or not. "They make a hundred on every test," Lottie said, "even the hard

ones, and I've never seen them crack a book. I do wish to God
Almighty that Peter Lewis was more like them. That boy is about
to worry me to death, and he knows it too."

"At least he don't have meanness in him," said LeRoy Redd.
He had reached his limits with the Overstreet twins, so he ap-
pointed a committee of four to discuss the problem with Isaac.

When the committee came calling, Bessie saw fire in their
eyes and refused to let them in. But they paid her no mind and
filed, one right behind the other, through the house and onto
the sleeping porch where Isaac was lacing his boots.

Just outside the window, Ruby and Coleta, sitting in an overgrown mimosa and crocheting from the same ball of yarn,
stopped for a moment to recognize the members of the committee:

"Easy Bottle, Wattle Wiggins, Tub o' Guts and Ole Twitch."
"Easy Bottle, Wattle Wiggins, Tub o' Guts and Ole Twitch."

The committee launched into a tirade of choral complaints.
Arms flew, fists shook and feet stomped the sleeping porch
floor. Heads waggled, and ears turned red and tongues leaped
out into the air and snapped up each other's words. Dust rose
from under beds, and chairs and between cracks in the floor.
The house that Isaac built in fourteen days shook on its foundation.

"I don't believe we know the same people," said Isaac, as the
committee cooled off. His boots were laced and he was ready to
go to the river. "I sure would hate to meet up with the kind of
people you entertain."

Then they complained to Bessie.

"Our children don't have time to be mean," she argued.
"They sweep out this house twice a day. They get their lessons,
and cook as best they can and go with me down the river. The
people we sell to want to keep them."

"Maybe you ought to give some credence to that," Izzie Burrow spoke before he thought.

Izella Wiggins changed the subject. "Does it take both of
them to push a broom?" she asked.

"Yes it does," Isaac answered. "If you want your floors to be
as clean as ours, it sure does."

"They do everything together," said Bessie. "It's a blessing really. They'll never know what loneliness is all about, will they?"

"Maybe you ought to have another child to keep the two you've got a little bit busier," said Izzie.

"Zeda Earl is on her way again," Bessie smiled. "I think she'll give Ruby and Coleta a lot of company."

* * *

The next day Lottie Faircloth heard about the visitation. She dismissed her morning classes and went straight to the lily gardens, where Bessie was getting ready to plant seeds from her latest experiment. A pain in her side was beginning to slow her down. "That's Miss Zeda Earl telling me something," she said to her pets. They were standing so close to her she could hardly move. "Something tells me the time isn't right again."

"Precious pets!" Lottie pointed to the birds. "How lucky they are to have you, Bessie." Then she started her advice. "I have come here to tell you that your daughters are perfectly and completely normal as well as brilliant, and you are not to listen to what those gossips have to say about them. Twins are supposed to be close. They're supposed to be clever, and they're supposed to be cute. Yours are just going through something right now and pretty soon they'll come out of it. My boy Peter is the exact same way, only the opposite. There's nothing we can do for them at this time in their lives. Listen to me! I'm a schoolteacher so let it be known that I know exactly what I'm talking about."

"You know a whole lot, don't you, Lottie?" Bessie poured some seeds into the palm of her hand.

"Yes, Bessie Overstreet, thank you so much, I do know a lot." Lottie Faircloth spoke without a trace of modesty. "I'm so glad someone around here appreciates what I have to say."

"I know a few things too," Bessie said, holding the seeds as though they were an offering. "I know that I have crossed these Ruby Reds with these Lavender Ladies back and forth, back and forth so many times I've all but lost count. Deep purple, almost black, is what I'm after and these seeds may be the very ones. I try not to expect too much, so if they don't turn out right, I won't be too disappointed. It's bad to spend your life being disappointed."

"Bessie Overstreet, I have always said the exact same thing myself. Let it be known that you have taken the words right out of my mouth."

"I had the feeling," said Bessie, returning to her planting, "that I was doing just the opposite."

"Well now, you know you weren't, so let that be known too," said Lottie. She was proud of her insight and wished more people would recognize her for it. "I'm glad I could be the one to set you straight, Bessie. You can always depend on me to do that."

After Bessie was alone again, Zeda Earl gave up. "This baby just refuses to be born," Bessie told her husband as he carried her home.

"She'll be born yet," he said. "I'm not worried."

They put the child in a jar, and the next day they buried her inside the fence of cypress knees. Isaac chose two stones to mark Zeda Earl's new grave.

From her classroom window, Lottie Faircloth was watching them. "Bessie's too old to be having babies," she said. "Wonder if anyone's told her that."

* * *

Ruby and Coleta didn't really care for Lottie Faircloth, they merely tolerated her. Behind her back, they called her Miss Let-It-Be-Known, and said she looked foolish with her hair braided with ribbons and pinned across the top of her head. They were bored in her classes, but they forced themselves to be nice to her anyway because she was Peter's mother.

They were both in love with Peter Faircloth, and swore they would never get over him as long as they lived. He was small and blond. His eyes were hazel, and his lashes were long. His complexion was bright, and the twins liked that. After searching for flaws they gave up.

"Pete can't be improved upon," said a sister to a sister.

"He's perfect the way he is," said the sister being spoken to.

But they didn't like his father one bit.

Peter's father's full name was Boyce Monroe Faircloth, but Ruby and Coleta called him "Worm." They hated him because he gave his flawless son a whipping nearly every other day. Boyce accused Lottie of passing bad blood onto their child because he was underweight, nervous and practically lived in the kitchen. It didn't take Boyce long to realize that Peter wasn't the son he wanted. He had dizzy spells, couldn't catch a ball, or throw it perfectly straight, and he showed no interest in guns.

Boyce thought the only way to *save* his son was to rough him up. "Boy, I can't imagine how we got stuck with you," he would say. "You wouldn't last a minute in my daddy's house." Then he would remove his belt.

"If that boy can live through everything I'm preparing him for, he'll make it just fine," Boyce told his wife. "If he can't, he just can't."

Lottie went along with her husband's ideas. She said it was hard being a parent sometimes because you had to do a lot of things that hurt you at the moment but, in the long run, were for the best.

Lottie had met her husband at a school dance on the other side of the river. Boyce had been a good dancer, and that was the first thing she had admired about him. Women would beg him to spin them just once around the floor, but Lottie had to give her approval first. She had just been certified to teach, and Boyce was looking for a job. He was hot-tempered in those days and ready to fight anyone who crossed him, but Lottie thought he would grow out of that. After marrying they discovered they were distantly related.

When Ruby and Coleta found out that Boyce and Lottie were second cousins, as well as husband and wife, they decided *that* was the reason why Peter was so sickly. They also decided he would forever need taking care of and they dedicated their lives to serving him.

Peter frightened easily, and at first the twins made his condition worse. They brought on his asthmatic attacks, coughing fits and fainting spells. Lottie thought it was disgraceful. "He's not really that weak," she told her class. "He just likes to aggravate his mother." She taught the first eight grades, and had patience for everyone except her son. She expected the world out of him, and he was always letting her down, especially in class. He had a nervous stammer, formed most of his letters backward or upside down and couldn't read a word. He said he couldn't help it, but his mother said he could.

"I want you to stop pretending you can't and start believing you can," Boyce told him. "We want you to make us proud of you, but right now you've got a long way to go."

"The pitiful part is no one's asking the impossible," Lottie whined. "I just want you to be a straight A student and well liked. I just want you to marry a wonderful woman and have lots of children. I also want you to make me a grandmother so bad I don't know what to do. I know it sounds silly, but I can't help it. Now if you were smart, if you were really, really smart, you'd pay close attention to one of those Overstreet girls. They both think the world of you, I can tell, and one of them would make a good mother, not to mention a wife. I really and truly don't care which one you choose; they are both the same to me."

Peter was convinced the Overstreet twins would turn on him at any moment, but they never did. Halfway through the fifth grade they decided to let him know exactly how they felt. Each day they moved their desks a little closer to his until they were practically sitting in his lap. He was trying his best to control his nervousness, and Lottie was beginning to be proud of him again when the twins whispered in his ears, "We're going to marry you, Pete. We're not going to wait till we're grown to do it either. And one day soon we're going to do to you all the things we've seen Sticky Pants do to her boyfriends. We've kept a list."

Hearing them whisper the same words into different ears was more than he could endure. He stuttered and wheezed and passed out at his desk, and that made Lottie so mad she cried in front of her class.

That night she asked her husband to give Peter another whipping for being so jittery, tongue-tied and scared of his shadow. Then she got him off by himself and told him that she was going to make him sleep in the woods if he didn't stop letting those sweet Overstreet sisters frighten the pants off him.

Billy Wiggins, the retarded grandson Izella was determined to raise to maturity, took it upon himself to protect Peter Faircloth from the Overstreet girls. He already hated them for slipping into his bedroom while he was sleeping and painting his face with lipstick and rouge. He was determined to get his revenge, so every time he saw them following Peter Faircloth around he would chase them with switches and threaten to set fire to their clothing. He pinched their arms black and blue and slapped their faces with a flyswatter he carried in his back pocket.

The twins were scared of Billy Wiggins. When he came too close they threw rocks and tantrums, cursed in identical gibberish and had been known to wet their pants at the same time.

"Something has to be done with him," Isaac said, coming to his daughters' defense. "Izella, if you can't think of something by tomorrow afternoon, I'm sure I can. And if I can't, Bessie will."

Before evening Izella had penned up her grandson with the chickens. Her chicken coop was under her back porch, which was high off the ground and fenced in with rabbit wire. Little did she know he would enjoy being there and want to stay. "You ain't nothing at all and never will be," she said, as she closed the wire gate behind her.

"That's what I been telling you all this time," said Billy, "but you won't believe me."

"I feel so sorry for him I don't know what to do," said Elsa Mae Broom. "He looks so lonesome sitting under there with the hens." She believed he was too deranged to know how to escape so she went in after him. "Come on out of there Billy Wiggins before you break my heart," she said. "I don't care how crazy you are, you don't need to be treated like this." It was the first time she had ever looked him in the eye and spoken to him seriously. He fell in love with her on the spot, and after that she couldn't go anywhere without him trailing her.

"I know who Elsa Mae is," he went around saying. "I've placed her, is what I've done. One day she'll know it too."

Elsa Mae was absolutely sure that Billy was a threat to her life and she told everyone so. It was thrilling. It gave her something

new to talk about and besides that, the attention made Billy
Wiggins very happy.

At last he was out of the way, and no one could have been
more pleased than the Overstreet twins. Now they could follow
Peter Faircloth all day long, if they wanted to. For a while at
least, Billy Wiggins no longer cared what they did.

Ruby and Coleta knew they had an adverse effect on Peter,
but they were convinced that they were good for him also.

"What makes you sick can make you well, Pete."

"What makes you sick can make you well, Pete."

His legs would nearly give out from under him whenever he
heard their voices, his breathing would become difficult, and his
head would swim. But the twins refused to let up.

Finally, they couldn't control themselves any longer. They
pinned him to the ground and kissed him until he cried and
almost passed out.

"We might kiss you and hug you and squeeze you, Pete, but
we're not about to hurt you."

"We won't give you whippings either."

"But we will give you all the babies you want."

"But we will give you all the babies you want."

"I don't like babies," Peter said. "I don't like kissing and
hugging either."

"You will," said a sister.

"We're not through with you yet," said the other.

They kept a close watch over him, could predict when he
would leave his house and when he would return. They practiced guessing when he dropped off to sleep, what he was
dreaming about and when he would wake up. Gifts were soon to
follow. They left them on his doorstep: chewing gum, shoelaces,
hair oil and shaving cream, even though he didn't need it.

One afternoon they followed him to the commissary and
waited for him to come out. They were thirteen years old, madly
in love and deliriously happy.

"Ruby Duby-Du wants to take you into the woods today," said
Coleta when Peter came out of the store. She could hardly speak
through her excitement.

"Sticky Pants showed us a good place to be alone in," said

Ruby, taking Peter by the arm. "She doesn't know she showed it
to us, but she did."

"Sister and I are going to show it to you now," said Coleta.

Peter Faircloth lost his breath. His face turned blue, and his
knees gave way. Clarence Pritchard carried him home, and Lottie put him to bed. All over the camp he could be heard gasping
for breath.

"Listen to that boy wheezing," said Izella Wiggins. "I don't
believe he'll live another day, but don't tell Lottie I predicted
it."

Doc Broom administered vapors and sharp slaps on the back.
When that didn't work, Brother Clovis resorted to the laying on
of hands. That didn't work either, so he put a Bible under
Peter's pillow and went back home.

That night Navasota Blackburn woke up hearing a human
breath trapped inside her house. "Who's trying to find his
breath of air?" she asked, throwing open her front door. She
stood on the porch and listened to the wind blowing off the
water. "There's a death rattle in that wind," she said. "I know
whose it is." She crossed the river in the dark and rapped on
Isaac's sleeping porch. Bessie awakened to see Navasota's face
in the window. "That boy's strength is about to play out," she
said. "Tell your girls to take him up the river. Let the water get
to him." She didn't wait for Bessie's answer.

The next morning the Overstreet twins appeared at Peter
Faircloth's bedside. They were all bundled up in black coats,
black stockings and high-top shoes. They each wore a yellow
mitten and a blue glove. Identical gray caps covered their eye-
brows.

"We can make you better, Pete," said a sister.

"But you've got to want us to."

"You've got to say you do too."

"You've got to say you do too."

Peter didn't answer. He no longer had the strength to resist.

It was almost dawn, and the sisters were in no mood to wait
around. They had made a soft bed in the lily boat and carried
him to it. "We're about to take a pleasant trip," said Ruby. "We

advise you not to worry about anything at all," said Coleta. "Let us do that for a change."

"The only thing that's wrong with you is you don't know how to relax and have a good time."

"We're here to teach you."

"We're here to teach you."

To combat the cool spring morning, they had brought along a fruit jar filled with a mixture of hot tea and their father's fishing whisky. They insisted that Peter drink half of it before they pushed off, and he did. They put a warm cap on his head, propped him up with pillows and took him up the river. The warm drink numbed him. And the rocking of the boat made him want to sleep, but he was too excited for that. When they reached Sabinetown, one of the sisters said, "We still got relations living up there, but they don't care about us, and we don't care about them. That's just the way it is sometimes." Next they came to the place where their parents had met. They stood up and pointed. "Right over there is where a whole lot of important things happened, Pete," said one.

"We better stop here for a little while," said the other.

They stopped the boat and stared toward a tree that grew over the water. That was how they recognized the place where Bessie had stood. In front of them, a blue heron dipped its wings into the river and made ripples that traveled toward the boat and gradually disappeared. Peter Faircloth counted them. The world was misty that morning. The water was calm and pearly gray, and when the sun tried to burn through the clouds, the river sparkled like a stream of opals.

"It looks so good it makes you want to drink it," one sister said to the other. Their teacup was dipped into the river. Sips were taken. "Still the same," said one. "Taste won't ever change, will it?" said the other.

Peter Faircloth took a sip and said, "I like what's in the jar a lot better." Another cup was poured for him.

Soon they were paddling slowly through fallen clouds so thick the riverbanks could not be seen, and the water around the boat seemed to be part of the sky. The twins rowed in perfect harmony. Their paddles reached out like wings and dipped into the river, pushing the boat on a little farther. Their rhythm was slow and unbroken. Peter Faircloth felt his bones melting into the river. Nothing else existed except the boat, the fallen clouds and the water.

Flying must be just like this, he thought.

"This is what the world looks like if you're a bird, Ruby-Duby-Du," Coleta whispered. The morning seemed to demand it.

"When you're way, way high up it looks just like this, Sister, I know it does," Ruby whispered back.

Peter Faircloth wondered how they knew what he was thinking.

For a long time they traveled through the dense clouds that seemed to protect them from the world they could no longer see. The boat sat low in the water and the river claimed it. Peter Faircloth convinced himself that the boat did not exist and neither did the world he had just left. He was flying, and, for the first time in his life, he did not dread the next moment.

Farther up the river the current became stronger, the clouds thinned out and the steel skeleton of a bridge that connected Texas and Louisiana could barely be seen. "This is what you call a river bridge," said a sister. "It connects one state to another state."

"There are all kinds of bridges," said the other sister. "Not all of them look like this."

The boat emerged from the clouds into a bright sky. No one felt the need to whisper anymore.

"I'm about dead!" shouted a sister. "All this paddling has just about killed my poor arms. Sister, I didn't know we'd be going so far. Not upstream, anyway."

"Sister, hush your mouth and paddle. Even if we'd gone downstream we'd eventually have to turn around and go upstream to get back again. Better to go upstream first and get it over with, don't you think?"

"Don't ask me, I'm too tired to think," came the answer.

They took their caps off at the same time and used them to fan their red faces. They had Buster Brown haircuts and wore matching barrettes over each ear. They wanted to stop and turn

around, but they didn't want to change directions in midstream
for fear of bad luck.

"We don't chase after bad luck."

"We don't chase after bad luck."

It pleased them when they said the same thing without planning to. They rolled back in the boat and laughed out loud. Fish
jumped out of the water, and turtles came up for air. A water
snake making a zigzagging path across the river stopped and
changed its course.

"Ruby-Duby-Du-Du-Du," said Coleta. "Straighten yourself
up and listen to this: Peter Faircloth has never set foot in another state. What do you say about that?"

"I say let's cross the river," said Ruby.

"I say you know what you're talking about," said Coleta.

Once under the bridge they turned the boat to face the Louisiana shore and started paddling hard. "O Susanna, O don't you
cry for me," they sang as they crossed the center current. "For
we're going to Louisiana with a banjo on our knee."

"I sure wish we had a banjo," said a sister.

For the life of him, Peter Faircloth didn't know which one. He
had never been able to keep them straight for very long.

"Well, we don't, Sister, so don't be crying over it," said a
sister. "That's all I can tell you." Their voices bounced off the
bottom of the bridge, and the riverbanks and the surface of the
water.

"I think I'd like to live under a bridge," said one, paddling as
hard as she could.

"You'd soon get tired of it," said the other.

"I think I'd like to live in a boat then," said the first. "But I
guess I'd get tired of that too."

"No you wouldn't, Sister," said her sister. "I know you better
than that. You just think you would but you wouldn't."

"Well, Sister, I guess I'd better take your word for it because
you seem to be the smartest one today. I wonder how come and
how long it will last."

Finally, they made it across the river to the Louisiana side.
They pulled the boat close to a rock and told Peter to put his
foot on it. When he did they clapped their hands and laughed

and squealed and dropped their paddles in the water. "Now you've set foot in another state," said a sister.

"In more ways than one," said the other.

"You'll never be the same again."

"You'll never be the same again."

"In that case, I think we can turn around now," said Peter. He was trying to fish the paddles out of the river with a broom he had found floating in the water.

"Wonder what that ole broom was doing way out here all by itself," said a sister. "I'm ready for the answer now. Sister, you have it on the tip of your tongue, I know you do."

"Sister, have you lost your mind or what?" asked her sister. "You are forever and always asking me questions, and what you don't seem to remember is that both of us know the exact same things and nothing more. Why put yourself to such trouble?"

"I don't know, Sister, I just do."

"Well, I can already see that nothing or nobody will be able to convince you of a single solitary thing today, so give me a paddle and let's get going."

They took the boat to the center of the river and relaxed as it floated downstream. Peter Faircloth had been breathing without effort for over an hour, and he was just now realizing it.

They returned to Camp Ruby under clear skies. But as they approached the sandy banks, they felt sad and almost frightened to return.

"Why can't we live on the water?" said Peter.

"Why can't we live in the sky?" said a sister.

"Why can't we live both places at once?" said the other sister.

Lottie Faircloth saw them coming down the river and ran to meet them. She was frantic. "What have you two kidnappers done to my boy?" she screamed. "He's sick. He's very, very sick."

"Not anymore he's not," said Coleta. "Ruby-Duby-Du's been teaching him that it's nice to have something to look forward to."

"And my sister's been teaching him that living's not nearly as bad as he's been led to believe," said Ruby.

"We've been showing him the world," said one.

"We even took him to another state," said the other.

"What a terrible thing to do," said Lottie. "You should have talked it over with somebody first." She took Peter home and put him to bed.

"You're sick," she said.

"No I'm not," he argued.

* * *

Peter Faircloth came to find out that the Overstreet sisters were his best friends. They read to him. They took him places, made him feel healthy and helped him learn to laugh. He enjoyed every moment they spent together and looked forward to their secret meetings. He even helped plan them.

"We don't care whether you can read or not," said a sister.

"We don't care whether you can write your name frontwards or backwards or upside down," said another sister. "We just want to make you happy."

On Woods Creek, a tributary of the Sabine, there was a wide pool surrounded by beech trees. It was secluded, and the Overstreet sisters liked it there. On warm days they would scrub Peter Faircloth's face and body, wash his hair and clean his ears. They would freshen his breath with sweet bay and take turns taking their time with him. They would slip around and meet in secret places here and there: Campground Cemetery during the early evening, or an empty house on the river. Sometimes they would hide behind a sawdust hill, or underneath the bridge that crossed Wood's Creek. If the moon was dark they would go no farther than the daylily beds, or the lily boat, and during warm weather they would retreat to the cool sand under Redd's store. But their favorite place, day or night, was the water tower. They pitched a tent on the narrow platform and called it home.

"When we get a little older, we'll live up here, I think," said one sister.

"There's a lot wrong with that idea," said the other sister. "This tent won't last a year, and it's awfully buggy way up here."

"The hornets will carry us off," said Pete, "but it's worth a try." Joining hands, they said together:

"We'll all be happy till we die."

"We'll all be happy till we die."
"We'll all be happy till we die."
They felt so comfortable with one another that it pained them to be separated for longer than an hour. When they were together all they talked about was how they would keep their house, a topic of conversation that inspired them to leap to their feet and dance jigs and reels to accompany their rhymes, which they wrote down to keep from forgetting. More than anything else they enjoyed singing about themselves and their future home:

"It'll be neat as a pin, we all three agree,
And so clean you can eat off the floor.
Every little thing will have its own special place,
And nothing will need to be looked for.
Oh how happy we will be, just us three, just us three,
Oh how happy we will be. Just you wait and see."

They sang on the tower, in the moonlight, down on the river-banks and dancing through the daylily beds. They sang in the boat Bessie bought them to travel around in. They even sang in their sleep.

* * *

Peter's asthma gradually vanished and his nervous spells became less frequent, but he never learned to read. That was impossible.
"It's not necessary for you to read word one," said a sister.
"We read quite well, thank you," said the other sister.
"We'll tell you what everything says."
"We'll tell you what everything says."
Now, there was only one thing that bothered Peter Faircloth. He still had trouble telling the sisters apart. They did not look *exactly* alike; Peter realized that. But they did act alike, and they did sound alike and to Peter Faircloth they were the same. "I don't know what to call you," he confessed as they were floating on Navasota's Lake, a wide part of the river that was calm and deep.

The twins were not the least bit distressed over his announcement. They knew a solution was in sight. "We can't change the way we act or think or look," said a sister to a sister.

"No we can't," said the sister being spoken to. "But we can change our names. Maybe that will help."

The renaming took some time and thought, but in the end it did work.

Ruby, who was named after the maroon daylilies, liked her name and didn't want to give it up, but Coleta, who was named after Isaac's grandmother, didn't like hers at all. She decided to call herself Jewel instead. Then Ruby decided she liked the name Jewel also and started going by that name rather than her own. Next, Jewel who had been called Coleta, decided that she would like to be called Ruby. So she renamed herself Ruby-Jewel. Then Jewel who had been called Ruby decided that she wanted her real name back, so she started calling herself Ruby-Jewel in spite of the fact that her sister was already going by the same name, which they both insisted upon hyphenating.

For a while everyone still attempted to keep them straight by referring to them as Ruby-Jewel-One and Ruby-Jewel-Two, but that didn't work either. Hardly anyone could tell them apart for very long.

"It doesn't matter which is which," the Ruby-Jewels explained. "We're both the same anyway. Besides, having one name has made it a lot easier on Pete."

PART THREE

Ain't Nothing At All

Izella Wiggins, originally from Monroe, Louisiana, married when she was sixteen and had two children. Her husband died when she was nineteen, leaving her with no means of support except peddling hot lunches to sawmill workers. She used a bucket to carry the lunches and a jar of hot water to keep them warm. Sometimes her children helped her. She had a son named Billy, but he called himself Bull, and a devil-of-a-daughter whose name was Kay Linda. Mexicans loved Kay Linda better than anything. They were always saying her name, and that worried Izella.

At the age of fifteen Kay Linda married a man named Fred Womble who came from a place called Pine Island. When they weren't getting along, which was most of the time, Kay Linda and her three children moved in on Izella. Izella liked that, especially after she lost her son. Bull had been her cross to bear, and she had always had trouble admitting it. "There wasn't a thing wrong with him except a little bit of meanness. He didn't do nothing wrong, and he didn't do nothing right either."

Bull had married a woman named Velma Barlow. He called her Velma B. and she called him Billy Bull. For years they tried to have children. Bull wanted a boy that looked exactly like him, but eventually he was forced to admit that they would never have a child. He blamed it on Velma B., and Velma B. blamed it on him. Finally, they resorted to kidnapping.

The town of Hotel Dew was full of families at that time, so they went there first and chose a baby by the way it cried. It had a laughing sort of cry that appealed to them. Another thing they considered was the size of the household. There were eleven children in that particular family, and they felt that one less mouth to feed wouldn't disturb anyone. As it turned out, they were right. They kidnapped the child in the middle of the night, took him home and named him Billy Wiggins.

"I guess they couldn't think of anything else," Izella said.

The child was about a year old. He had bright red hair and large ears, fleshy lips and a wild-eyed stare. His new mother and father worshipped him, but not for long. A month after the kidnapping, the proud parents were on a fishing trip upriver. Isaac Overstreet was on the water that day and watched their boat vanish into a whirlpool that suddenly appeared from no-where. The river was like that, especially in the spring, and especially that year. The Year of the Rains was how it was re-membered. The boat went down as though some creature had opened its mouth and swallowed it. Bull and Velma rode it down, but they didn't ride it back up again. The boat surfaced without them, and a day later their bodies washed ashore near Navasota Blackburn's sandbar and she buried them in a secret place.

That left Izella with the kidnapped child to raise. "You ain't never going to amount to anything," she would tell him when he misbehaved. "You ain't nothing at all, and never will be nothing at all, because you don't want to be nothing at all." Eventually, he became accustomed to hearing that.

"That's right," he would say. "I ain't nothing, and I'm glad of it. I wouldn't want to be something for anything."

Mary Twitchell kept saying, "Izella, I believe that boy's half-way retarded."

But Izella refused to admit it. "My grandbaby's real smart," she said. "He'll be able to understand a lot of things most people have trouble with."

As soon as she considered Billy Wiggins old enough to know

about his parents, she tried to set him straight. "Some people have two sets of parents," she told him, "and you're one of those people who do. Your parents who were not your parents were swallowed up by the river, and your parents who are your parents are living somewhere nearby, but no one knows just where or how to find them." Billy Wiggins asked which set was the best and Izella told him, "Your parents who were not your parents were the best by far."

Billy grew up with that in mind, and when he was almost thirteen he decided it was time for him to see the place where the boat went down. Isaac took him not far upstream where the river had broken through one of its meandering curves. An oxbow lake was on one side and a break in the trees on the other.

"It was right about here where they went down," Isaac said, pointing with his fishing hat.

Billy Wiggins hung his head over the side of the boat. He had the feeling he was seeing all the way to the bottom of the river, but he wasn't. The water was too deep for that, too muddy too, but Isaac let him believe what he wanted.

"I see them down there," said Billy. Before Isaac knew it, the boy had jumped in. He went down and stayed down a long time. Then he came up and went down and came up and went down, and finally Isaac grabbed him by the hair and pulled him back into the boat. On the way home, Billy Wiggins said he went all the way to the bottom of the Sabine and opened up his eyes. Down there he saw a catfish twice as long as Isaac's boat. "On the back of that old fish I saw my father who's not my father and my mother who's not my mother," he said. "And I got to know them too. I got to know what they look like, and I got to know what they think like and I got to know a lot of other people who look and think just like them. Now, the place where all these people are living has its own name, a name you wouldn't naturally think of as being the name of a place. They call it Ain't Nothing At All, and the people who live there are called Ain't Nothing At All People, but if you don't have time to say their full name or just don't want to say their full name you can call them Not People just to get it over with. Now here's the way it is:

Every Halfway Not Person who dies and goes to Ain't Nothing At All gets a chance to become more of a Not Person than he could ever become just walking around on dry ground."

"I don't get it," said Isaac. His head was swimming from listening too hard.

"Then let me tell you another way," said Billy. "Some people have two sets of parents. That's the first thing you got to understand. There's the parents who bring you into this world, and they don't count. They don't count because they leave you alone and don't care a thing about you. Then there's the parents who take you out of this world, and they're the ones who do count. They do count because they're Not People. And because they're Not People, they're the very hardest ones to understand. Right at first it might seem like they don't know what they're talking about, but they do. Ain't Nothing At All is what's on their minds, and Ain't Nothing At All is what they're always talking about anytime they're talking."

"You lost me a long time ago," said Isaac, as they drifted down the Sabine. "I guess you're too smart for me today."

"I might be too smart for you every day," said Billy, "but that don't matter to me if it don't matter to you."

Isaac accused him of having too much mud on his brain, but Billy Wiggins said that he didn't have a drop of mud up there and never would because he knew what he knew, and he also knew what he didn't need to know.

What his knowing came down to was this: His father wasn't really his father and his mother wasn't really his mother, but they were more like his mother and father than his real mother and father would have ever been. No one had to tell him that, he just knew it. "There's a kind of kin that's a lot closer than blood kin, and that's the kind of kin we were to each other." He knew what he was talking about. He understood. And for a long time he wondered why no one else did.

Then he learned a new word. Lottie Faircloth, attempting to help him understand himself a little better, told him he was a *special* person. After that Billy Wiggins went around telling everyone exactly how special he was and how special he was sure to become. He said that he was not just special, but special in a special sort of way. *'Specially special,* he sometimes called himself, and was constantly on the lookout for anybody who came close to being 'specially like him.

Lottie Faircloth said that she felt like a complete failure because she had taught Billy Wiggins the meaning of a word he didn't need to know. But Billy Wiggins was certain that he needed to know the word because it was another way of describing people who were on their way to being Not People but didn't know it. He was one of those people, but he knew it, and that made him a halfway Not Person, or a 'Specially Special Person.

Oh how tired Lottie was of hearing it, and how she wished she could stop listening, but she couldn't. Billy Wiggins wouldn't let go of her ears. He told her there were a lot of people halfway like him, but not all the way like him. He kept a list of the people who hit the halfway mark, and from time to time he put them to test, just to make sure his instincts were correct. The list was kept in his head, and the test was never the same. "You can't test everybody the same way, and you can't test the same person the same way twice in a row." That was the rule he followed, and that's what he told Lottie.

"Billy Wiggins, don't you dare stand up and tell me how to test somebody." Lottie Faircloth just hated for anybody to lecture to *her.* "I happen to be a schoolteacher, and let it be known that I know how to give a test."

"So do I," said Billy Wiggins. "I just gave you one. I told you something you were supposed to understand, and you didn't understand it, and that was your test, and you didn't pass, and now, I can't give you another one because you failed too bad."

"Well, that's the only test I've ever failed in my entire life," said Lottie. "And I'm glad I failed it too. If I had to take it over again, I'd try to give the exact same answer, whatever it was."

* * *

There were people Billy Wiggins tested over and over, and there were people he never tested at all because he could tell with one glance that they would never measure up. Of those who were tested, almost all of them failed, and for different reasons. Redd kept too much loose change rattling around in his pockets. "Anybody who cares about Ain't Nothing At All can't care that much about money," Billy Wiggins said. He added Redd's name to the list of failures. The list also included Izzie Burrow because he picked up empty bottles. "If he was the kind of person he ought to be, his bottles would have something in them," Billy said. That made Izzie a complete, nonretestable failure. Mary Twitchell was in the same boat. She talked too much and told everything she knew, and Peg Leg was partially to blame because he allowed her do it. Boyce was too mean to measure up. Bunyon Bostic's feet were too ugly. Brother Caldwell read the Bible too much, and Doc Broom failed because he was messy and smelly and wore a hairnet to control his thoughts.

"People ought not to be behaving the way they do," Billy said.

Izella Wiggins didn't have the slightest idea what he was talking about. Now she was certain that he was perfectly crazy and to be pitied, and that put her way below the halfway mark on Billy Wiggins' mentally kept list. "The boy thinks he's the smartest human who ever walked the earth," said Izella. "And here he is running around without a brain. He don't know nothing."

But Billy took up for himself. "You're talking about another kind of knowing," he said. "My kind of knowing is different. I know things without having to be told I know them, and that's the important thing. That kind of knowing is the only kind of knowing that's worth anything. That kind of knowing gets passed down from your people who are not your people, not from the people who are your people. It gets passed down some way I can't explain real good. It just does." He waved his arms in the air when he talked this way, and his eyes sometimes rolled back in their sockets.

LeRoy Redd was sure Billy Wiggins was epileptic, but he had never had a seizure. "All he does is talk wild talk," said Izzie Burrow. "We've got that to be thankful for. Some days he's just like his father who wasn't his father, and other days he's just like his mother who wasn't his mother. Some days he looks like both of them at the same time and acts like them too. That's the puzzling thing. Makes you wonder how it happens."

But what was puzzling to Izzie wasn't puzzling at all to Billy Wiggins. He had everything figured out and was on his way. "Once you know what I know, you have to help these things get better known and stay better known." That was what he lived by. His father, Izella's only son who was not his father, would have wanted it that way, and his mother who was not his mother would have wanted it that way too. That's why he tested people. He had to find out who *was*, but what was more important, he had to find out who was *not*.

Occasionally, someone would come along he wasn't sure about and he didn't know how to test. Isaac Overstreet was one of them, but eventually Billy Wiggins found a way.

* * *

Isaac was fishing upriver when a limb from an overhanging tree fell on his boat. He was knocked unconscious, and when he woke up, he was on Doc Broom's kitchen table having a gash in his head sewn up. Bessie was holding his head steady. And Peg Leg, who had seen Isaac's boat floating downriver, was inspecting the doctor's work.

"You go easy on Isaac now," ole Peg instructed. "Don't be doing one of your rush-up jobs like you did on me."

Doc Broom always performed his "slightly surgical operations" in the kitchen. He did everything except open the abdomen. That he had no interest in doing. He also had no interest in removing appendages, but John Twitchell had been an exception. Years ago, Mary's husband had been trapped under a log for half a day. When Doc Broom inspected the damage he said that he had no choice but to saw off the leg just above the kneecap.

"You could have left me more leg than what you did," Peg Leg said, while watching the doctor thread his needle again. "That's why I'm standing here. Isaac needs all the brains he's got."

"Who taught you how to sew?" Bessie said. "All you know how to do is lose your thread." She took the needle away from the doctor. "I can do that myself. I don't know why we came here." Bessie removed Doc Broom's stitches. She cut Isaac's hair on both sides of the wound, sterilized it with alcohol and started sewing. "This is the way it's done," she said. "You better watch." Her stitches were small and evenly placed. The gash started at Isaac's forehead and ended at the back of his neck. It took her eighty-eight stitches to close it.

Isaac's recovery was slow. He was plagued with dizziness and blackouts. Walking in a straight line was sometimes impossible, and headaches became a daily occurrence. It was too dangerous for him to be alone on the river, so he took a part-time job at the sawmill. "People can keep an eye on you there," Doc Broom told him.

Lester Jenkins hired Billy Wiggins and Isaac on the same day. Billy's job wasn't really a job, but it gave him something to do and kept him out of the way. "My job is part of somebody's test," he said. He was supposed to walk around and make sure all the men were wearing their hats while working in the sun. Billy took his duty seriously and so did Isaac. Lester had hired him to grade lumber with a blue pencil, which Isaac kept needle sharp.

"All you have to do," Lester had told him, "is inspect every board that comes out of this mill. Make a check on every piece of lumber that's ready to be carried down to the river and loaded. If it's an odd size, mark a line through the check. If there's any kind of flaw in the wood, mark a line through that check too. All the bad pieces get loaded last."

Isaac thought he could handle that. He was proud to be working for a company and determined to do his best. He said it was the first real job he had ever had, and he meant to take it seriously. But the pressure of grading the lumber accurately was, at times, more than he could endure. During the heat of the day he suffered headaches that slowed him down. Black spots swarmed before his eyes. "Where did all these flies come from?" he would say, swatting the air with both hands. From the corners of his eyes he could see rainbows, and just above his head there was always movement of some kind, but he wasn't able to focus on it. Occasionally, he would sit down before he fell down, and sometimes he would see his thoughts in the air before he was aware of thinking them. He no longer enjoyed a restful night's sleep. He had nightmares about boatloads of lumber getting away without blue markings.

Doc Broom said that Isaac was going to run himself down if he wasn't careful, so he prescribed a tonic to produce both mental and physical stamina overnight.

Bessie took a sip of it and said that it smelled like creasote and tasted like kerosene and would certainly ruin the healthiest of minds. She poured it out.

"It's supposed to make a new man out of me," said Isaac.

"The old man was just fine," Bessie assured him. But Isaac was determined to show his wife that he could be successful in something other than fishing.

"Fishing is plenty good enough," she said. "Your place has always been on the water, and pretty soon you'll be able to return to it. You can be yourself there."

But Isaac disagreed. He continued taking his sawmill job to heart, going over and over every plank to make sure it was marked with a check that was not too large and not too small and always in the same place, a thumb length from the end of the board.

Billy Wiggins studied the way Isaac held his pencil. He used all four fingers and a thumb to steady it and made deliberate checks that cut into the wood. He sharpened the pencil after each time he used it, and that impressed Billy until he took a closer look at the damage done to the boards. That told him a lot. "Mr. Overstreet's bearing down too hard. He's trying to learn something he ain't supposed to know and don't ever need to know."

Billy Wiggins gave Isaac some advice: "When you find out what you're supposed to do, and where you're supposed to do it, and what you're supposed to know and when you're supposed to know it, you'll be a lot better off because then you can be relaxed about doing things. Right now you're still looking for your natural place. You don't know nothing about the place I know about, and you ain't supposed to know about it either, but you do have it in you to know about another kind of people and another kind of place. Everybody's got to know his place, and I do and you don't, and that's the big difference between us."

"I'd say that's a mighty big difference." Isaac painstakingly graded a board and spoke without looking up.

"Even if I don't know nothing about the place you're supposed to know about, I can still help you know about it." Billy Wiggins smiled, showing his swollen gums and little round teeth. "I can help you a lot."

But Isaac didn't want Billy's help or anybody else's, except Doc Broom's. "Your big problem," Broom told him, "is a bad case of the blahs coupled with a total lack of self-confidence. Confidence is something that's mighty hard to find and impossible to look for. I don't imagine your accident helped you much, either."

Because Isaac worried constantly about his job, Doc Broom prescribed a tonic to help him sleep and told him to come back if it didn't work. Isaac promised to take the proper dosage, but most of the time he drank straight from the bottle. The tonic didn't make him sleep, it kept him awake, kept him pacing the floor and worrying about his job. Now, it would often take him an hour to examine a plank and grade it. Often he would grade the same board four times without realizing it. Finally, Lester Jenkins told him to go back to fishing, which he did, but only when he needed money for Doc Broom's remedies.

He would buy several bottles of tonic at once and hide them from Bessie, but she would usually find and empty them. It exhausted her to keep up with all his hiding places, all the tree stumps, the loose boards, the hollow logs. He even hid bottles under the house where the Rhode Island Reds were being fattened. But when he started burying them in the sand and river mud, Bessie gave up the search.

The weight of supporting the family had fallen upon her shoulders. Zeda Earl was on her way again, and this time it was Bessie who wasn't ready. "If there's anybody in the world I'd like to kill," she told her pets, "it's Doc Broom."

A few days later, Zeda Earl changed her mind for the third time. Bessie told no one. She buried the child next to the other two. "Zeda's got a lot of graves waiting for her," Bessie said. "But one day, she'll finally make it."

Along about that time, Doc Broom changed the ingredients in Isaac's tonic. He stopped worrying, stopped pacing nervously to and fro and at night he would go to sleep and wake up in the same position. He laughed frequently, meditated on the clouds and sat quietly while his daughters entertained him.

The Ruby-Jewels read their poems to him, and he liked that, but more than anything else, he enjoyed hearing Bible stories about angels. At times, after they had read to him for hours, he would close his eyes and see the archangels circling his house.

Then he would take a bottle of Doc Broom's tonic down to the river and sit under a certain mimosa whose branches fanned out in all directions. There he would wait for evening, when the mimosa's leaves would slowly begin to close up for the night. A fragrant moisture would then drop from the pink flowers and the sleeping leaves and fall onto Isaac's upturned face.

The tree's roots formed a perfect chair. Isaac called it a chariot. And on days when the leaves went to sleep in the late afternoon and the night winds blew up earlier than usual, Isaac would command the chariot to move and it would. Taking the entire tree as a canopy, the chariot floated above the river on its way to nowhere.

Soon Isaac and the flying mimosa attracted the attention of a very old angel whose sense of navigation was no longer what it had been. The angel's attention span had diminished to a paltry state, and his lack of wing-to-wing coordination sent him crashing into the river when he saw Isaac and the flying tree gliding with the nighthawks over the Sabine.

"You better watch where you're flying," Isaac said, fishing the angel out of the water with a branch.

Mary Twitchell heard the commotion and leaned out her bedroom window. "Isaac's out there beating the river with a stick," she told Peg Leg. "It seems like ages since he's been in his right mind."

The angel settled himself on the tree roots, while Isaac lit a cigarette and held it so his wet visitor could take long puffs.

"Poor ole Isaac's offering somebody a cigarette, and there

ain't nobody there." Izzie Burrow was standing on his back porch taking it all in.

Billy Wiggins was drawing water from the well. "There ain't nobody there you can see," he said. "But that don't mean there ain't nobody there."

"Boy, you're sure smart today, ain't you?" said Izzie.

"At least you know that much, but still that's not enough," Billy answered.

Down on the river Isaac was lighting another cigarette. This time for himself. "I believe you got yourself a new friend," he said to the angel. "I don't know what I'll do if you're not friendly, though, teach you to be, I guess."

The old angel turned out to be quite a talker and that suited Isaac just fine because he was a listener. Before long they were constant companions. Each evening they would sit side by side under the raining mimosa or upright in bed. The angel's feathers were always ruffled and muddy, and his once-fine raiment was threadbare, but Isaac didn't mind. "I'll still be seen with you anyway," he said. "I'm not proud." Neither was the angel. He willingly admitted that he could no longer fly like he used to. His joints were stiff with arthritis and his eyesight was bad. He was forever tripping over his feet or scratching for fleas in public. And, since his banishment to earth, he was unable to control his temper, so he warned people that he sometimes threw fits, and other things, until he felt better.

"It's hard being a divine creature," he told Isaac, "because people have forgotten how to commiserate. Everybody on earth expects too much of me these days. They don't even like the way I play the Jew's harp anymore." He claimed he had not been able to settle in a single place for very long without being run off. "They threw eggs at me over in the other county," he shouted, flapping his wet wings and stirring a breeze in the branches of the mimosa, which had already gone to sleep. "Can you imagine anyone doing a thing like that in this day and age? Nobody, but *nobody*, respects an angel anymore. All they want you to do is shine, and be a good example and carry an important message."

The old angel said that he could not remember his heavenly

name, but on earth he was called You-So-'n'-So, a name he didn't understand at all. Every time he slept in flower beds or sprawled over watermelon vines, he'd wake up to someone calling him that name. But he didn't like the sound of it so he changed it to Saint So-'n'-So. This made him feel more important and brought him a few friendships that were short-lived.

By then he had developed a terrible odor, and a petulance that only Isaac could tolerate, so they became the best of friends. For hours, they would sit under the mimosa and sing, "This world is not my home, I'm just apassing through."

In the evenings when the mimosa dropped its fragrant rain, Bessie would sometimes feel the need to sit with her husband and hold his hand. She would join him under the tree, and listen to him singing with the angel, but she would not sing with them. "Musical ability is not a gift from this world," she said. "It comes from someplace else."

At times she could almost hear the angel's voice. She could not see the divine creature, but unlike everyone else she did not deny the old angel his existence. "I have always believed in the visitation of angels," she told her neighbors. "Sometimes they come through our doors when we least expect them. Sometimes we don't know they're angels until they've said good-bye. I believe the Bible has that in it somewhere."

"Bessie seems to be getting more like Isaac every day," said Izzie Burrow. "I think his state of mind is rubbing off on her."

"Makes you wonder if it could happen to the rest of us," said Izella. A chill ran up her spine.

"I'll be able to see that ole angel one of these days," Bessie told her husband as they sat beneath the tree. "At times, I can already hear him, and that's the first step. When he trusts me like he trusts you, he'll let me see what he looks like, and if he's as dirty as you say, the first thing I'm going to do is give that Saint So-'n'-So a cake of soap and a tub of hot water. That'll fix him."

"We think angels can take care of themselves, but that's not always so," said Isaac. "The Bible says they were created a little bit higher than man, but not much."

"Poor ole Isaac's lost all concern for life," Izzie Burrow said.

"Grading lumber will do it to you every time. That's why I had to give up the job. It got to me pretty quick."

"I'm afraid Bessie's not far behind him," said Clarence Pritchard, who was still a bachelor. "It's pitiful what's happening to that woman."

"Ain't pitiful neither," said Billy Wiggins. "Anybody who can get along with flowers and birds can't be pitiful. And Mr. Overstreet too. He just passed the test he once failed so bad. Anybody who can talk to an angel the way that man does, don't need no more testing."

* * *

There were two people Billy Wiggins refused to test. One was Elsa Mae Broom. He refused to test her because he was afraid she'd fail, and he didn't want her to. And the other person he refused to test was Bessie Overstreet. He refused to test her because he was afraid that she would outmeasure him, and he wasn't ready for that, because for the longest time he was the only one there was, the only one he wanted there to be. He was more than halfway. He was almost equal to his father who was not his father and his mother who was not his mother. Now he was realizing that there were others, if not just like him, almost just like him. He was not alone. He could sometimes find comfort in this.

Without having to be told, Billy Wiggins knew, beyond a doubt, that Bessie Overstreet didn't come from Ain't Nothing At All. She came from some other place, some place that was just as good. At times, he wondered if her place was better than his. That it might be worried him. He decided the only thing to do was to learn as much about her as possible, so he began following her around. He carefully matched his feet with the footprints she left in the sand, studying each print as he inched along from one to the next. His feet were almost twice as long as hers, and when he stepped into her tracks and looked behind him, they weren't her tracks anymore. This was his way of getting to know where she came from. "Pretty soon now, I'll find out," he would say to no one in particular.

Bessie kept a close eye on him. She watched him watching her and wondered if he was as aware of being watched as she was. Each day he came a little closer, and finally, he was standing on the edge of her gardens and mentally recording her every move.

Occasionally, she would stop hoeing, bend down to pick up a feather and put it in her hair. Her pets were molting, and every time they dropped a feather she would save it. She had jars and envelopes filled with feathers she didn't know what to do with but refused to throw away. Even the bun on the back of her head had feathers in it.

"I'm trying to think the way you think, Mrs. Overstreet," Billy said. His eyes were burning a hole through her. "But you're not letting me, are you? You got too many feathers in your hair to let me see your thoughts."

"Why would anybody want to see my thoughts?" asked Bessie, using her hoe for support.

"I'm trying to see who you really are and where you really come from," Billy Wiggins said. His eyes didn't move. "I'm trying to place you." He wanted to blink, but his eyes were fastened to Bessie's, and he refused to break the connection. To blink at a time like this, he felt, was a sign of weakness, so he squinted instead. "I think I'm ready to know about you now."

The cranes, old and nearly blind, stood between them and spread their almost featherless wings as if to protect their keeper from Billy Wiggins' bloodshot eyes.

"I'm going to give you something to look at and study," Bessie said, plucking a single flower, a Lemon Lily she had developed to the size of her hand. "What do you see here?" she asked.

"Nothing," Billy answered.

"That's not so," Bessie said. "Tomorrow when it closes up it will seem like nothing, but today it's one day away from seeming. Today it's in its glory."

Billy Wiggins examined the lily. It now seemed small in his overgrown hands. "You can look inside a flower and see everything in the world, can't you, Mrs. Overstreet?"

"I can look inside a lily," said Bessie, "just any lily out here, and see *you*. That's what I can see. Every time you aggravate somebody, I can really see you. I want you to remember that, especially if you take the notion to start chasing my girls around again."

"If you'll teach me how to look inside one of your flowers and see Elsa Mae Broom, you'll never have to worry about me aggravating nobody, no matter how mad they make me."

"For you that won't be too hard," Bessie said, stooping to collect another feather. "But you won't be able to see Elsa Mae right away. You'll have to prepare yourself, and that might take some time. The first thing you have to learn is how to be still long enough for your mind to go blank and then start filling up with pictures. It helps if you have something to look at while you're sitting. It doesn't have to be much, a dot on a piece of paper will do. Oh, you'll start off saying, 'Well, this is just a dot on a piece of paper,' but if you look at it long enough it won't be a dot anymore. The more you look at it, the more you'll see what's not there but really is. Sometimes when you study something long enough, especially something that doesn't have much to it, you can take your understanding a step or two beyond where you thought your understanding could go—maybe it's a step or two you never even thought about taking. Sometimes you don't see pictures, you just see your thoughts. Thoughts look different than pictures. Sometimes I look at a lily just opened up and petals are all I see right at first. Then I let my mind settle down, and I see a whole lifetime in something that only lasts a day."

"I hope one day seems a lot longer to one of your flowers than it does to me," said Billy.

"Sometimes a day can seem like a very long time," said Bessie, "especially if something's troubling you. Then at other times a day is very short. Everything has its deceiving side. Tomorrow another lily will open up and take the place of the one that's bloomed today. Tomorrow's lily will bloom on the very same stalk, almost in the very same place, and at first you're liable to think it's the same flower, but it's not. The spirit is the same, but the flower is different. Still, I can look inside it and see you anytime I need to. I've been studying you all this time. You didn't know it, though."

"Did you know I come from a place called Ain't Nothing At All?" Billy asked, throwing back his shoulders.

"Oh yes," said Bessie, "I knew that. Ain't Nothing At All is a good place to come from. If you start out with nothing, you're bound to find something along the way. It's just like that dot on a piece of paper I told you about. You either have to start out studying nothing until it becomes something or you start out studying something until it becomes nothing. Either way you end up with the same thing."

"I believe I need something to study that reminds me of Nothing At All," said Billy. "You've got yourself something to study, but I don't."

Bessie handed him another lily, this time a bright orange one. "This ought to keep you busy for a while," she said. "Just start studying it and see what you see."

For days Billy Wiggins spent all his time thinking about Elsa Mae and dreaming into the center of a lily. "Whatever he's doing, I'm thankful it's harmless this time," said Lester Jenkins. He dismissed Billy from the sawmill job. "It seems to me like you've got other more important things on your mind," Lester said. "You better go tend to them." Billy thanked him kindly and retreated with a bouquet in hand to Izella's back porch.

From her gardens, Bessie could see him fidgeting. "It's very hard to sit still, Billy," she shouted to him. "But if you don't be still nothing good can ever happen to you."

That afternoon her gardening gave her more pleasure than it ever had, because at last everyone in her world seemed to be happily occupied at once. Not far away, under the mimosa that had not yet started to rain, Isaac was telling the oldest living angel that a bath in hot soapy water would restore luster to his wings.

Inside the store Redd was counting his money out loud. If he counted silently he would forget his totals, but if he spoke the numbers into the air they did not escape his memory, even on a hot day. On the sandy ground under the store, directly beneath Redd's feet, the Ruby-Jewels were watching Elsa Mae Broom please Clarence Pritchard. Peter Faircloth was with them. He hated it under the store. There were too many dirt dobbers, sand fleas and wasps buzzing about, but the Ruby-Jewels wouldn't let him leave. They said that Elsa Mae was about to teach them something that they needed to know.

Everyone was doing something. Lottie Faircloth was writing a letter. Izella Wiggins was baking a cake. And Doc Broom, wearing nothing but underwear and a hairnet that Mary Twitchell had lost in the store, was sitting on his porch. His portable laboratory was spread out on an ironing board balanced on his lap. Herbals were left open and scattered around his feet.

Down on the Sabine Izzie Burrow had just found a bottle with a dollar bill inside it and was looking for another one. Boyce Faircloth was shooting turtles as they came up for air. And not far away, Brother Caldwell was reading the Book of Revelations to his chickens. He was sure that the word of God would make them start laying again. Mary Twitchell had taken the afternoon off to dye her hair. Red was her favorite color.

At the mill the saws were buzzing away. The smell of pine and cedar settled over Camp Ruby like an intoxicating cloud that pushed away the problems of the afternoon. It seemed to Bessie that the entire world was busy doing something, and she was glad. "It doesn't matter how important it is," she told her pets, "just as long as we're occupied, otherwise we might forget how to reason."

For days on end everyone stayed busy and out of everyone else's way. There was energy in the air. Bessie could touch it with the tips of her fingers. No one else noticed it enough to comment on its being there, but everyone was caught up in a storm of activities. Chores that had been postponed were now being tackled. Old linoleum was ripped up and thrown away and floorboards were scrubbed with sand and hot water until they glistened. Porches were leveled, and rooftops were patched. Screen doors were mended, and new curtains were stitched up and hung in place.

When the frenzy let up, Billy Wiggins emerged with a nervous feeling of being unoccupied, so he looked for something else to challenge his mind. Flowers were not the answer. "They don't do for me what they do for Mrs. Overstreet," he said. Flowers wilted too fast, and he was always having to break his concentration by getting up and picking a fresh one. That annoyed him, so he decided it was time to go on to the next step. He asked Redd for a blank piece of paper, but Redd wouldn't part with a scrap. Billy settled for a used brown paper sack instead. On it he drew a dot with a piece of coal, and for days he did nothing but stare at the dot until his eyes crossed and his head ached. That's when he joined Isaac on the river.

Isaac was rolling cigarettes and listening to the old angel complain. The mud-spattered creature was searching for fleas in his feathers while recounting the story of his banishment to earth. He said he had taken up residency in the city of Sodom, and as punishment for his week of debauchery, he had been sentenced to a place called Hell on Earth. "Before I knew it, the lights on my halo went out," said the angel. "My feathers turned a dull brown, fleas got bedded up under my wings and I haven't been able to get rid of them to save my life. Now my toenails are growing. And nobody's razor is sharp enough to trim them."

"You haven't found the place where you can calm down and be yourself and learn a thing or two about your new life," Isaac told the angel.

"Oh, yes I have," said Billy Wiggins, settling himself next to Isaac. "Right now I'm trying to go one more step. I'm trying to find a place that reminds me of my place, because my real place is somewhere I can't get to real fast, so I've got to have something that reminds me of it and makes me think I'm there."

"Well, I'll try to put up with you while you're looking," Isaac said, still speaking to the angel.

"I 'preciate that," said Billy. He was holding the brown paper bag, but the dot was nothing more than a smudge.

"Just let me remind you of a few things," Isaac said, lighting two cigarettes at once. "You didn't mean nobody no harm when you took up with the wrong crowd, in the wrong place—that can happen to anybody once in a while—and the only reason you get yourself run off every time you settle somewhere is because you've stumbled into somebody else's place, and it reminds you of your own, but it's not."

"I don't have a place of my own anymore," the angel complained. "Nobody likes me. Nobody wants me around for very long at a time."

"Complain, complain, complain," said Isaac. "That's all I can get out of you anymore. It's enough to drive a sensible person out of his mind, so you better move on now. Go wander around until you find your own quiet place and calm down. You've made this place too noisy, but just remember, you can come back when you don't have so many bad memories."

The world's oldest living angel took Isaac's advice and flew away across the river. And for the longest time, he was not seen again.

Billy Wiggins took Isaac's advice also. For days he wandered aimlessly until he found a place that meant something to him. Bessie was the first to know about it. "I better come look at this place you're talking about," she said, dropping her hoe and cradling all three pets. They walked downriver to Rocky Shoals, and from there they waded to Whisky Island, where an abandoned still was covered with vines.

The island was overgrown with cypress, saw brier and sweet bay. Rattan vines hung from every tree. Spider lilies were blooming near the shore and snowy orchids in the shadows. On a sandy point Billy stopped abruptly as if something Bessie could not hear had told him to. They sat down on the wet ground. The cranes, fighting for a place on Bessie's lap, whistled in high, windy tones until she gave them bread crumbs from her pocket.

"I'm fixing to tell you about me now," Billy said, pointing upstream. "Way, way up there where you can't see good is a little piece of place where the trees thin out, and the water, and the ground and the sky nearly touch but don't. It's a little bitty silver piece of a place that ain't water and ain't sky and ain't ground. Ain't Nothing At All is what you call it. Now this is the way it goes: Every Not Person is born there. He spends his first life on the ground. He spends his next life in the water. He spends his third life up in the air. Then he gets to go home to that piece of a place where all three places are the same place. That's sometimes called the Home Place, or the Starting Off Place, or the Ending Up Place or you can just call it Ain't Noth-

ing At All and get it over with. So you see, now I have something
to look at that reminds me who I am, and why I am and where I
am going next."

Bessie thought for a long time before she spoke. "What will
you do . . ." She hesitated before deciding to go on, ". . .
when the trees grow up and the earth, and sky and water don't
touch anymore?"

"If that happens," Billy said, "I won't have nothing to look at
that reminds me of where I come from."

At that moment Bessie saw into the near future. The door was
opened only wide enough for her to see a small slice of what was
to come. "Oh, Lord," she said out loud. The fatigue of knowing
passed from her body into the cranes and their necks drooped
like wilting vines over her shoulders.

Every spring and summer, for the next few years, she would
travel upstream in her boat. She would find the place where the
sky, water and earth almost touch and clear away the under-
growth, the saw briers, the saplings and the youpon. The Ruby-
Jewels usually accompanied her. All day they would work hard
until every tree, bush and blade of grass had been cut and
burned.

Drifting downstream after all the work, Bessie would lean
back in her lily boat and dangle her long legs in the water. She
would again remember aloud to her children the first day she
had seen Isaac. She would again point to the very spot where
she had stood and where his boat had come ashore. She would
remember how happy she had been to be riding off with him,
and how she had known in her heart that she was doing the right
thing. She would also look toward Sabinetown and try to imagine what it would be like to still be living there. She would
wonder what her sisters were doing, and how many children
they had. But she had no desire to see them. Approaching the
sandy cliffs that had become her home, she would think of Billy
Wiggins sitting on the sandbar, staring upriver to the place they
had just cleared. And she would hear him in her mind: "Ain't
Nothing At All is what you call it because there ain't nothing

there except where I used to be and ain't no more, so there's
something there after all, but it ain't nothing really."

And she would smile and say to her children, "We've made
him happy a little while longer."

PART FOUR

*Just Like It,
Only Better*

On a stifling afternoon in July, Bessie conceived again. The river was low. Fish were floating on their sides, or washing up dead on the parched and cracking mudbanks. No breeze could be felt, and hardly a creature stirred. Lottie Faircloth came down with a sick headache. "Now you see what kind of suffering Daughter's been doing with her head," said Doc Broom. He was practicing medicine on his front porch that day. It was the coolest place he could find. He examined Lottie's eyes and listened to her heart. Then he sent her home with an envelope of powders. "That ought to make her sleep about eight hours," he said, stripping down to his underwear.

"Fourteen if she's lucky," came Elsa Mae's voice from inside the house. She was trying to calm her boys as well as her nerves.

Across the way, Isaac was dreaming beneath the mimosa, and the Ruby-Jewels were napping under the store. Peter Faircloth was with them. They were hiding him from his father, who was angry because Lottie was sick.

Lester closed down the sawmill. The workers and their families gathered in the commissary. It was like a cool cavern on hot days, but Redd still found the need to wrap a wet towel around his neck. "Dog days are coming early this year," he said, marking a few cents off on items he wanted to get rid of.

Everyone was going in slow motion except Bessie. Her cranes

had just died, and to keep from missing them too much, she had been spending long hours in her gardens.

The cranes had lived twenty-two years. "That's three years less than what Navasota says they're supposed to," said Bessie. "I wonder if I didn't feed them right."

At the very last the three birds had lost most of their feathers. Bessie had wrapped them in chicken down and soft flannel and had fed them by hand. But there was no way of saving them at that point. "They're too old," she had said. "It's more merciful to let them die." She stopped feeding them for a day and the weakest bird died the next morning in her arms. But the other two had more energy than ever. As Bessie held the dead crane in her arms, she wondered if it had bequeathed some of its last remaining strength to the other two. Late that evening the survivors began whistling in a low, windy voice that Bessie had never heard before. "They're using their extra strength to grieve themselves to death," she told Isaac. "Grief will just about kill you every time. It's best to get ready for it way in advance. But who can do that?"

The last two cranes died in her arms also, and the next morning, Bessie buried all three birds just outside Zeda Earl's fenced-in cemetery. "Tell Miss Zeda Earl that we're still looking for her," she said as she covered the birds with sand. "Tell her it's not too late yet."

She was lost without her pets, but she refused to mourn. "There are better things to be done," she said, stirring the ground around her lilies. "Three more eggs have to be found and hatched. These plants have to be watered. The Jewels need new dresses. Isaac needs just about everything I can think of. And I sure would like to paint this house before it rots down."

She looked up at the sun. It was bone white. She had been gardening nonstop since dawn, and she wasn't through yet. The lilies were in full bloom, and she was selecting the strongest plants and pulling up the rest. Only the hearty were allowed to live. Bessie worked with a cold eye. Her judgment was stern. Down on her hands and knees with her notebooks at her side, she examined a Maroon Night. "These lilies are too small," she said, still talking to her pets. She compared the flowers of two plants. "They're just alike in color, only this one is bigger, better shaped and healthier too. This plant can stay. But this one has to go." She pulled it up by its roots and threw it onto a pile of others just like it. On and on she went, from one color to the next, culling out the lilies that would weaken the strain.

Toward midafternoon she stood up to puzzle over a sudden drop in temperature. Her skin tingled, her mouth dried out and what felt like an autumn wind blew a cold shiver across her back. Before long she lost her reasoning, and when she started regaining it again, she was sitting on Doc Broom's steps. The whole world seemed to be spinning without her.

"I feel drunk," she said, not knowing who she was talking to. Doc Broom, hurrying to put on his pants, replied, "Well, Bessie, maybe you are and don't know it yet."

"I'm too dizzy to stand up anytime soon," she said.

"Good," he told her. "I don't want you to." Then he started scratching his double chin and pacing the porch. "Dizziness," he said, "can be a mighty serious thing if allowed to go undiagnosed, so I suggest we start off with a full examination. Won't hurt a bit."

He walked her through the house, sat her on the kitchen table and gave her what he called a mild medicinal dissolved in a full glass of water. "Drink it all in one swallow while I listen to your heart." He adjusted his stethoscope. "If you get any dizzier just fall back on the table. That won't hurt you none."

After Bessie drank the water, she passed out on the table. Then, Doc Broom tiptoed into another part of the house, where Elsa Mae was trying to catch her two sons. "Daughter," he whispered, to keep his voice from traveling too far. "Bessie Overstreet's out in the kitchen, and I'm about to give her a full-fledged examination from head to toe, so promise me you'll leave us alone for a little bit, you hear?"

"Have fun," said Elsa Mae. She was feeling a bit dizzy herself and wondering if it would hurt her any to take another aspirin. She had already taken eight dissolved in a bottle of Coke.

According to her father, Elsa was suffering from broken skin and thin blood, coupled with a weakness in her Lady's Department. He was sure her system couldn't be straightened out, but he was determined to keep experimenting with tonics and regulators until he stumbled upon a cure. "Whatever it takes to settle you down is all right with me, Daughter," he had told her, "just as long as it don't involve more children."

On the afternoon of Bessie's examination, Elsa Mae was about to have a screaming fit, and her two sons, Virgil and Robert Douglas, were making matters worse by throwing rocks inside the house.

"God, just promise me you won't let anything bad happen to my boys until I get my nerves back in shape," she said, locking her sons in their bedroom. All she wanted to do was sit on the front porch and nurse her headache. But she didn't get to. On her way to the steps, she caught a glimpse of that sandy-haired fisherman she'd been just dying to meet. He was rowing upriver, and on seeing him, her interest in life returned. She ran down the hill and stood kneedeep in the water. "You better stop and pay attention to me this time," she shouted, waving her arms in the air. That day the fisherman responded. He rowed toward her. She waded out to meet his boat, and pulled it ashore.

"I'm about to show you my promise, whoever you are," she said, taking the man by the arm and leading him to the back of Redd's commissary. "If you want to see my promise as bad as I think you do, you'll have to crawl."

Billy Wiggins watched her disappear under the store. The fisherman followed her. And when they reached a place where Elsa Mae was fairly sure no one could see them, she unbuttoned her dress and took it off. She wasn't wearing anything else. Then, she leaned back and slowly opened her legs, gradually revealing her promise a little bit at a time.

The fisherman tore off his clothes. Elsa Mae helped him. And when he was completely undressed, she said, with disappointment, "I thought you'd be more promising than that." She pointed and squinched up her face. "But now that we've gone to all this trouble, I guess you'll have to do."

"I ain't never seen nobody as white-skinned as you," he said, totally amazed. "You don't have no color." She answered by licking her lips all the way around. "Your tongue don't have no color on it, either."

"Look at yourself and see if you're perfect," she said, putting an *I don't care about you one bit* expression on her face. That was all it took. He fell upon her like a starving animal, and she squealed and kicked the bottom of the store. That thrilled Peter Faircloth and the Overstreet sisters. They were just waking up from their naps.

"Sister, my sister, this is the second time Elsa Mae's acted up under the store."

"She don't care where she acts up, Sister. You know that. Elsa Mae's got bees turned loose inside her. Be glad you don't."

"Now, Sister, you know perfectly well I don't intend to find myself in that kind of a fix."

"I am so thankful to hear you say that, Sister, because whatever kind of a fix you find yourself in, I'm liable to find myself in the very same one."

And they said together:

"Poor ole Elsa Mae."

"Poor ole Elsa Mae."

"Her promise is running away with her again."

"Her promise is running away with her again."

"I don't want to watch her anymore," said Peter Faircloth. "She's not at herself."

"When was she ever at herself?" asked a Ruby-Jewel.

"Never in her life," came her sister's answer.

They explained to Peter that Elsa Mae was giving a demonstration on what not to do, and what not to say and that he would profit by opening his eyes as well as his mind. With their thumbs and index fingers they forced Peter's eyes open and told him not to make a sound.

Not far away, Billy Wiggins was rounding up all the stray dogs and chasing them toward the store. "That man can't give Elsa Mae what she needs," he told the dogs. "But I can. And one day I will." Pretty soon every hound in Camp Ruby was under the store. They sniffed, and barked; ran their cold noses along Elsa Mae's legs and neck.

"I can't do this with dogs staring me in the face," she screamed, pushing the fisherman off her. "They got me out of the mood."

"I'm through anyway," he said.

"You were through before you ever got started," Elsa Mae informed him. She put on her dress, almost as fast as she had taken it off, told the man she had misjudged him something awful and the next time he wanted somebody's promise he could go looking for it under another store. She crawled out on the front side of the commissary. The fisherman followed her. She brushed herself off as best she could and said that she better go see about her children.

"I'd like to give you another one," he said. Mary Twitchell, sitting on the front steps, heard him.

"You probably already have," Elsa Mae answered. "It would be just my luck." Then he tried to kiss her good-bye, but she wouldn't let him.

"Never cared nothing about kissing," she confessed, and started back to her father's house. She had cobwebs in her hair, sand and chicken feathers stuck to the backs of her legs, but she didn't care. She needed another aspirin fast.

Mary Twitchell had heard it all. "Nine months from today." She counted on her fingers, while Billy Wiggins followed Elsa Mae home.

"You shouldn't let that man do to you what I'm supposed to do to you, Elsa Mae." Billy Wiggins grinned, showing his purple gums and little white teeth. "I'm the only one you're supposed to let do that."

She slammed the door in his face and locked it. He ran to the back, and that door was locked too. But the kitchen window was only partially covered. He could see all the way inside.

The medical examination was nearing an end, and Bessie was waking up. She was still lying on the table. Each leg was resting on the back of a chair, and a sheet was covering her. Doc Broom was under it. When he realized she was awake and trying to sit up, he patted her on the thigh and said, "Examination's almost over, Bessie. You don't need to stir around so quick. Just relax while I take this instrument out of you."

Elsa Mae stuck her head through the door and said, "Daddy, Billy Wiggins is watching you, I hope you know." Then she released her sons.

Doc Broom didn't hear her. He slipped out from under the sheet and pulled up his pants. He was redfaced and winded. His white hair was standing on end, and his fingers were trembling as he rearranged the sheet over Bessie's body. "I realize this is a terrible thing for a woman to have to endure," he said. "That's why I covered us up. You never know who's going to be looking in, or dropping in, or listening in, what with all our houses squeezed up so tight." He shooed Billy Wiggins away from the window. "Privacy is something that's missing in the world these days, Bessie. Ever stop to think about that? If you haven't, you ought to."

Bessie tried again to sit up, but Doc Broom handed her a pillow and told her to relax while he elaborated on his findings. "Bessie," he said, mopping his face with a corner of the sheet, "I'm tickled nearly 'bout to death to be able to tell you that you're the healthiest woman alive. I shined a flashlight all the way up to your lungs, and I tell you right now, you're clean as a whistle. Not a thing the matter with you. But if you want me to, I'll go back up in there with another kind of instrument and make double sure."

"I know what kind of instrument you're talking about," said Bessie, "and the answer is 'No.' " Her voice was very weak.

"Dreams, dreams, dreams," said Doc Broom, prancing around the table. "I don't have one patient who don't dream his head off. Never could tell fact from fiction could you, Bessie?"

"I can tell pretty good," she answered. She was still light-headed, but she managed to sit up, and a few minutes later, she was on her feet again. Reluctantly, Elsa Mae parted with an aspirin and walked Bessie home.

Mary Twitchell was still sitting on the steps of Redd's store. Inside, everyone else was discussing the heat that had descended upon them like the Devil's breath. "What they don't know," said Mary, "and what I ain't telling, is that it's now cooler outside than it is inside." Then she saw Elsa Mae walking Bessie home. "I wonder what Bessie was doing at Doc Broom's," she said. "She's walking like she's had some kind of operation. Must be the heat."

* * *

The thought of having Doc Broom's child disgusted Bessie. And she was certain that it was his. She felt the truth in the marrow of her bones, and in her joints that ached at night. Truth was revealed through her dreams, through a crying voice heard when her back was turned and through a stale odor that remained on her body through many washings. She knew the truth.

She prayed for an accident of some sort, just anything to keep from telling Isaac what had happened. In the first weeks of her pregnancy she jumped off porches and fell down steps. She bound herself with rags and tight corsets. She took long walks, starved herself to the bone and worked in the lily gardens till midnight. Still, the child in her womb thrived.

In the second month, she broke down and consulted Doc Broom. On the day she made this decision, the doctor was sitting on the porch with his portable laboratory. He was wearing a stained lab coat buttoned to his bare knees. Tuffs of white hair were springing through a black hairnet pulled over his ears.

Bessie, standing at the foot of his steps, waited for him to see her. Although he was aware of her presence, he kept right on working. Two herbals were propped open on his lap. They were both dog-eared. Pages were marked with strips of paper, pencils and bobby pins. Sentences were underlined again and again, and some were crossed out completely and rewritten to his liking. Notebooks were stacked at his feet. Test tubes were scattered around in buckets and tin cans and wire holders. On a small table to one side, fruit jars containing liquids and powders were arranged according to the date on their adhesive labels.

Doc Broom was bent on finding a way to regulate Elsa Mae's sexual drive and stop her headaches at the same time. So far, he was an admitted failure, but that afternoon he felt close to a new discovery.

Why, Bessie wondered as she stood on Doc Broom's run-down porch, should she be consulting someone she had no faith in, a man who had caused her more misery than he was worth? "I don't know who's in worse shape, Broom," she said. "You for sitting there like you don't know what's going on, or me for thinking you might be able to do something decent for a change?"

Doc Broom didn't look up from his work, but Elsa Mae stuck her head out the door and said, "Don't mind him, Mrs. Overstreet. If you didn't know no better, you'd think he knew what he was doing, but he don't. Just sit right down, and he'll look up when he gets good and ready."

Bessie sat down on a pine bench in front of Camp Ruby's only doctor, who was pretending to be buried in his favorite books. When he glanced up to turn a page, she leaned forward and said in a low voice, "I got something I want you to get rid of."

"So's Elsa Mae," he said, looking all the way up. "How in tarnation do women like you get yourselves in that kind of shape?"

While waiting for her answer, he turned his attention back to his herbals. And when he was sure she wasn't going to leave until he suggested something, he closed his books and said, not to Bessie but to the test tubes at his feet, "Well, maybe it's too late, and then again, maybe it's not. We'll just have to see, won't we?"

They moved into the living room where he went straight for the kerosene lamp. He removed the globe and the wick, poured some of the oil into a drinking glass and added equal parts vinegar and water. He handed Bessie the mixture, and when she refused to drink it, he suggested the next best thing: "We'll just have to wash a little bit of it up in you, Bessie. Won't hurt a bit. It's what I call slight surgery."

"I've had enough of your slight surgery," she snapped. "That's how I got in this shape."

"Bessie, Bessie, Bessie," said Doc Broom, more concerned over picking the dead skin off his elbow than what he was saying, "I don't know what I've done to make you say such a hateful thing as that."

"It's useless to talk to a fool, unless you're just as foolish," Bessie said. "I should have known that." She walked out without uttering another word. Doc Broom, his pregnant daughter and two grandsons stood on the porch and waved, but Bessie didn't look back.

"There goes the best woman in the world," Doc Broom said. "Trouble is she don't know it. I wonder how in thunder she got herself in such a fix."

"Bet you do," said Elsa Mae sarcastically, but her father pretended not to hear.

A few days later, Bessie paid a visit to Navasota Blackburn. Her energy was low that day, so she asked Billy Wiggins to row her across the river. "What you going to see ole Navasota for?" asked Billy when they started out.

"I have something I want to give her," said Bessie.

"She ain't taking it," Billy said. "Not if it's that baby you got."

"How do you know what it is?" asked Bessie.

"I can guess pretty good," said Billy. "I can also see pretty good, and I seen through the window. I seen Broom when he give it to you. I was there. I know when it happened, but I ain't told. Nobody else would understand if I told."

"Understand what?" asked Bessie.

"They wouldn't understand that your baby's got two fathers already. She's got the father who's not her father and the father who is her father. Just like me."

"Then let's let it be our secret, Billy," Bessie said.

Billy smiled as he rowed. His mouth seemed to cover most of his face. "I can talk to you like you got good sense, Mrs. Overstreet."

"I'm glad someone is smart enough to realize that," said Bessie. Her eyes were on a dark cloud that was moving in fast. Halfway across the river, a wind carrying the smell of rain almost forced them to turn around, but they persevered and kept on rowing. The waves were like hounds teeth, sharp-pointed and white, but the cloud moving in was black. Soon the water matched it. Lightning touched the earth on both sides of the river, and a walking rain blew across the water like a curtain of silk. Bessie watched it coming. She didn't hide her face from the rain, but Billy Wiggins buried his entire head in the neck of his shirt until the thunder that seemed to split the earth in half passed them by. The storm only lasted a few minutes, just long enough to charge the air and leave the world clean and crisp.

"I always did like the way the air feels after a storm," said Bessie. "So full of sparks, you can hold it in your hands." She watched the dark cloud following the course of the river. So did Navasota. She had kept her eye on the boat the entire time.

It was said that Navasota knew how to stop the throbbing of a tooth, hemorrhaging and headaches, although she had never been able to cure Elsa Mae Broom for more than a day. It was also said that she could put her hands on your abdomen and cure anything from indigestion to appendicitis, but when she heard about Bessie's problem, and the solution she wanted, Navasota turned her back and walked across the sandbar. When she reached the edge of the woods, she turned around again and said, "Bessie, I ain't never killed nothing on purpose, but that's not to say I don't know how to."

Then Navasota sat down on the sand and thought. Bessie sat down with her. Billy Wiggins, still watching the storm, remained in the rocking boat.

Navasota's head was tied up with a rag the color of dawn. She tightened the knot, and with the tip of a long fingernail she drew three circles in the sand. She sprinkled tobacco on top of them and, while studying the circles, she rolled a cigarette and smoked. The veins in her neck enlarged, and the wrinkles around her mouth deepened. "I can tell you how to make this child change father's in your womb, Bessie." Navasota was staring over Bessie's shoulder at a rainbow that was gradually beginning to form on the other side of the river. "Get back into you boat and do your own rowing in this direction." She drew a map of the river on the sand. "Follow this current. You'll recognize it. The boat will pitch. Let everything inside you get stirred up and mixed up and tangled up. Let yourself get sick. Then let yourself relax until you get to the island." Again she drew on the sand. "Get out and start looking for a big nest in the cypress. Billy Wiggins can get the eggs. You need three. Don't let them get cold."

For a little while she did not speak. When she finished smoking, she sprinkled more tobacco on the map and drew again.

"Take an old dress with long sleeves and fold it like this." Bessie watched Navasota's fingernail slice through the firm sand. "Put the eggs inside it and tie the dress low around your waist." She made a fist and touched her lower stomach. "Here," she said. "Tonight, give yourself to Isaac. But don't break the eggs. You will both dream dreams, and if the eggs hatch, the dreams will come true."

Then Navasota stood up. She took a few steps and disappeared into the woods. Bessie watched her vanish, as if she had dissolved into air and light. The woods were almost impenetrable at that point. Only Navasota knew the hidden paths. Bessie could not see her, but she could hear the movement of branches and the sound of twigs breaking underfoot.

When she returned to the boat, Billy Wiggins was still watching the storm move slowly up the river. In the distance lightning flashed and thunder split the world in another place.

"It's my turn to steer," Bessie said. "I don't mean to make you do all the work." She paddled until the current Navasota had described began rocking the boat.

"Don't be going this direction, Mrs. Overstreet," said Billy Wiggins. "Water Devils live out here. They got horns on their heads and long tails."

"Yes, and we're going to shake them up," said Bessie. The boat pitched and rocked. The current carried it sideways down the river, and soon it began to spin. Bessie felt as though her whole body was coming apart. Sickness swelled up inside her. She hung over the edge of the boat, her arms dragging in the rough water.

"Mrs. Overstreet," cried Billy Wiggins. "We don't need to be here, Mrs. Overstreet." He tried to row to calmer water, but the paddles splintered in the whirling current. Bessie was now lying on her back. The rainbow that Navasota had seen from the sandbar was completely formed. It stretched from one side of the river to the other and seemed to be circling the entire world.

"What a good sign," Bessie said as the boat drifted into peaceful waters. Soon it came ashore on Whisky Island.

The tops of the cypress were white with nesting birds, and the limbs were bending over with the weight of many eggs and young. "I sure miss my pets," Bessie said, waiting for her head to stop spinning. "I didn't realize how much I missed them until right now. Let's see if we can find some eggs; I want the best ones up there."

They tied the boat to a cypress knee, and found a fairly dry place to lie down. Above them were dozens of nests. Slowly, their eyes moved from one to the next until they had seen them all. "I believe that's it," said Billy, pointing to the nest that he thought was the strongest and most shapely.

"I believe you're right," Bessie said. "That's the best-looking one up there, so it has to have the best eggs in it. I sure can't afford to get stuck with sickly birds."

Billy climbed the cypress tree while Bessie, still lying on her back, watched him go. There were five eggs in that nest. Billy chose the three largest ones. He wrapped them in Spanish moss and tied them up in his shirt. Bessie kept them warm all the way home.

Alone in the sleeping porch, she tied the eggs in an old dress and strapped them to her body. That night she gave herself to Isaac, and the eggs remained unbroken.

"It won't take long for them to hatch," she told her husband before they went to sleep. "I can already feel some movement."

"When they peck their way out," said Isaac, "they're liable to take up with the first person they see. But I don't want to be the one they fix on, for I sure don't need three birds following me around."

That night they both dreamed of Zeda Earl. And the next morning Isaac said, "Do you think she could be on her way again?"

"Yes I do," said Bessie. "This is her last chance, and this time she'll make it. I dreamed about her too."

While the Ruby-Jewels took charge of all the cooking and cleaning, Bessie lay in bed hatching the eggs and dreaming of Zeda Earl. The twins wanted to assist with the hatching also, but Bessie refused. "I'm the first one they need to see," she said. "If they think there's somebody else in this house just like them, they won't ever be discontent. I know how to make them think that."

While she kept the eggs warm, Bessie passed her time by sewing all the white feathers she had collected onto an old winter coat. When she finished, the coat was completely covered with white plumes. She put it on and appeared briefly on the front porch.

Billy Wiggins was the first to see her. He ran all over the camp shouting, "Mrs. Overstreet's done turned into a bird!"

"I knew this was going to happen," said Izzie Burrow.

"You did not," screamed Lottie Faircloth. "Nobody did, not even me."

"Our Dear Bessie's about to have three birds and a baby," said a Ruby-Jewel.

"The baby's going to be our sister," said another Ruby-Jewel. "Papa said so."

Before long, the Overstreet house was filled with neighbors who didn't wait to be invited in. Bessie was in bed keeping the eggs warm, and her coat of feathers was hanging from a nail on the sleeping porch wall. The women stood around the coat, not knowing exactly what to say. The men remained at a distance.

"I can't help wondering what would happen to me if I tried it on," said Mary Twitchell. "Something tells me I might not want to know."

"If you put it on, you'll turn into a bird," said Billy Wiggins. He was standing outside a window and looking in.

"I'm not going to be one to disagree with that," said Peg Leg.

"Do you think this new coat will keep you warm, Bessie?" Izella inquired with some hesitation.

"It's not for warmth, Izella," Bessie answered.

"Well what's it for then?" asked Elsa Mae Broom. She was not yet beginning to show.

"It's for feeding the birds," Isaac said. "Bessie got three eggs strapped to her. And when they hatch she'll put on the coat, and they'll feel right at home with us."

"That's true, they will," said Lottie Faircloth. "I read it in a book a long time ago."

"She did not," said Boyce. "She's just saying that."

"Friends and neighbors," said Brother Caldwell, "if I could think of the right prayer, I'd pray it. But right now words won't come to me." He left the house shaking his head. For once he couldn't think of a thing to say, not even to God.

After a long silence on the sleeping porch Bessie announced that Zeda Earl was on her way again. "I'm determined she's to be born this time."

"And Zeda Earl's determined too," said Lottie. "And so are we."

"My daddy says your baby and my baby are going to be born at the same time," said Elsa Mae. "Maybe on the same day."

"How does he know that?" asked Izella.

"He figured it out some way," said Elsa Mae.

"I wonder if I know how," said Mary Twitchell. "Bet I do."

As everyone left the Overstreet house, Izella turned to Elsa Mae. "Wouldn't it be awful if Zeda Earl turned out to be a boy?"

"Wonder how Bessie would get herself out of that one," Elsa Mae said.

"That's not going to happen," Lottie Faircloth spoke up. "But if it did, Bessie would think of something, I'm sure."

In eleven days the cranes pecked their way out of the eggs, and Bessie put on the coat of white feathers to greet them for the first time. Then began the long arduous task of feeding. Clad in her feathered coat, Bessie raised her new pets on soft-spoken words, tender strokes and affectionate caresses with both hands. She fed them oatmeal and bread crumbs along with beetles and moths crushed and blended with warm milk. When they were big enough she gave them small tomato worms and slivers of sun perch. Just as she had planned, they refused to take food from anyone else.

Isaac, still happy from the concoction that Doc Broom continued to supply, brought food to the cardboard nest many times each day, and Bessie prepared it for the cranes. As they grew, so did Zeda Earl.

* * *

At three o'clock in the afternoon on the twenty-sixth of March, a baby came into the world. Elsa Mae Broom gave birth to a boy who was to remain nameless. She just couldn't decide what to call him. Her new son, born two weeks early, according

to Doc Broom, had eyes like the sandy-haired fisherman. "I
know who the father is," Elsa Mae was proud to announce. It
was the first time she had had that privilege. "Just don't anyone
ask me his name. I know him, but I sure don't know him that
well."

Almost a week later, on the last day of the month, Bessie went
into labor. The moment the child dropped in her womb a March
wind forced its way down the stovepipe and put out the fire in
her living room. At dawn, when Zeda Earl was born, the house
smelled of cold dusty ashes. And that, Bessie would always say,
was the reason why her third child was so cold-natured and why
her personality was on the chilly side, too.

Zeda Earl came crying into the world on an Easter Sunday
that fell on the first day of April. Around two in the morning a
storm with wind in it came racing up the river and deposited hail
and heavy rain on the tin roofs of Camp Ruby. Houses trembled
on their blocks, and lightning struck the mimosa growing in
Izella's backyard, split the tree to its roots and electrified the air.
Suddenly Izella's house was filled with light. She woke up instantly, thinking that her bed was on fire. Another thunderclap
sent her running to the store in her nightgown.

The store was considered the only safe place to weather wind
and heavy rain. Redd already had the front doors open and the
kerosene lamps burning. All over the camp, neighbors were
bundling up their children and entering the downpour. Screen
doors could be faintly heard slamming behind them.

Down on the Sabine, waterspouts were forming. Everything
on the surface of the river was sucked up into the air and deposited on land. Minnows, mud and sawdust fell from the night sky.
The temperature dropped suddenly and a cold, damp wind
drifted through Isaac's open windows and into his face while he
dreamed of deliverance.

A little while later, he was awakened by thunder and a commotion of voices outside. Everyone was hurrying to the store to
weather the storm. As they spoke, Isaac, even in a half sleep,
could recognize every one of them.

"Who threw all these little fish on the ground is what I'd like
to know?" That was Elsa Mae Broom.

"They just come falling out of the sky every once in a while."
That was her father. He was suffering a head cold.

"It just about always comes a cold snap around Easter." That
was Mary Twitchell. She was carrying a kerosene lamp.

"This is the night Elsa Mae's been waiting for, but she don't
know it yet." That was Billy Wiggins. He was standing on Izella's back porch and shouting into the night. The storm had
awakened him from a deep sleep. He had been dreaming of Elsa
Mae. "This is the night Elsa Mae's supposed to forget everything she knows about and go to remembering everything she
don't know about. She's about to find out who she is and where
she comes from. She's about to find out all about her and all
about me. She's supposed to."

His words carried into the sleeping porch, but Isaac couldn't
understand them. Unaware that Bessie had gone into labor, he
drifted back to sleep, but the Ruby-Jewels were awake and rush-
ing to get dressed. "This is the night we've been waiting for,"
they assured each other.

They had already chosen their clothes for the occasion and
had set them aside: shirtwaist dresses of ticking, bright red
scarves to be tied around their necks and black caps—they had
knitted them themselves—to be bobby-pinned in place, slightly
off center.

Dressed and ready to go, they went to their parents' bedside.
"Papa won't move an inch," said one. "But Our Dear Bessie
better get up and go with us," said the other.

"This house is safe enough," said their mother. "You girls
run on to the store and look after Peter. Don't worry about us if
we don't make it this time. When you come back I'll have a
surprise for you."

They put brown paper sacks on their heads, oilcloth over
their shoulders and raced to the store, where they waited, not at
all patiently, for Peter Faircloth. This was to be their first full
night together. After they left the house, Bessie moved into
another bed to wait for Zeda Earl. A light hail began falling
followed by more rain and wind.

Out on the porch, Redd was ringing a cowbell to wake everyone up. "It's liable to come a twister," he shouted over the bell ringing. "Everybody better hurry."

Everyone was hurrying except Elsa Mae Broom, and she was about to have another nervous fit. Her two sons were acting up again, and she wished to God Almighty they would disappear.

Virgil picked up a little fish off the ground and put it in his mouth. Down it went, without any trouble at all. His brother, Robert Douglas, saw him and told Elsa Mae what had happened.

"I'll be the happiest person in the world when I can find a good home for all three of you," Elsa Mae screamed, trying to talk above the sound of rain pounding on tin. "Now run on up there and tell 'That Virgil' if he don't spit whatever it is out real soon, I'm aiming to reach my finger so far down his throat he'll choke to death, and then he'll spit it out for sure."

Elsa Mae was convinced that her children were out to wreck her life. Her nerves were running away with her something awful, and she was still weak from childbirth. If only her head would stop hurting, she would feel better, she knew she would. The very top of her scalp was so tender she could barely stand to run a comb through her hair. It was sticking out in all directions, and she was soaked to the bone. But her nameless son was perfectly dry and sound asleep. She was carrying him in a roasting pan with the lid on tight and was proud of herself for being smart enough to think of it.

"I'm in so much pain, I'm about to die, and nobody cares," she said, shifting the roaster from one hip to the other.

"It's all in your head, Daughter." Doc Broom was holding a hot-water bottle close to his chest and trying to button his pants while he walked. He had a high fever. A piece of checkered oilcloth was draped over his shoulders and two lozenges were dissolving in his mouth. "What you've got to do, Daughter," he advised, "is get your mind on somebody else's problems, and you can start with 'That Virgil.' I do believe he's swallowed him a little bitty fish."

"I don't care if they swallow poison and die on me," said Elsa Mae, "because they're going to end up in the penitentiary if they live. I can't wait to get to the store and turn all three of them

over to Lottie Faircloth. She's the only woman alive who can
make 'That Virgil' behave."

All over the camp, dogs were whining under the houses, and
windows were being slammed shut. The Collymores, the Spur-
locks and the McQuirters were on their way. Bunyon Bostic and
his family of six were just getting ready to leave, and the
Durhams, the Prescotts and the Kirklands were dressing their
children. Puppies being carried into the rain were letting out
little sharp cries that made Elsa Mae remember the baby chickens she had left behind.

"Will you boys run back to the house and bring me that box of
biddies," she shouted to her sons. They ignored her. "Oh,
Lord, you have slapped me in the face with future convicts, and I
deserve better." She tightened her grip on the roaster. "All I ask
is that you deliver me from some of this burden or make me
strong enough to stand up to it, one or the other; I don't care
which."

Just then Billy Wiggins, galloping like the red-haired stallion
he thought he was, whizzed past her. "If I make her look at me,"
he said, "she'll know who she is forever. She'll know who I am
forever too." It was his intention to beat Elsa Mae to the commissary so he could stand on the porch with Redd and ring the
cowbell. Redd had told him that he was the best ringer in the
world, and now Billy wanted to prove it to Elsa Mae.

When he reached the store, Redd gave him the bell and he
rang it as loud as he could. There were all kinds of things he was
dying to tell Elsa Mae, but he didn't know how to get her
attention without making noise, so he kept on ringing the cowbell. He used both hands and both arms as though it weighed a
ton, and was hoping that Elsa Mae was admiring him. "It's hard
to ring it right," he said. "It's Elsa Mae's fault that it's so hard.
She don't want to hear what I'm supposed to tell her, but she's
about to hear it anyway."

"You're ruining my ears with that infernal bell ringing!"
screamed Lottie Faircloth. Her voice could barely be heard over
the storm. She was sidestepping puddles with her husband and
her mother-in-law, Bertha, who was visiting from Louisiana.
Peter was lagging behind due to the water and sand in his shoes.

"Children are my passion," shouted Lottie, trying to hang on to three sacks of toys and storybooks, "but that Billy Wiggins is one I've failed on—never been able to get inside that head of his and help him see the light of day."

"That's because he don't have no head to get inside of," said Boyce. He was carrying quilts to sleep on, and they were already soaking wet.

"I can't hear what you're saying," yelled Bertha. "Speak up!"

"I think that boy's what they're calling a nitwit!" Boyce spoke directly to Lottie.

"I don't care what you call him," Lottie screamed. "I'm not going another step until he puts that bell down. I'm the most sensitive woman in the world, and that's why I hate a racket worse than anything." She was drenched. Her braids were coming apart, and her eyeglasses were sliding down her nose, but she didn't have a free hand to push them up. "You'd think someone would have the good grace to help me," she said, glaring at her mother-in-law, who was standing up to her ankles in water.

Billy stopped ringing the bell until Elsa Mae, roaster in hand, started up the steps. Then he decided to show off. "Elsa Mae," he said proudly, "I'm about to let you see my Most Specialest Thing. I'm about to let you see it for the first time." He pulled off his shirt, dropped his pants and started ringing the bell again. "Now you see me, don't you, Elsa Mae?" He pranced around in front of her. "Now you see who I am."

He had a narrow chest, broad hips and rolls of flesh hanging to his sides. What he called his Most Specialest Thing was exactly that. Elsa Mae had never seen anything quite like it, and neither had Mary Twitchell.

"I have never known a mentally retarded boy yet who wasn't bigger in the private parts than what he ought to be," said Mary. She had already shredded her hairnet and thrown it down. Now she was nervously attacking her earlobes. "Billy Wiggins is about to establish a world's record, if you're asking me."

"No one is asking you," said Elsa Mae. For a few seconds all she could do was stare at the Billy Wiggins she had never known. "You've been hiding yourself from me," she accused him. That set him off. He laughed and rang the bell and danced right out of his pants. Then Elsa Mae went to pieces. "Billy Wiggins," she screamed. "You're about to give me a bad case of the shivers, and I don't want to have them right now because I've just had a baby, so quit it."

Her head was throbbing worse than ever, and her knees were weak. She ran back into the rain. "Here!" she said, forcing the roaster into Lottie Faircloth's arms. "Take it, it's yours, baby, bottles and all."

Lottie took the roaster but dropped all three sacks of toys and storybooks while doing so. "Here," she said, handing the covered pan to Boyce, "take Elsa's bottles while I pick up my books. Somebody get down here and help me get them before they're ruined in the water." No one lifted a finger.

Boyce, already loaded down with quilts, passed the roaster to his mother, whose arms were free. "Every time I come visit, I have to do all the cooking and heavy lifting," she complained, passing the pan to her grandson. "Here," she told Peter. "Breakables. You set them down right over there until we get ready to go in."

"I done give Elsa Mae a case of the shivers," Billy Wiggins shouted into the rain. "She'll let me give her another case too."

Elsa Mae was hiding behind a stack of lumber that was ready to be sold. She was trying not to look toward the store, but she couldn't help it. From the waist down, Billy Wiggins was so much like an animal she could hardly take her eyes off him. "God," she prayed out loud, "give me a pill to turn myself off."

"No such medicine exists right now," shouted her father. "But I'm still working on it."

Billy Wiggins was so proud of himself he couldn't be still. "Elsa Mae's got the shivers," he shouted. "And I helped her get them. After she has them real, real bad I'm liable to tell her something she needs to know about, and after she knows that, I'm liable to show her something else, and after I show her *that* she won't never be the same again."

"There's only one thing to do in a case like this," said Izella Wiggins. She knocked her grandson over the head with her walking cane and told him to put his pants back on. He just stood there as if he hadn't felt a thing, and she hit him again. "You ain't nothing," she said, "you just make out like you are."

"I already know that," he answered, puffing out his chest. "Ain't Nothing At All is what makes me so special."

"You'll think *special,*" said Izella. Again she whacked him over the head, but Billy refused to dodge or fight back.

"Izella, you really put that boy in his place," said Izzie Burrow.

"She sure did," agreed Billy, "but the pitiful part is she don't believe in the place she put me in, and I do." He put on his pants and marched inside ahead of everyone else.

Gradually, the store filled up. The Ruby-Jewels had entered through the back door and were waiting for Peter Faircloth. When they caught sight of him their hearts fluttered. They squealed and clapped their hands and jumped up and down. They adjusted their hats, buttons, belts and scarves. They squeezed their hands and fingers and hugged each other for good luck.

Before the excitement of the storm had died down, the twins led Peter to a back room where Redd had kept a coffin on display. The coffin had been shipped upriver in an outer box made of cedar. The box was empty and the Jewels had already decided that three people could easily fit inside it. Weeks before the storm, they padded the bottom with sacks of flour, and fastened a latch to the inside.

"This is what you call a hideaway," they told Peter. "We planned it with you in mind and nobody else." While bedding down for the night they could hear a few muted voices drifting through the back room and into their secret chamber.

"It's as wet inside as it is outside," Peg Leg complained. His voice could barely be distinguished inside the box.

"One of these days Redd will be forced to break down and spend his money on a new roof," said Bunyon Bostic. His voice carried into the back room but no farther.

"That day will never arrive," said Mary Twitchell. "He'll let this store float away first."

There were at least a half dozen leaks in the store, and the sound of rain dropping into pans of water reminded Lottie

Faircloth of a harp being plucked at random. "It's the most heavenly music in the world," she said, taking all the children and babies who needed attention off to a far corner where she put pallets, books and toys on the floor. She slipped on a Halloween mask, a clown with fluffy orange hair. Then she sat down on the floor with the big children and played her heart out, while the babies slept on a mattress Redd had never been able to sell.

Everyone left her alone to play.

Elsa Mae made herself a bed under a checkout counter that was boxed with sliding doors. She closed herself in and went to sleep while Billy Wiggins pranced around the store and told everybody that he was going to give Elsa Mae Broom another case of the shivers. "What for?" Redd asked him. And Billy said, "Because I like it when she looks at me." Then he bounced a basketball off the back door until the noise got on everyone's nerves and Boyce Faircloth, along with Bunyon Bostic, tied him up and left him in the back room where the Ruby-Jewels were secretly entertaining Peter Faircloth.

Everyone settled down after that. Families began claiming their spots and bedding down on the floor. Brother Caldwell made himself comfortable on the barber's chair, and Clarence Pritchard unfolded a cot he had brought from home. Doc Broom sat by the fire and tied slices of onions to the bottoms of his feet. "This is the best way to break up a head cold," he said, carefully putting his socks back on. "I recommend it for just about everybody."

Outside the wind blew up under the store and stayed there for a long time as if it were about to lift the building straight up in the air. Lottie Faircloth, watching the children sleep, just sat there glassy-eyed, her false face in her hands. She had read four stories aloud and had sung every bedtime lullaby she could remember. Now she was listening to the wind whistling around the houseblocks as though telling a forgotten story.

Toward dawn, the rain stopped and the wind died down. The world was suddenly very still. Nothing was moving, not even the mimosa's long branches that usually scraped against the back window. Nothing could be heard but Redd's alarm clock ticking away on a shelf behind the barber's chair.

The storm seemed to have passed. On the other side of the river, fallen clouds were hugging the earth, and trees coming out of them were leafless and black. The sun, struggling to show itself through the haze, filled the morning with a sickly yellow glow that turned the river the color of tarnished brass.

"Jaundice," Mary Twitchell kept saying, running first to the front door and then to the back. She didn't want to miss a thing.

Gradually, the yellow light creeped into the store. Doc Broom told everyone to tie handkerchiefs and scarves over their noses so they wouldn't come down with yellow fever.

"Yellow fever, my hind leg," said Mary Twitchell, watching her neighbors tie rags around their faces.

Lottie Faircloth put the Halloween mask back on. "It's real good for filtering the air," she said. "I sure wish I had enough of them to pass around because we certainly don't want to get sick."

"Only an idiot would listen to an idiot," said Mary Twitchell. "It's about to come a terrible windstorm, that's all."

"Well keep your eye out for a funnel cloud, is what I ask," said Elsa Mae. "But don't tell me if you see one, because I sure don't want to know about it until after it's come and gone." She put a brown paper sack over her head and refused to leave the check-out counter.

The light changed from yellow to greenish gold. Nothing moved, not a branch, not a blade of grass, not even Redd's best blanket, left out on the line by mistake. But down on the river something was going on. "I've never seen it so calm," said Mary Twitchell. When the fish came to the surface and made ripples in the water she said, "They got to find out what's going on, just like me." Then she saw Elsa Mae's worst dread, a swirling cloud dropped out of the sky and churned the surface of the river, sucking up everything in its path. The cloud lifted, and a hard muddy rain began falling in front of the store. Minnows fell with it. Minnows and sun perch and mudcats as big as a hand.

Redd untied Billy Wiggins and gave him a bucket. He told him to go outside and pick up all the fish that were big enough to sell and bring them in. Billy Wiggins threw back his shoulders and strutted through the store. Along the way he cast malicious glances at everyone. When he reached the front door, he slammed it open and slammed it shut, but he didn't stay outside long. He got distracted by something and came back right away.

"I got something that Elsa Mae wants and can't have no more," he said, looking happier than Lottie Faircloth had ever seen him.

"You march yourself right back to where you found that pan and apologize to Elsa Mae for taking it," said Lottie, speaking through the mask. She tried to rock to her feet, but she had two children weighing her down. "It's about time for Elsa to feed that child. I'd do it for her, but she don't seem to want me to. Lord, have mercy, that precious little thing must be starved to death by now."

"It sure is," said Billy Wiggins. He marched up to Lottie's rocking chair and bragged. "I never took this pan away from Elsa Mae. That boy of yours had his hands on it the time before me. I seen him when he set it down outside."

"Well, I told him to set it down," said Bertha, noticing that the pan was wet. "But I sure didn't tell him to leave it out there overnight. Goes to show you you can't depend on nobody no more, not even a grandchild."

"I guess I'll have to give that boy another whipping," said Boyce. "But I'll wait until I have my good belt to do it with."

"That's not important right now," Lottie said, trying to remain calm. "What's Elsa Mae's baby been eating all this time? That's what I'd like to know."

"Nothing," Billy answered as he carried the roaster to the back of the store to find Elsa Mae.

She was still sleeping under the checkout counter with the paper sack over her head. Billy Wiggins put the roaster on the floor and removed the lid. "Lookie, lookie, look, Elsa Mae," he said, almost singing. "What'd you go and let something like this happen for? If you'd of had the kind of baby you were supposed to of, this never would have happened in a hundred million years. When you can't think of a name to give a baby, you know right then it's not the baby you're supposed to have."

Elsa Mae rolled over and removed the paper sack. At first she believed she was still sleeping, but Billy Wiggins' sour breath made her realize that she wasn't. There in the roaster were the bottles, the pacifier and a piece of pink blanket she had used to pad the bottom. But that's all she could recognize. The child had shriveled. The winter cap had swallowed his head. The booties were half on and half off, and the baby's face was gray and wrinkled.

"That's not my baby," Elsa Mae said, knowing with her heart that it was. She reached out and touched her son. He was hard and cold. "You take that rubber dolly right back to where you found it," she screamed, "and tell Lottie to bring me my real baby."

"This here's it, Elsa Mae," said Billy, "and it's dead too. Just as dead as it'll ever get."

"Lottie wouldn't do that to my baby." Elsa Mae spoke in a crippled voice. "I know because I know Lottie. I been knowing Lottie for all my life." She touched the child again, uncovered his hands and saw the blue ribbon she had tied around his wrist. "He *is* dead," she whispered.

"He ain't never breathing no more," said Billy. "But you don't have to worry none, Elsa Mae, because I promise to give you another one just like it, only better. I cross my heart and hope to die if I don't. But right now I got to throw this one away."

Elsa Mae crawled to the middle of the counter. Billy Wiggins watched her roll into a ball in the dark space.

"Oh, Elsa Mae, you're stunned, ain't you?" he said. "You're stunned that you let this happen, ain't you? You're plumb stunned out of your wrong mind and into your right one."

"What's stunned you, Baby? That ole Billy Wiggins again?" Lottie Faircloth came running through the store with two children in her arms and a Halloween mask blocking her vision. Billy Wiggins met her with the open pan. "This is what stunned her," he said.

"Oh, my Lord Jesus," screamed Lottie, squeezing the three-year-olds so hard they woke up coughing. "Elsa Mae told me she had baby bottles in there."

"Well, I guess she told you wrong, didn't she," said Mary Twitchell, gazing into the pan. With one finger she touched the child's forehead as though she were testing a cake. "That baby's froze," she announced, not quite believing herself.

"Dead!" screamed Lottie Faircloth.

Before anyone could stop him, Billy ran out the back door. He was holding the roaster over his head. Lottie bounced the children higher on her hips and ran after him. "He's got Elsa Mae's dead baby in that pan, and God only knows what he'll do with it," she screamed.

"I'm fixing to throw this baby in the river," Billy Wiggins shouted. "And when I get done doing it, I'll turn right around and give Elsa Mae another one just like it, only better. That's my promise."

The McCormicks, the Bostics and the Collymores followed Lottie out the back door. The Pullens, the Prescotts and the McQuirters were right behind them, but no one could catch Billy Wiggins, not even Mary Twitchell, who was the fastest on her feet.

"You better not do nothing bad to that baby!" Peg Leg yelled from the top of the hill. But by then, there was no changing Billy Wiggins' mind.

"It was dead when I found it out in the road," he said. "Lottie's boy left it there. He did just exactly what he was supposed to do." Then Billy Wiggins threw the pan, bottles, baby and all, into the swollen river. For a while the roaster with the baby still in it floated downstream. Billy Wiggins watched it until it was sucked under. "I ain't nothing at all," he said, "but that baby was something after all, and that's why it had to freeze to death." Then he ran out in the woods to hide.

Everyone stood silently on the banks of the Sabine, and watched the whirlpool that had taken the roaster. The sun was burning a hole through the clouds, and three white cranes were gliding like lost angels over the river, but no one saw them. Logs and pieces of houses floated by. A rowboat with nobody in it traveled sideways through the debris, and someone's old Christmas tree with silver tinsel still clinging to the bare branches was caught in the current as well. Slowly, these things disappeared too.

Then, as if there had been some unspoken warning, or as if everyone had thought of it at the same time, all eyes turned toward the Overstreet house. The sand shifted out from under it, and the house lurched forward. The sand shifted again, and the house slid off its blocks. Every chicken penned underneath it was crushed to death, and every slat but two fell from Bessie's bed. It was then that Zeda Earl was heard crying for the first time —but far from the last.

"Oh precious morning star!" exclaimed Lottie Faircloth, still packing the two children on her hips. "When the Lord takes a life, He gives a life." She pushed the Halloween mask to the back of her head. "Now I can see again," she said, running toward the fallen house, the clown face laughing behind her back.

It was then that Brother Caldwell woke up on his barbershop bed. He stood on the back porch of the commissary and reminded everyone it was Easter Sunday and that he intended to preach on the crucifixion as it pertained to present day.

"We don't need to hear about no crucifixion today," said Mary Twitchell. "Switch your topic to something more inspirational. We got Elsa Mae to worry about."

It took three men to pull Elsa Mae from under the counter. "I don't feel good, and I don't feel bad," she said as she was being carried home on a makeshift stretcher. "I don't feel like nothing at all." Those were the last words she uttered for five days.

Later that morning, while the Overstreet house was being jacked up and leveled, the Ruby-Jewels and Peter Faircloth emerged from the box. Boyce was looking for them. "So you disappeared last night, did you?" he said. "We got a few things to straighten out right now."

For leaving the pan outside, Peter was given a whipping that he would never forget, and the Ruby-Jewels predicted that it would be the last one he would ever receive.

While Boyce was punishing his son, Isaac took Zeda Earl in his arms and introduced her to the neighbors. That day he was totally himself. His head wasn't aching. His thoughts weren't swimming around before his face. The old angel had gone back to the high, high clouds to watch over him and, for a while, he didn't even need Doc Broom. All he wanted to do was walk Zeda Earl, but she cried every time he picked her up. "This is liable to get on a man's nerves," he said. "She don't seem to know when to stop."

Zeda Earl was a large child. She had thick black hair, dark skin and a strong voice. Everyone said she was Isaac made over. Everyone except Mary Twitchell, and she wasn't so sure, so she didn't say.

* * *

Elsa Mae blamed herself for her baby's death, and for almost a week she didn't speak a word or utter a sound louder than a sigh. She could talk, she knew she could, but she just didn't want to. There was too much to think about. She convinced herself that she would never have a moment's rest until she gave her child some kind of burial. She believed she would eventually find the body.

On the fifth day after "that terrible tragedy," as everyone was calling it, Elsa noticed something floating in the river. She hoped it was the body of her baby boy drifting ashore, but it turned out to be nothing but a burlap sack full of dead kittens. "Poor ole kitties," Elsa Mae said, raking them out of the sack with a stick. "Nobody wanted them, did they?"

The day was unusually warm, so she waded knee-deep into the river. She stood there until she felt the current pulling her. "If I find my baby," she said, wading downstream, "I sure hope it looks better than them little cats did."

At Rocky Shoals she waded into a cove where water spiders were scurrying across the scum that was collecting along the shore. She was wearing a flour sack dress with no sleeves. It was white with printed blue flowers fading all over it. Even though it was her favorite dress, she didn't think to lift the skirt out of the water. She was too busy letting her eyes drift around and fall where they may. She was certain she was about to be led to her baby.

When she looked up, Billy Wiggins, standing on a sandbar,

was watching her. He had been living on Whiskey Island and had not once returned to the camp. "I know what you're looking for, Elsa Mae, but you won't never find it," he said.

Don't be cutting your eyes at me, Elsa Mae wanted to tell him, but she didn't. She enjoyed not talking to anybody. It made her life easier.

"I been following you, Elsa Mae," Billy said, twisting on the straps of his overalls. "I been following you and thinking at the same time."

That must be pretty hard for you, she said to herself.

"I been thinking about that promise I made to you, and today is the day I'm thinking about keeping it." Then he laughed a kind of sucking-on-air laugh and said, "Elsa Mae, the only way you'll ever forget about that baby that froze is to have another one just like it, only better. You heard me promise you that, didn't you?"

She shook her head yes.

He waded toward her.

She watched him coming but didn't move.

He took her hand. "You're part of a bigger plan than you know about right now," he said. There was a solemn urgency in his voice that was soothing. "Brother Caldwell talks about a bigger plan all the time, but my plan is bigger than his. And you're about to know it. One day you'll know everything that I know, and all your babies will know it too. If they don't, they'll get thrown away."

For the first time, Elsa Mae almost felt comfortable with him. He seemed to understand something about her that she didn't understand at all.

"I'm about to show you where I come from," he said, leading her through the shallows to Whisky Island. "All this time you been thinking that I come from the same place you come from, but that ain't right, Elsa Mae. You come from the same place I come from, only you don't know it yet, and it's been left up to me to make sure you do know it."

He took her across the island to the sandy point from where Ain't Nothing At All could be clearly seen.

They sat down on the wet ground. Billy Wiggins put an arm

around Elsa Mae's shoulders and said, "I'm fixing to tell you about me now."

Elsa Mae gave him a stick of gum to sweeten his breath.

"Way, Way up that old river," he pointed, "is a place where the water, and the sky and the ground nearly 'bout touch but don't. And that's what we call Ain't Nothing At All. Now if you go up there, you won't see it. But that don't mean it's not there. It is there, but this is the only place you can see it from, and this is the place I been calling Our Place. That means my place and your place too, Elsa Mae."

Elsa Mae studied the point on the river where the water, and the sky and the ground almost touched but didn't. She stared at it until her eyes relaxed, and her mouth fell open and her mind stopped trying to understand. She did not see what Billy Wiggins saw, but he thought she did.

"I knew you'd see it too, Elsa Mae," he said. "I knew because I already figured it out for you. You heard people say to your face, 'You ain't nothing at all and never will be nothing at all' and all this time you didn't have the slightest idea what they were talking about, but now you know. They were just trying to put you in your place, that's all."

What he said made little sense to Elsa Mae, but she listened anyway. She had always wondered if she had been born with a mission to fulfill. Brother Caldwell had told her that she would never be content until she had found her place on earth. But the place he chose for her wasn't the place she wanted for herself. His place was filled with don'ts, abstinence and repentance. That didn't interest her a bit. She saw no sense in it. "I may as well be dead as live that way," she had told him. But with Billy Wiggins, it was different. His place just might be her place after all.

Billy gave her neck a squeeze and continued. "It took me a long time to start figuring all this out, but once I got started I couldn't stop. I came out here every day and started figuring and figuring, and pretty soon, I figured out where we came from Elsa Mae. The only difference between you and me is that I have a better recollection of the place than you do. Your memory ain't as fresh as mine is, and that's why I'm getting to tell you all this, and that's why your little baby had to freeze to death and that's why I'm getting to give you another one just like it, only better."

He stood up ceremoniously. "Elsa Mae, it's that time now," he said. "It's time for me to keep my promise to you." He reached down and pulled off her dress by the shoulder seams. She leaned back on the sand. He unbuckled the straps of his overalls, and they fell to his feet.

"Oh, my God, Billy Wiggins," Elsa Mae said, in a tone reserved for prayer. "Just looking at you gives me the shivers so bad I don't know what to do."

"You know what to do," said Billy. "You know how to talk, too."

"Now, I'm about to show you something you haven't ever seen before," Elsa Mae said, slowly opening her legs. "You're right. It is time for you to keep that promise you made me."

Billy Wiggins was almost too nervous to speak. "Elsa Mae," he managed to say, "I got to tell you something first. I got to tell it right now too." He stared up at a cypress as he spoke. "Elsa Mae, I ain't never kept a promise like this before because I ain't never found nobody who wanted the kind of promise I have to keep."

"Well, now you have," said Elsa Mae.

"That's what makes it so hard to talk," he confessed. "I'm finding out it's real scary to be all by yourself with somebody. I'm also finding out that if you'd talk more, it'd be a whole lot easier for me to keep my promise."

"Just lean over me on all fours," she said. He did. She wrapped her legs around his waist. "I want you to make me feel like somebody's pouring me out of a big ole drinking glass," she said. "I know you can do it, Billy."

And she was right. That day, Billy Wiggins made the river flow all the way through her and out again. He made her fly above the clouds and the stars and look down on a ball of dirt that was called earth. "That ain't nothing at all," she said when she saw the size of her world.

"That's what I been telling you all this time," said Billy.

"You make me see things I've never seen before," said Elsa Mae. "Why has it taken me so long to open my eyes?"

Gradually, she entered Billy Wiggins' world and accepted her place in it. Gradually, almost everything he said made sense to her, and what she didn't fully understand was at least comforting to hear. She left her sons in her father's care and moved into the whisky still with Billy Wiggins. No one tried to stop them. "I believe they deserve each other," was all Doc Broom said. Izella agreed. So did everyone else. Billy Wiggins and Elsa Mae Broom were a perfect match.

When they were together sparks flew. Izzie Burrow saw them. And at night, he swore that the island was filled with light.

"It's taken me a long time to find my place," said Elsa Mae, "and now that I've found it, I wouldn't think of giving it up."

Billy Wiggins made her feel things she had never felt before. With him, she was light as air. When his Most Specialest Thing was inside her she was outside her body, outside her mind. She was in the high, high clouds looking down on everything that was, and on everything that was not. "I feel like liquid!" she would scream from the heavens. Her voice would carry through the camp, and Redd would appear on his porch and say, "I believe those two have found happiness. Why can't that be everybody's case?"

"I feel like air!" Elsa Mae would scream. Her voice could be heard all along that stretch of the river. "Billy Wiggins you make me feel like nothing at all."

Life with Billy Wiggins completely changed Elsa Mae's way of thinking. Her headaches vanished. Her broken skin cleared up. And she never took aspirin again. She didn't need to because when she was with Billy Wiggins, stars fell from the heavens. Navasota Blackburn counted seven in one night, and one fell into the river.

In less than a year, Billy Wiggins' promise was born. Elsa Mae gave birth to a son with bright red hair. They named him Rooster, but everyone else called him Billy Wiggins' Boy, or, Billy-Wiggins'-Boy-By-Elsa-Mae-Broom.

Billy Wiggins took care of his son. He fed him and clothed him and taught him all he wanted him to know. He didn't want

Elsa Mae to do anything except have one baby right after another, and, when she realized how well behaved her promised son was, she agreed.

In comparison to her other children, Billy Wiggins' Boy was no trouble at all. "That baby's in a good mood all day long," she told Mary Twitchell. "He eats everything his daddy puts in his mouth. Not like my other two were. If I'd only known then what I know now, I'd of thrown 'That Virgil' and Robert Douglas in the river the very minute they were born, because it's my mission to populate the earth with Nothing People."

"I thought that's what you were doing all this time," said Mary Twitchell.

"Well you thought wrong," said Elsa Mae. "I didn't know a thing about Ain't Nothing At All until I saw myself in Billy Wiggins. Now I know where I belong."

Over the years, she happily gave birth to fourteen pale-skinned children, although some people claimed to have counted as many as twenty-six. Some were red-headed, others were blond. "There's only one of us that's dark," Billy Wiggins would tell his sons and daughters. "But it's going to take her a long time yet to realize who she is." He was talking about Zeda Earl.

His ears were tuned to her almost constant flow of tears, especially on winter nights when the air was thin and even the wings of an owl could be heard slicing the dark. On those cold nights when the air was too still to breathe, Billy Wiggins would sit on his island and listen to Zeda Earl crying in her sleep. Her unhappiness would travel across the river and settle like a flame in his heart. He would listen carefully and hear her other voice. "Her voice that's trapped inside her voice" is what he called it. "She's too mad at herself to let it out."

He took it upon himself to capture Zeda Earl's discontent in brown paper sacks which he hung from long poles placed along the river. When the wind blew the bags open he would tie them shut and burn them on the sand.

"Zeda Earl won't ever be happy until she realizes where she came from," he would say while burning a portion of her discontent. "When she knows what I know, she won't never need to cry no more."

PART FIVE

Kiss Them Good-bye

Not long after Billy Wiggins kept his promise to Elsa Mae Broom, Peter Faircloth, who had just turned fourteen, announced his plans to live with the Ruby-Jewels. "You'll do no such of a thing," Lottie informed him. "You can marry one and live with one, but you cannot marry both and live with both, and you cannot live with both of them unless you're married to at least one of them. You'll never be happy if you do, and neither will I. Am I making myself clear?" She tore off her apron and threw it on the kitchen floor. "You have made me sick," she said. "You have driven me crazy. You have pushed me to the very edge of my nerves over those twins, and I wish to God Almighty they had never been born."

"They're special," Peter reminded her.

"I believe I've heard that before." Lottie left the kitchen and Boyce took over.

"I guess I'll have to beat you with my fists this time. My belt didn't hurt enough did it."

"I can't imagine how I got stuck with you," Peter said, throwing his father's words back in his face. "You wouldn't last a day in *your* daddy's house."

"That's the last time you'll mock me." Boyce took off his shirt to beat his son, but Peter escaped. He had never run so fast.

He hid in the Thicket for the rest of the day, and toward

evening, when Billy Wiggins was burning paper sacks filled with Zeda Earl's discontent, he spotted Peter hiding in a tree. "You better ask ole Navasota to give you some protection of some kind," said Billy. "Your daddy's looking for you. He's done asked me where you were. I'd give you some protection myself, but I ain't got time. Zeda Earl's crying too much. See here? I got her tears in these sacks. Navasota told me how to burn them. She told me nobody else could do it but me. So you better ask her for something to keep you alive."

After dark he took Peter Faircloth across the river and left him on the sandbar near Navasota's house. "She'll be along to get you real soon," he said. "Every time somebody stops here, she knows it."

Alone on the sandbar, Peter listened to a clock striking somewhere nearby. Soon a flickering light could be seen moving through the woods. It first appeared high up, as if in the tops of the trees, and then it started a meandering journey down the riverbank to the sandbar, where it stopped. Navasota, carrying a lantern with a green globe, asked, "Whose there tonight?"

"I need some protection," said Peter. He could hardly speak. Navasota approached him. She held the lamp over her head and a circle of light fell around her visitor.

"I can see you do," she said. "It's your daddy again."

"How did you know?" Peter spoke through his fear.

"I can hear things coming off the river," said Navasota. "Anybody can if they listen."

She took him up a steep, winding path that ended at the door to her one-room cabin. The cabin was made of logs and covered with vines. Trees growing against the outside walls hemmed it in on all sides. "There's a current of wind that blows through here regularly," Navasota said. They were standing on her porch. "Nothing can stay in its path very long, even the tree branches grow around it. That's why you can stand right here and see the river, and the sandbar and a whole lot of other things."

Inside, dried herbs hung from the ceiling. Pictures of angels and clouds covered an entire wall, and on another, scarves of many colors hung from nails and wooden pegs. "Those scarves contain magic in their threads," Navasota said while adjusting a lampwick. "But you have to know how to speak to them. They won't help you unless you know the words they like hearing."

"How do you know the right words?" asked Peter.

"The words come to you," said Navasota. Then she thought for a moment. "Oh, just any words will do. But you have to know how to say them. That's the part that takes practice."

A bowl of sage, smoldering on a center table, filled the room with fragrance. "Smoke Spirits," Navasota said, as she stirred the burning leaves. She always kept a flame in the house, usually a candle, or a kerosene lamp, sometimes a log in her mud fireplace.

On another wall was a collection of clocks. "None of them work," she said. "At least not the way most clocks work. They don't tick or go off until I need to know something and sometimes not even then. Sometimes they forget, just like the rest of us."

"I'm glad they didn't forget tonight," said Peter. He was studying a picture hanging on the wall of clocks. It was an old, yellowing poster of an Indian princess standing on the back of a galloping stallion while balancing the sun on one palm and the moon on the other. In the background were bareback riders, and sharpshooters, carnival tents and an indistinguishable figure crossing a ravine on a sagging rope.

"Who is that?" asked Peter.

"Wouldn't a whole lot of people like to know," answered Navasota. She asked him to sit down and talk about something else. "Talk about what's here," she said, drumming on her chest with a fist.

"Elsa Mae's baby got left outside," Peter said. "That's always on my mind. I can't . . ."

"I found that baby," Navasota interrupted him. Her smile seemed to reach to the back of her neck. "It washed up to me. They almost always do; anything that wants to be buried, I mean. I just about always find them. That baby's been put down in the bottom of a hollow tree."

She played with the strings on her moccasins and stared at the floorboards while she spoke. "Sometimes when a tree rots from the inside it loses its spirit, and you have to find another one to put back inside it. That's what I did. I hope somebody does the same thing for me."

Peter Faircloth wanted to thank Navasota for doing what she did. But he didn't know exactly what to thank her for.

"No blame has been cast," she said. "So you can take the rocks out of your shoulders right now. They're not heavy anymore. See, there they go." She pointed to something floating through the room. "Those old burden rocks are lighter than air. I see them trying to leave." She opened the door for them. "Kiss them good-bye, Peter Faircloth," she said. "And be glad they're going. If you're not glad, who will be, besides me?" She was excited now. Her voice was higher-pitched and more youthful too. She giggled like a young girl in love, while blowing kisses through the open door. "If you don't kiss your troubles goodbye, Peter, they'll come right back."

Peter stood in the doorway and blew kisses into the dark. A cold chill starting at the base of his spine traveled to the top of his head. He felt it leave his body.

"It always makes me happy when somebody gets rid of something they don't need," said Navasota. "It makes me want to put on a skirt again and go dancing the way I used to." She took a scarf off the wall and tied it around her head. She laughed into her hands like a shy schoolgirl who was waiting for someone to ask her to dance. Navasota: overalls and string tie, moccasins and magic scarf, starched shirt and wrinkled face, she was anything but young, and yet, to Peter Faircloth she was all ages at once. Navasota curtsied low. She pantomimed lifting her skirt with one hand and holding it between her thumb and index finger. Her arms were poised in the air, beckoning Peter to take them. He had never danced before, but he didn't think of that. He took Navasota in his arms and twirled her around the room. She was light on her feet and fast. Her steps were executed with the precision of someone who had danced all her life. Around and around they whirled, stirring up the dust, the spiders and the Smoke Spirits.

Suddenly Navasota stopped. "I just saw your father," she said. "He was a good dancer too, wasn't he? That's how he met Lottie. I just saw him in this room." The schoolgirl left her face but was still present in the way her hands caressed the ends of the scarf tied around her head. "Seems to me your daddy's got too far outside himself, or something. I can't quite see it yet. I better go think now."

While Peter tried to sleep, Navasota sat on her back porch and listened. Hours later, when dawn was creeping through the trees and the sun seemed to be rising from the middle of the river, she lit her pipe and smoked. The aroma of sweet tobacco drifted into the room where Peter waited. Navasota continued to smoke while watching daylight sneaking up on the world like a thief.

"Everybody better be staying off the river awhile," she said, just as though someone were sitting beside her. "I'm telling you, everybody better be minding Navasota this time." Her eyes were fixed on the Sabine. It was blood red, and the edges were black and the sun rising from the deepest channel seemed to be ripping a hole through the earth.

She hurried down the path and stood on the sandbar. "Everybody better be going home now," she called to the fishermen who were passing. "This ole river ain't no place to be today." She warned everyone in shouting distance until she no longer felt safe that close to the water. Then she returned to her house to wait.

"You can't go home yet," she told Peter. They sat on her porch for the rest of the day and listened to the ivory-billed woodpeckers drumming in the trees.

Navasota kept her eyes on the river, and toward evening when the water, to her way of seeing it, had still not returned to its natural color, three fishermen from Village Mills were shot from their boats. The next morning Boyce was captured and locked up in the back room of Redd's store.

"Something's happened," Navasota told Peter. "Your mama's about to need you now." She took him across the river.

"You see what you made me do," Boyce said when his son entered the storage room. "You made me so mad I killed somebody."

"Three somebodys." Peter sat beside his father. "Mind if I dispute your word?"

"It'll be your last chance," said Boyce.

That night he hanged himself in the back room. He used a roll of barbed wire to cut through the ropes that bound him. He also used the wire to form the noose.

"He was the meanest man in the world," Lottie told her son after the burial at Campground. "He should have been locked up a long time ago. Those three weren't the only ones your father killed. Over across the river, I know of two more, but he was just a kid then and didn't mean to kill *them*. Just showing out with his gun, that's all."

That night she told her son a little more: "You father was a handsome man. He was proud of his strength. All the women admired him. He could shoot a gun like nobody else, and he was the best dancer I ever met. But that's about all he could do, now that I come to think of it."

Peter Faircloth felt no grief. He wondered if he should. He breathed deeply. The air wasn't the same; it was lighter and no longer felt heavy inside his body. He imagined a large rock floating before him. It had his father's name on it, and it dissolved into the sky. Then grief came to him.

"Rocks are sometimes necessary things to have around," he heard Navasota say, but he could not see her. "You have to live with them a long time in order to appreciate their absence. Every time you get rid of a burden rock you must respect what it has taught you. Then you just kiss it good-bye so it won't ever come back."

* * *

A week after Boyce hanged himself, Peter and the Ruby-Jewels decided to live on the water tower. They replaced rungs in the ladder and rigged up a rope and pulley to hoist lumber, provisions and Zeda Earl to the platform. The Ruby-Jewels carried their baby sister with them almost everywhere they went. It was the only way to stop her crying.

"We'll still do the cooking at Our Dear Bessie's house," said a sister, as she pulled scraps of lumber to the platform.

"Papa's going to think he's about to lose us, but he's not."

"Sister, we'll have to think of some way to get him up here. He'd like it once he was."

"He might not," said Peter. "It's awfully high, you know."

The water tower was higher than Redd's store, and, from the platform, they could see the faint skeleton of the river bridge, and the high banks where Navasota's house was hidden from sight. They could look down on a maze of logging roads like a fisherman's net hurled over the Thicket. Here and there the main road to Splendora would emerge from the timber and pass through areas where the trees had been cut down and transported by rail, by oxen or by barge to one of many new sawmills.

"Pretty soon," said Peter Faircloth, "there's not going to be much of anything left." Zeda Earl was crying in his arms. Peter turned her toward the river and a pole of brown paper sacks. Some of the sacks were already open. Billy Wiggins was tying them shut and burning them on the sand. "Ole Billy Wiggins has captured all our troubles," said Peter, bouncing Zeda Earl in his arms.

From the window of her classroom, Lottie Faircloth could see her son standing on the very edge of the platform. "Peter Lewis Faircloth! You're going to fall and break your neck," she screamed, completely disrupting her class. "You're all I've got left, whether you know it or not. Now come down from there." She abandoned her teaching to find Bessie.

"You can't make something grow in dirt it don't want to grow in, Lottie." That's what Bessie told her. She was tying cloth bags over the flowers she had just pollinated by hand. She put down her journals and pollen samples, took her three young cranes in her arms and followed Lottie to the base of the tower.

"Grow up and face the facts," shouted Lottie. "Two of you can get married and live together, but the other one will have to find somebody else."

"Impossible," came three voices from the top of the tower.

Then Bessie threw back her head and shaded her eyes. "It's a long way up there!" she said. "Farther than I thought." She straightened up again. "We can't stop them from doing what they think they got to do, Lottie. But we can help them do it a better way."

Again Bessie threw back her head and shaded her eyes. She sent her voice climbing every rung of the ladder. "You can't live up there," she shouted. No one, not even her own children, had ever heard her raise her voice. Everyone in Camp Ruby stopped to listen. "You have to think about my happiness as well as your own. You know perfectly well I can't climb. How will I ever visit you, is what I'd like to know? Think about your father. He can barely make it down the steps on a good day. Think about Zeda Earl. What if you were to drop her?"

Without another word, Bessie carried her pets back to the gardens. She had succeeded in developing a bright lavender lily with a scarlet throat. It had taken her years. And now she was wondering how to deepen the color. "Maybe if I mix it up with a Maroon Night," she said. "Wonder how that would come out?"

* * *

The next day the Ruby-Jewels and Peter Faircloth decided to live in an eight-room house the McQuirters and their eleven children had abandoned one year when the river sent them running. Most of the rooms were sitting on dry ground, but some of them extended over the water and were supported by cypress poles. The back porch, attached to the house with ropes and chains, was nothing more than a raft covered with a tin roof. During floods, it rose with the water level.

When they moved into their new home, the Ruby-Jewels balled up their auburn hair, the style they intended to wear it for the rest of their lives. They sewed identical housedresses of ticking, their favorite fabric, which they used for Peter's shirts as well. They made all of his new clothes, including his pants, and kept them starched and ironed. They always wanted him to look his best, even when scrubbing the floors, or sweeping out spiders and water snakes that found their way inside.

While cleaning up the old house, the Ruby-Jewels began calling Peter Faircloth "Brother." Likewise, Peter began referring to them as his sisters. It seemed perfectly natural to do so.

"Sisters, what are we going to do today," he said at the start of their second week together. "Give me the plan."

"Brother, you're impossible to get along with these days,"

said a sister. "Are you too happy or what? All you want is a plan a minute."

"Brother just wants to be entertained by his sisters, Sister, that's all he's after. We've spoiled him rotten, is what we've done."

"The plan today," announced a sister, "is to clean up the back porch so we can have a comfortable place to fish. Won't that be fun."

"Yes it will, Sister," said a sister. "And on days when Papa's at himself he's liable to want to do some fishing too, so we've got to fix a way for him to get back there without killing himself. You don't want that to happen, do you?"

"No, I most certainly do not, Sister. I'm so sorry if I gave you the idea I do, because I don't."

"Isaac's bound to like it here," said Bessie when she inspected the back porch. "Only thing is, it's not as strong as I'd like it to be."

For days she abandoned her lily gardens to help her daughters furnish their house. While the cranes perched in a window and Zeda Earl cried until someone held her, Bessie stitched up curtains and covered old chairs. She wanted to paint the house too, but the sisters wouldn't hear of it.

"Nobody else's house is painted," said Peter. "Why should ours be?"

The more Lottie watched them work, the more guilt she felt for not lending a hand. Finally, she broke down and planted wood fern in tin cans and lined them up on the front steps. "Don't get the idea that I'm doing this because I agree with what's being done," she said. "All I want is a *proper* grandchild, and something tells me I'll never get it."

"Not from us you're not," said a Ruby-Jewel.

"Brothers and sisters can't have babies."

"If they do they'll be retarded."

"Besides . . ."

"The pleasures of the flesh no longer intrigue us."

"The pleasures of the flesh no longer intrigue us."

"Too messy to bother with," said Peter, inspecting his pants for wrinkles. "But how will we ever explain this to Elsa Mae without hurting her feelings?"

"I don't know, and I don't care about Elsa Mae Broom or whatever she's calling herself these days," said Lottie Faircloth. "You sisters just better promise me one thing." She pointed her finger at the twins posed in ticking, identical sunbonnets and work gloves. "Don't let my boy starve to death. That's all I ask of you."

The Ruby-Jewels had no intention of starving Peter Faircloth. Cooking for him became their greatest pleasure. When frying, or stewing or coming up with sauces from scratch, they would each hold the handle of the same pan and stir with their fingers wrapped around their favorite wooden spoon. They washed and peeled vegetables together, cleaned fish together and passed eggs through their hands to separate the yokes. Their cooking pots were polished inside and out. Their woodburning stove was kept immaculately clean, and their woodbox was always filled to the brim. Brother split their logs with a long-handled ax, and often his two sisters helped him while Zeda Earl, strapped into a chair, watched or cried.

Zeda Earl practically lived with them. While Bessie worked her lilies, and Isaac studied the formations of the clouds, or fished from the banks of the river, Peter Faircloth and the Ruby-Jewels looked after Zeda Earl, the most restless member of the family. Nothing suited her. Nothing pleased her. The Ruby-Jewels said she was the most disagreeable, the most hateful-talking and the most uppity child they had ever known, but they were forced to love her and take care of her anyway because she was their sister.

*   *   *

By the time Zeda Earl learned to print her name, only Isaac had the patience to put up with her. Zeda would sit at the foot of his bed and listen to his stories for hours on end. Over and over he told her about the old angel he had banished from the river-banks. The angel was forever on his mind. "I do miss that talkative devil sometimes," he would say. "He always had something to complain about, though, and that can get on your nerves fast."

Occasionally, the angel would send a message down from the high clouds where he was happy and free of all complaints. "I can't come back right now," was the usual message. "Life's too good up here in the sky."

"That's where I'm going one day," Isaac would say, pointing to the clouds framed by the sleeping porch windows. "Daughter, don't you want to come too?"

"Don't talk that way Papa," Zeda would say. "You don't need that ole angel anymore. You've got me."

After he had sent the angel away, Isaac had been attacked by a loneliness he had not felt since marrying Bessie. To fill that vast emptiness that not even his wife could enter, Isaac had soothed his mind with Doc Broom's tonics. He had placed himself entirely in the old doctor's hands, and had taken whatever new remedy Broom had asked him to try out.

"I sure hate to charge you for my medicine, Isaac," Broom would say, "because when I discover whatever it is I'm looking for you'll go down in history for being my human guinea pig. You're liable to get all the credit too."

To fill the void left by the old angel, and to banish the sick headaches that swept over him, Isaac spent his days taking Doc Broom's *medicine* and fishing from the riverbanks. After a few years, he no longer had to go to the river to do his fishing. The river came to him. He no longer had to leave his sleeping porch to wet his hook. He fished off the side of his bed. Zeda Earl fished with him.

They used cane poles and perch hooks, heavy sinkers and light bread for bait. They would drag their hooks over the sleeping porch floor until they snagged something. That gave them a thrill. If they didn't catch anything on the floor, they would cast their lines through a hole in the window screen at the foot of the bed. There was always something outside to snag a hook. Once it was Izella's tomcat. Twice it was a Rhode Island Red, and several times they lost their bait to mockingbirds, or Isaac's imagination. When the fish weren't biting, Zeda Earl would go outside and hook shoes, socks or coffee cups on Isaac's line. Anything to make him happy.

While fishing, Isaac would sip from a bottle of Doc Broom's tonic. The dependence was expensive, and Bessie came up with every cent it took to keep her husband happy. She started advertising her lilies in almanacs and mail-order catalogs, and soon, a steady stream of orders arrived each week. But there was barely enough money to meet their needs. For a long time, she told herself that Isaac didn't really depend on Doc Broom's tonic. "He just enjoys the taste," she told Lottie Faircloth. "It makes him happy to drink it. I know it smells like poison, but it's not. There could be worse things to live with."

Finally, Bessie was forced to admit what she had known for a long time but had never been able to admit, even to herself. Finally, she accepted the inevitable: Isaac couldn't live without his *medicine*. His body would quiver and jerk when he ran out. His face would draw up with pain. But under the influence of Doc Broom's concoctions he was the calmest, most forgetful person around. He was happy and content, and Bessie did not have the heart, not then, not at that time in his life, to deprive him of what he needed to dream another hour, to sleep another night, to live one more day. Life without her husband: She refused to think about that, but there were times when she could not control her thoughts.

Once, on a hot afternoon when the air was heavy with humidity and the river was sinking low into the earth, she walked away from her gardens and stepped into the vast emptiness that had plunged Isaac into a life of forgetfulness and dreams. "I know what he's been through, now," she said fanning the still, hot air with her hands. "I feel like I could smother to death all cut off from the world like this." It was as though something she could not see was separating her from everyone else. "I'm so confused today," she said, "I guess it's just the heat. It's mighty hard to walk through heat like this. The air is so heavy right now."

She rested on her front porch until the day cooled off a bit, and the emptiness she had entered left her. "I have neglected Isaac," she said. "He must feel as though I've forgotten all about him." It was then that she decided to bring her husband back.

"All you need is to stay out of that empty place," she told him. "Doc Broom is keeping you tied to it."

She was determined to force from her life anything that would harm her husband. She gradually reduced the amount of tonic he consumed each day. She spent hours sitting in bed and holding his hand. The Ruby-Jewels read to him, and Peter Faircloth took him back to the river to fish. But Isaac continued to beg for his *medicine* and the more he begged, the less Bessie gave him. "I think what I am doing is for the best," she told her children, but the Ruby-Jewels weren't so sure.

"It seems like he's better off happy," they said, "no matter what it takes to keep him that way."

Finally, Isaac's body rebelled. His fingers quivered, and his eyes rolled back in their sockets as if looking for a place to rest. He slept very little, and when he did, his sleep was fitful, filled with dreams and agony. He would awaken with his body on fire. He would see the flames burning through the sleeping porch and feel them racing through his veins. He would moan and howl, and beg for water to extinguish the burning.

Navasota Blackburn brewed herbs in rainwater, and Bessie spooned the mixture into Isaac's mouth. But still the flames burned. Isaac could be heard howling all over the camp. Neighbors lined up at his front door to ask what they could do. Doc Broom sent over a new concoction free of charge, but Bessie poured it out. Isaac continued to beg for relief of any kind.

"I don't know what to do now," Navasota said a few days later. "Isaac seems to have willed himself to Doc Broom. After a person wills himself, there's not much anybody can do."

"I can't stand to see him suffering," Bessie said. "I don't want Broom to control him, and I don't want him to die either. I don't think I could go on living without Isaac."

Finally, she broke down and gave her husband as much of Doc Broom's tonic as his body demanded. And again, he became calm. Clouds drifted through the sleeping porch windows, and the river visited him in his dreams. The fish bit his hook again, and occasionally, he would glimpse the old angel smiling down from the high, high clouds.

"Papa is better off this way," the Ruby-Jewels assured their mother.

"At least he's not in pain anymore," said Peter. "That's the main thing."

Bessie carried a silent rage against Doc Broom. There were days when she found herself wishing death upon him. But she retracted those wishes. "Right now," she said, "Isaac needs him too much for him to die."

A lot of other people needed him too. Doc Broom operated a cash and carry business which was thriving on both sides of the river. He now employed his two grandsons as his assistants. He mixed the ingredients himself. Robert Douglas filled the bottles, and Virgil made the deliveries. He also went around collecting the empty bottles. Most people saved them, but Isaac did not. He pitched them through a hole in the window screen at the foot of his bed, and he rarely missed his target. Outside lay the evidence of his dependence as well as his steady aim: a pile of broken bottles. Sometimes Bessie would bury them, but before she knew it, they would stack up again. Sometimes Isaac would catch one on his hook and pull it through the window. "That ole river is getting mighty low on fish," he would say to Zeda Earl. "Something's got to be done about this."

That's when Isaac started carving. Zeda Earl would bring him scraps of lumber or odd-shaped roots, and he would sit in bed and carve sun perch, buffalo fish and mudcats. He would carve long, slippery water snakes, snapping turtles and alligator gar. Zeda Earl would run the carvings down to the river and throw them in the water. Sometimes Isaac would accompany her. "These are not real fish," he would explain, "and they won't turn into real fish when they hit the water, but they'll remind the river that it's got a job to do that it's not doing. It will be a terrible thing if this ole river runs out of fish."

"We're helping the river," said Zeda Earl, "and we're helping the fish too."

She printed her name on each wooden fish before throwing it

into the water. "I want that river to know who I am," she would say. "I want everybody to know who I am."

She would spend afternoons staring at her name, printing it over and over on Isaac's carvings. The Ruby-Jewels had taught her the alphabet, but the only letters she was interested in were *her* letters. She developed what was to become a lifelong fascination with her name, and Lottie Faircloth was held accountable.

"It's such a pretty-sounding name," Lottie said when Zeda started to school. "The kind of name that looks good on paper too."

Zeda printed her name on all her textbooks and on every scrap of paper she could find. She would often sit in Lottie's class and stare at her name, wondering what it meant, if anything at all.

"Are names supposed to mean something," she asked Lottie one day.

"Everything means something," Lottie replied. "Especially a name. But it's up to the individual to discover the meaning." Lottie was proud of her answer. She hoped that it would encourage Zeda Earl to study harder.

But Zeda Earl wasn't interested in studying, and therefore, she wasn't a very good student. She had trouble with math and science and thought history as boring, but she could draw better than anyone. Because she controlled her pencil so well, Lottie decided to teach her penmanship early.

"A name like Zeda Earl deserves something fancier than printed letters," Lottie said. She taught Zeda Earl the *written* alphabet and showed her how to connect one letter to the other. Then she encouraged her to write her name with swirls and curlicues and decorative dots carefully placed. It was her first name that intrigued Zeda Earl the most, and she practiced writing it in as many different styles as she could think of.

"That child's trying to write something out of her system," Lottie said. "I wonder what it is." She told Bessie the only thing to do with Zeda Earl was leave her alone and let her grow out of whatever it was she had grown into. But she never did. As she grew older, the fascination with her name increased. She wanted everyone to know her, so she wrote her name on the sides of houses, on trees and rowboats. When Lottie Faircloth saw what Zeda Earl had done, she said she was sorry she had ever taught the child to write.

"Besides my own son, I have had only two students who have been hard if not impossible to teach," Lottie confessed, but only to herself. "One was Billy Wiggins and the other is Zeda Earl, but I haven't completely given up on her yet. Thank God Almighty I don't have to teach Billy-Wiggins'-Boy-By-Elsa-Mae-Broom. If I had him in class I'd never be able to give Zeda Earl the attention she deserves. I have counted my blessings that Billy Wiggins' Boy is too dumb for school. He can stay on that island until the world comes to an end, I don't care. That's a good place for him."

Elsa Mae's son by Billy Wiggins was his father made over. He was born three months after Zeda Earl's first birthday, and by the time he was ten years old he had *discovered* Zeda Earl. He took a special interest in her and went out of his way to make their paths cross, but Zeda refused to notice him. He repulsed her, and she wouldn't even throw a glance in his direction. Determined to gain her attention one way or the other, Billy Wiggins' Boy began chasing Zeda Earl around the camp. He would catch her and kiss her on the cheek, and sometimes pull her hair until she screamed. "I like it when she looks at me," he would say. He aggravated her constantly.

"I hate Billy-Wiggins'-Boy-By-Elsa-Mae-Broom," Zeda Earl told Lottie. "I hate him more than this house I'm forced to live in and more than this place that's not my home."

"Hate is a very strong word," Lottie said. "Perhaps you mean dislike."

"No," said Zeda Earl. "I mean hate."

"In that case," said Lottie, "you will stay after school and write the word "love" on the blackboard until there's no more space left."

Zeda Earl wasn't the only one who hated Billy Wiggins' Boy. Prissy Way Barlow hated him too. Prissy Way, one year older than Zeda Earl, lived upriver and came to school in a rowboat. Prissy and Elsa Mae were distant cousins, but Prissy didn't claim her. She went out of her way to let everyone know just how much she disliked Elsa Mae and everyone else associated with her. She started an ongoing game of tag, inspired by Elsa Mae and her white-skinned children.

"You're a Dirty Ole Broom," Prissy would say, slapping one of her classmates on the arm or back. Then the Dirty Ole Broom would relinquish the title by tagging someone else.

The game was forever interrupting Lottie's classes, and, after she had endured more than her nerves would allow, she prepared a sermon. "Pupils!" she said. "There's nothing I can do for you but pray to the Lord Jesus who died on the cross that one day you will all outgrow your pitiful prejudice."

Zeda Earl interrupted her. "I will never outgrow my prejudice, Mrs. Faircloth. So don't you ever suggest such a thing again. Prissy Way Barlow, who used to be my best friend, has tagged me too many times for me to forgive her. She's got everybody believing I'm a Dirty Ole Broom when I'm the furthest thing from it. I'll have to move forty miles away from here in order to live down my horrible reputation."

"Zeda Earl," said Lottie, "I intend to forgive you for disrupting my class whether you want to be forgiven or not. It is my Christian duty to do so, but you will not get away with this without being punished."

Lottie sent Zeda Earl to stand in the corner where she wrote her name fifty times on the wall. When Lottie saw what Zeda had done she made her scrub the wall clean and stand outside until the end of the day when she received another lecture.

"Zeda Earl," Lottie said, "I want you to know that I have taken into consideration the fact that you are going through a very difficult period that we have all experienced. You have grown too tall too fast. Therefore, your mind is not capable of keeping up with your body. Already, you're the tallest girl in this school, and I know that's not easy for someone like you."

Zeda Earl was not only tall, her bones were big, and she didn't have much flesh on them. Her nickname was Broomstick. The Ruby-Jewels taught her to fight anyone who called her that, especially Billy Wiggins' Boy. Zeda Earl learned to slap, or bite or use her fists; it didn't matter to her. What did matter was her name. She was not a Broom. And she was not an Overstreet.

Bessie wasn't her real mother. And Isaac wasn't her father either. She was certain of that, and so was Billy Wiggins' Boy.

"Who do I belong to?" Zeda Earl asked her mother.

Bessie, standing in her gardens, studied the Lemon Lilies for a moment and said, "Children belong to the parents who love them the most. You're Zeda Earl, and you're my daughter. You're Isaac's daughter too. I saw to that."

"Then why do I feel like I've been born in the wrong place and to the wrong people? I don't think I asked to be born."

"I didn't know there was any asking to it," said Bessie. "Maybe we decide to, but I don't think we ask to."

For a while that satisfied Zeda Earl, but Prissy Way Barlow's game of tag continued, and Zeda Earl usually ended up the loser. That always made her angry. The other children enjoyed seeing her lose her temper, so they tagged her and kept on tagging her.

There were days when Zeda Earl would come home so unhappy that Bessie would do anything in her power to raise the child's spirits. She sewed evening gowns for her to wear around the house, and eventually around the camp. Zeda Earl liked that. It made her feel important to wear taffeta or dotted swiss. Long skirts were her greatest pleasure, so Bessie kept her fingers sewing and her eye on inexpensive yardage. She would rip up almost anything to make Zeda Earl a new frock.

The Ruby-Jewels added their say. They encouraged their little sister to wear makeup, and they practiced new styles on her long black hair. "This is probably what you will look like by the time you get married," said a Jewel, adding a beauty mark to Zeda Earl's colorful face. They had her believing that she was already an adult in the sixth grade.

Peter Faircloth made her an elaborate paper crown and turned a window curtain into a long train which he tied around Zeda Earl's neck. The Ruby-Jewels and Peter lifted the curtain off the ground as the new queen pranced around the camp. Zeda Earl ate up the attention. She became so accustomed to being made over that she pitched fits until Bessie broke down and allowed her to wear makeup and long dresses to school.

"Why do I give in so quickly?" Bessie said as she watched her daughter get ready for class. "Nobody else would put up with this, I don't think."

Often Zeda Earl would go to school wearing a face filled with color, a crown on her head and a long skirt that swished when she walked. "One day you'll all look back and remember knowing me and be glad I was in your class," she would say, sitting perfectly straight in her chair. That kind of talk caused the pupils to aggravate her even more. They would steal her crown, and mess up her hair and tag her a Dirty Ole Broom. Zeda was constantly having to relinquish her dignity by chasing someone down in her long skirts. Her feet were flat and her ankles were weak. She could hardly run at all, and the moment she tagged someone, she would be tagged right back again. She was always a Broom.

"Maybe she is Broom's child after all," said Bessie. She was talking to the earth. Down near the lily gardens, and not far from Zeda Earl's three little graves, Bessie dug a hole, a deep one, and into it she spoke her doubts. "Children are almost always the first ones to figure things out, especially things you wouldn't think could be figured out." She remembered to the earth what had happened on that hot afternoon when the sun had seared her reasoning and she had found herself on Doc Broom's steps. She remembered how much she believed everything that Navasota had told her. "Now," she said, whispering so low even the earth had trouble hearing her deepest thoughts, "I don't know who Zeda Earl is. Why should I expect *her* to know who she is? I should have stuck to my promise and given Isaac only two children. Promises like that should never be broken." Then she buried her head deeper into the ground and listened to what the earth had to say. A cool, moist air bathed her face. While digging the hole, her shovel had sliced through sassafras root, and now that sweet essence came to her with a voice that was unmistakably Navasota's. "Be good to your troubles. Kiss them good-bye, or they'll come right back on you."

Bessie took the advice. That day she buried her doubts, and for a while they did not trouble her. But the next spring, reeds grew over the place where the doubts were buried. They seemed to have grown up overnight. Suddenly they were there, and one day, before Bessie had noticed them, a wind came and blew low across the earth. The wind rattled the reeds, and they whispered her secrets for all to hear.

Mary Twitchell, who took pride in knowing the lives of others, was sleeping with her head near a window. A breeze blew into her bedroom, ruffled her sheets and awakened her with a voice she had never heard before. "I think somebody just told me something I'm not supposed to know," she said, sitting up in bed. She couldn't decide if she was still sleeping or not.

"You ought never to sleep on a hot afternoon," said Peg Leg. "It's not good for you."

"Somebody just told me something about Bessie," Mary said, rubbing her eyes. "I'll be damned, if I can remember what it was."

She looked out the window. Bessie was pulling up weeds. She was pulling them up by their roots and burning them. Then she tied a pillowcase on a pole and walked around the camp sifting the air. "I'm collecting some things that got away from me," she told Izzie Burrow when he inquired. He thought that somebody's honeybees had flown away, and she was out to capture them.

But Mary Twitchell said, "No, that's not it. I think she thought something that she had no business thinking. And now she's trying to take it back. I think I heard her thinking whatever it was she thought. Only thing is, I can't recall what I heard."

Bessie collected, in her pillowcase, and in her heart, all her troubles, all her wandering doubts and all her misgivings, not only about Zeda Earl, but about her husband, his failing health and his dependence on Doc Broom. She buried all her troubles deep within the earth. This time she was determined that they would never escape.

She could now look at Zeda Earl and see her daughter again. She could look into Zeda Earl's face and see Isaac, a healthy man with many years left. And that made her happy. But when she stared too long into her daughter's eyes she could also see more discontent than could be contained in all the brown paper sacks hanging from dozens of cane poles that Billy Wiggins had placed along the Sabine.

Billy-Wiggins'-Boy-By-Elsa-Mae-Broom was determined to help Zeda Earl know exactly who she was. His father had said that was his mission, and his mother had said so too. Elsa Mae had taught him to write four words: Ain't Nothing At All. It had taken him a long time, but finally he had mastered the order of the letters. Elsa Mae told him that one day he would be called on to write those four words in a place where they would do the most good. Soon he got his chance.

Zeda Earl had written her name on all sides of Mary Twitch-ell's house except one. The day she was correcting her over-sight, Billy Wiggins' Boy slipped up behind her and took the brush out of her hand. After her name he wrote, "Ain't Nothing At All." "You're the part of me you don't know nothing about yet," he said. "But one day you'll know that part of me and like knowing it too."

"Billy Wiggins' Boy, I'm about to beat you slam to death," Zeda Earl said, attacking him with her fists.

"You ain't nothing at all and never will be nothing at all," he said, standing up to her blows. "You better realize that your world ain't nothing to be something in."

She was about to slap his face on both sides when he dropped his pants and peed on her feet. "My daddy says if I pee on you enough you'll go to changing colors. You'll get real white-skinned like me."

"I'll never be white like you," she said, running toward her sisters' house.

"Thank God Billy Wiggins' Boy doesn't have the sense it takes to pull up his pants," Zeda Earl told Peter Faircloth after she locked the door. "If he did, I'd never have outrun him. He's trying to give me white spots, and I already have one."

Peter Faircloth took off her shoes and examined her feet with a magnifying glass. "I count three white spots," he said. "Sisters, come see."

The Ruby-Jewels, wearing identical dresses of ticking, took the magnifying glass and examined Zeda Earl's ankles. They inspected her toes and the bottoms of her feet, and they both agreed that their sister was developing "little white blemishes."

"Don't worry yourself ugly, Miss Throw-a-Fit."

"We won't let that boy wet on you another time."

The sisters armed themselves with sandpaper and flyswatters, their favorite weapons. They caught Billy Wiggins' Boy and beat him with the swatters until their arms hurt. They rubbed sandpaper on the bottoms of his feet, and then they abused him with words.

"You goddamn sonofabitchin' bastard-boy."

"You think our sister's just a toy."

Mary Twitchell threw a pan of dirty dishwater on them and the twins turned on her.

"You crazy ole red-headed crooked-nose witch."

"You're nothing in the world but a mean ole bitch."

Then they picked up their flyswatters and chased Billy Wiggins' Boy all the way back to his island.

"Don't you ever come around our sister Zeda again."

"She's got more important things to think about."

"And one of them's herself."

"And one of them's herself."

When they returned to their house by the river, Zeda Earl was crying again. Her voice carried up and down the Sabine. She almost never stopped that day. "I can't wait to get away from here," she screamed. "Nobody knows who I am."

* * *

By the time Zeda Earl had entered the eighth grade, all she talked about was Splendora. "When are we going to Splendora?" she would ask Isaac, and he would say, "I don't believe I've left anything there, so why should we go?"

"When are we going to Splendora?" she would ask her mother, and Bessie would say, "Oh in a day or two maybe we will."

"When are we going to Splendora?" she would ask her sisters, and they would say, "What's wrong with where we are?"

Redd was held accountable for Zeda Earl's craving for life in the town. Each week he gave her the county newspaper to read, and that's all it took. She wanted to know those streets, and those houses and wear those clothes worn by the ladies whose pictures were in the *Star Reporter*. She also wanted to see her name in print.

"Wouldn't you know?" said Mary Twitchell. "The Sears and Roebuck catalog *would* be next. Zeda Earl can't fix her attention on anything sensible."

Redd allowed Zeda Earl to look at his catalog, but he did not allow her to take it home. He knew he would never see it again if he did. So she would camp out in the store almost every afternoon and compare the fashions in the newspaper with those in the catalog. Everyone said she was bound to become a seamstress, but Zeda Earl said, "No. I wouldn't think of it. I intend to employ my own seamstress, and a very good one, too."

Her ambition was to become a housewife, but not just any housewife. She wanted a rich husband, two daughters and a big brick home with a proper bathroom and as much hot water as she could stand. She wanted clothes closets she could get lost inside, and a dressing room with a vanity table and lights around her mirror. She wanted a double garage, and two cars and someone to drive her everywhere she wanted to go. She never wanted to scrimp on anything. She never wanted to worry about having enough money to buy up-to-date clothes, or to take spur-of-the-moment trips. Her dream was to be able to walk into a beauty parlor and walk out as a completely different human being. She was sure her needs were basic, that she wasn't aiming too high and that one day she would see her dreams come true. That was why she had decided to attend the county high school whether Lottie Faircloth thought she was qualified or not. One way or the other, she had to get to Splendora fast.

After passing the eighth grade, Lottie's students were eligible to attend secondary school in Splendora, but to her disappointment, no one ever bothered. It was too far away.

"I have taught some brilliant students who should have continued their studies, and didn't," Lottie said. "Then there's Zeda Earl. All she wants out of school is a husband to support her."

"That won't be hard," said Mary Twitchell. "She's pretty enough."

"I can't dispute you there," said Lottie. "But Zeda Earl can and will. She thinks she's the ugliest thing that ever walked."

Zeda Earl was ashamed of her looks. Her high cheekbones and dark complexion made her afraid that people would think she was an Indian. And, that wasn't all. She despised her hair. It was coarse and thick and had never taken a curl of any kind. She hated her eyes too. To everyone else they were large and black with heavy lids and thick lashes, but to Zeda Earl they were much too small and deeply set, like her mother's, and she swore she didn't have any lashes to speak of. She would give anything, even half her life, to be able to make herself over. She was too tall. She just knew she was. Her legs were too long. She just knew they were. Her nose was too thin. She was convinced of it. And her feet were too flat to wear a fashionable shoe. To hear her talk, she was ruined forever.

She was afraid she was ordinary-looking and that her skin was bad. She was afraid she would wrinkle early, that her eyelids would sag and that she would get those little up-and-down lines around her mouth like her mother had. She promised herself that she would never look old no matter how long she lived, and that one day she would be so rich she could have the white spots on her ankles removed by a doctor who knew what he was doing.

Bessie assured her that those spots were nothing but pigmentation blemishes and that they ran in the family. But Zeda Earl was convinced that hers were getting bigger, and she prayed to God that He would make them go away, or move them to a more private part of her body, just anywhere as long as they were out of sight.

"This could ruin my life," she told her mother.

"There are many things that could ruin your life," Bessie said. "Those spots are the least likely."

* * *

Each morning Zeda Earl walked a mile along logging roads to the blacktop where the school bus picked her up. In high school she excelled in home economics. She was the fanciest pastry cook in her class. She could decorate a cake in record time, plan a menu faster than anyone, including Miss Sam Westly, her teacher, and as a seamstress, there was no one better. Zeda Earl could sew up the frilliest party dress in less than an afternoon, but she always had trouble with simple everyday housedresses. They were just too ordinary.

Oh how she hated the word "ordinary" and prayed that no one would ever apply it to her. She had a fear of anything common, and a love of all things modern and for that reason she couldn't wait to finish school and move to Splendora, population seventeen hundred. It was the place of her dreams.

"It's hard to live in a place that embarrasses you in front of your new friends," Zeda Earl told her mother. They were sitting on opposite sides of the dining room table. A crane was in Bessie's lap, and two were sitting at her feet. "I wouldn't want anybody in town to see where I live. I wouldn't want anybody to see you and your birds and Papa and his fish. And I wouldn't want anybody to see this ugly house. This sorry old place is about to age me beyond recognition. We don't have running water. We don't have electricity. We don't have anything. One more year around here and I'm bound to be dead."

"One more year of listening to you, and I'm bound to be dead too," Bessie said, trying to laugh off her daughter's discontent. "So you better figure out a way to move on and get it over with. Anybody who wants to do something that bad had better do it. Just don't forget to come back every once in a while and let me know you're still living. We'll try our best to recognize you."

"Well, I wish you would say that without laughing," Zeda Earl said.

"Sometimes I don't know what else to do, Zeda Earl." Bessie's voice was very heavy now. "I don't know what would make you happy anymore. If we could give you all the things you seem to want, you'd still be miserable. I'm sure of that."

"Sometimes I wish I had never been born," said Zeda Earl.

"Sometimes you almost make me wish that for you," said Bessie. She had absorbed so much of Zeda Earl's unhappiness she felt like one of the brown paper sacks Billy Wiggins was still hanging on poles along the river.

"One of these days," she told him, "I want you to make one of those poles for me. I think I need it worse than Zeda Earl." The next day Billy planted a cane pole in the lily gardens. The sacks hanging from it were for Bessie. And when the wind blew them open she tied them shut herself and watched them burn.

"It's funny how much better this makes me feel," she said as she watched the grocery sacks turn into ashes.

From the back of the store, Lottie Faircloth was watching her. "Bessie Overstreet!" she screamed. "What are you doing down there? Behaving like Billy Wiggins?"

"Well, I've got to do something," said Bessie as Lottie led her home. "Zeda Earl is the most unhappy child I have, and I include Peter Faircloth in that count. I wish I could find a good place for her, even if that place was somewhere far away."

* * *

Zeda Earl saw her opportunity and she seized upon it. In her junior year, she entered a beauty contest. All she wanted was the prize money. It would be enough for her to move away from home and establish herself. The Miss Hello Contest was a preliminary competition for all girls in Southeast Texas who desired to vie for the state title.

Zeda Earl spent weeks preparing herself. Her talent was dressmaking and her specialty was fancy buttonholes. Her motto was "A Woman's Place Is in the Home," and her Bible scripture was First Corinthians 13: "Though I speak with the tongues of men and of angels, and have not charity, I am become as sounding brass, or a tinkling cymbal . . ." She learned the entire chapter by heart just in case someone quizzed her. Her favorite bird was the singing canary, her favorite color was royal blue, and her favorite tree was the flowering dogwood because it had been used to make the cross on which Jesus was crucified. Her philosophy of life was: Success and achievement come through preparation and hard honest work.

"This is exactly what everyone wants to hear," she told her sisters, "especially the judges."

She felt secure with her wardrobe which she designed and sewed herself. She felt comfortable with her makeup, her hairstyle and talent entry. But she was insecure about her walk.

"I'm too tall and gangly and ungraceful," she told the Ruby-Jewels. "My feet are too big, my arms are too long and when I move I look like I'm coming apart at every joint. The girls who always win these contests know how to walk gracefully, but I don't know how to walk because Mama never taught me. Sometimes I just hate her for it too."

" 'Bessie-the-Best' can't know everything in the whole wide world, Sister, so hush your mouth," said a Ruby-Jewel.

"Miss Strut-Your-Stuff, we're tired of listening to you now. Don't you know it?"

The twins and Peter Faircloth were working on their first patchwork quilt that afternoon and didn't want to bother with Zeda Earl, but she was persistent. Finally, one of the Ruby-Jewels put down her end of quilting and prissed across the porch several times. "Notice how I swing my arms, Sister," she said. "This is what you call walking gracefully."

Her twin put down *her* end of the quilting and prissed behind her. "It's much easier if you put both hands on your hips," she said, swinging her elbows back and forth. "I believe this looks better too."

"Well, Sister, we've got this walking business down pat," said her sister. "And in less than a minute too. Do you think we've set a record?"

"Maybe *we* should enter that contest, Sister. I bet we'd win the graceful part anyway."

"Graceful walking can't be too hard," said Peter, "but if you make it real hard now it will seem easy when the time comes to really do it."

"Well, that's exactly what we'll do then," said a sister.

"We'll make it hard."

"We'll make it hard."

They took Zeda Earl to a place in the Thicket where a tree had fallen across Woods Creek. Peter Faircloth carried their quilting under his arm and sat down to watch.

"If you can walk across that old log with high heels on, Sister Zeda, you can walk across anything as gracefully as anybody," said a Ruby-Jewel.

"You just have to keep practicing and practicing until you've got it in your blood, Sister. That's all you do."

The log was slick. It crossed the part of Woods Creek known as Lily Hole. Everyone swam there, and because the log was springy, it made a good diving board. Zeda Earl strapped on her high-heel shoes and made it halfway across the creek before she lost her balance and fell into the water. Her sisters forced her to try again. Over and over she tackled the log, and each loud splash made Navasota Blackburn, who was fishing nearby, wonder what was going on.

After each fall, Zeda Earl's sisters forced her to try again.

"Practice makes perfect," said a Ruby-Jewel.

"We have proven that to be true," said her sister.

On the other side of the creek stood Navasota Blackburn. She seemed to materialize from the bushes and wood fern. Her white shirt was starched and ironed, but her overalls were wrinkled and rolled up. Her hair was tied in a red bandana, and her logging boots were covered with mud. "Let me show you how it's done, Sweetie Pie," Navasota giggled. "I bet I still know how." She crossed the log without a slip. "I've been called on to walk across more than slippery logs in my lifetime, haven't I Peter Faircloth? I believe you're the only one who knows that fact. I believe that piece of news won't go any further either." She took off her logging boots and put on Zeda Earl's high heels. She asked for the quilt top Peter was holding, and he turned it over to her. "This should put me in the right frame of mind," she said, wrapping the quilt around her like an evening gown. Then with one hand extended, her fingers slightly curled, and the other hand resting on her hip, she glided, almost floated across the log. On the other side she turned around and struck a pose by slightly lifting her patchwork skirt and glancing seductively at Peter Faircloth.

The Ruby-Jewels clapped their hands and squealed.

"I've got to learn how to do that," said Zeda Earl.

Navasota glided across the log several times. She walked with the most grace and femininity Zeda Earl had ever seen. "When you start walking across that stage," said Navasota, "you've got to put your eyes where your feet are so you can see where you're going. And that don't mean you walk around with your head down either."

For a moment she lost her balance, but she regained it fast. "I'm a little too old and out of practice," she said. "I was thinking about myself then, that's why I almost slipped. To be really good at this sort of thing you can't think too much about what you're doing. You'll mess up every time if you think."

Zeda Earl practiced for weeks. She practiced, with Navasota watching her, until she mastered the log. After that, walking across a stage, even in front of hundreds of people, seemed easy.

She did not win Miss Hello, but she did win first runner-up, and with the money she won, she moved to Splendora.

Lottie arranged for her to live with a family who had a spare bedroom. That was all she wanted. It was two blocks from school.

"This has made me very happy and very sad," Bessie told Zeda Earl. They were sitting on opposite sides of the dining room table and sewing new blouses and skirts to be worn in town. The cranes were resting their heads in Bessie's lap. "It's a blessing to see you move on to whatever it is you feel like you need. I did that too, but I was a lot older than you at the time."

"I'll come back, Mama," said Zeda Earl. But it would be a long time before that promise was kept, and Bessie knew it.

*   *   *

Zeda Earl's departure was followed by a silence that seemed to hover over the river and seeped into every household. "Our home is real quiet," the sisters said when the silence showed up at their front door. But it was too quiet. Especially the first day. The house on the river seemed too lonesome and empty to be lived in. Every moment they expected Zeda Earl to knock on their door. They missed her complaining, and her demands and her daydreaming out loud.

Finally, they attempted to distract themselves by making punch and roasting pumpkin seeds, but that didn't lift their spirits at all.

"There's only one thing to do," said a sister reaching for a tambourine. "When the sun goes down and the moon comes out we'll clap our hands and start to shout."

"Sister, my sister," said her sister, "I happen to know a dance that goes with that very song. Yes I do."

While the Jewels danced, Peter Faircloth played the spoons, and when his hands got tired he joined his sisters on the dance floor.

They danced and sang till the moon came up and went down again. Bessie stayed up late listening to them:

"We've done good,
We've done fine,
We've lived our lives
Without a dime.
Oh how happy are we three,
Yes sirree . . ."

* * *

For the next five years, the Ruby-Jewels and Peter Faircloth would live in that cluster of tiny rooms stretched out over land and water. During that time the only thing they ever fought over was a bed slat. How long to saw it was their difference in opinion.

The Ruby-Jewels didn't grow apart, but they did have days when one didn't know what the other was thinking.

"I don't know what you're going to say anymore," said a sister. They were fishing off their back porch and had caught a bucketful that day.

"Most of the time, I don't know what I'm going to say either," said the sister being spoken to.

"It's all right," said Peter Faircloth, pulling another sun perch out of the river. "I can just about always tell."

While Bessie kept busy filling mail orders for her fancy lilies, and Isaac replenished the river with fish, Peter Faircloth and his sisters sat on their back porch and made patchwork quilts. That was one of their greatest pleasures. Izella said they made the strangest-looking crazy quilts she had ever seen and wondered where they got their scraps.

"They wouldn't give away a secret like that if their lives depended on it," said Bessie. Her furniture was covered with quilt tops and so were her walls.

The Ruby-Jewels were good at working with their hands, and they passed their skills on to Peter. They excelled in cutting out tiny shapes and somehow fitting them together without a pucker. "They just have patience, that's all," said Izella. She inspected their stitches and pronounced them masters of the craft. Finally, they got up the nerve to enter their work in the Tri-County Fair. The crazy quilt division was the only category that appealed to them.

"Crazy quilting suits us, somehow," they said, after winning their blue ribbon. "This is our first year to compete, but we can assure you, it will not be our last."

No one had ever seen anything like their prizewinning quilt. "The patches are so small and odd-shaped it makes you dizzy to look at it," said one of the judges. "That's why it won."

After winning their first ribbon, nothing could hold them back. They took the prize every year for three consecutive years, and they also made personal appearances. Newspapers all over East Texas ran pictures of them holding their quilts or blue ribbons, or demonstrating the proper way to thread a needle. "Hold the needle away from the light," was their advice. "If you hold it up to the light, you'll never find the eye."

"Now we're expected to make an appearance at the fair every year," Peter said as they worked on their fourth entry.

"Because we've won three times in a row," said a sister.

"We've become celebrities."

"We've become celebrities."

"We've become celebrities."

"Everyone wants to know if success will change us," said Peter. He was cutting odd-shaped patches from a tablecloth no one wanted. "They also want to know if we'll change the way we dress. Sisters, you know everybody thinks we will, eventually."

They had special traveling suits which they wore only to the fair and had no intention of being photographed in anything else. Their outfits were made of ticking and topped off with long moss-green sweaters they had knitted themselves.

After they won their fourth blue ribbon for crazy quilting, Peter was asked to explain what they were wearing. "Ticking, ticking and more ticking, right along with our Moss Greens," he said. "We figured out a long time ago what we like to wear and we've stuck with it all these years."

"We've been blessed with the good sense it takes to come up with a combination like ticking and moss green," said a sister. "Most people wouldn't think of that."

"We not only know what we like to wear," said her sister, "we know what we look good wearing, so that's what we wear. It's as simple as that."

"We also know that our Moss Greens contain magic in their threads," said Peter. "They keep us warm in the winter and cool in the summer, and that's why we hardly ever take them off."

Then they started talking one right after another, so fast no one in the crowd could tell one voice from the other.

"Don't ask us to explain how these sweaters work because we flat don't know."

"We've got sense, but, fortunately, we don't have that much sense."

"We'd have to get scientists in here to explain it to us."

"And then we still wouldn't be able to understand what they were talking about."

"Plus, it would cost somebody a fortune."

"So it's better not to fill our minds with such foolishness."

"It might run us crazy."

"It might run us crazy."

"It might run us crazy."

The next year they did not enter the fair, although they did complete their entry, another crazy quilt, but this time it was made entirely of ticking. That was the autumn of many rain- and windstorms. The river was almost never calm, and that worried Bessie. Every time a storm blew up, she would watch the ramshackled house on the river as though her constant stare would hold it together a little longer. "That old house is bound to wash away one day," she would, on rare occasions, admit to herself. "I just pray my children aren't in it when it goes." She knew it wouldn't do any good to talk them into moving. They would never be happy anywhere else. And in that respect, she sometimes envied Lottie Faircloth, who was constantly trying to persuade them to move to higher ground. "It seems like it's harder," Bessie said, "to sit back and keep your mouth closed."

During those autumn storms she refused to go to the store with her neighbors. She couldn't see the house on the river from there, and, besides that, Isaac never went beyond the front porch except to deliver fish to the river. Through all bad weather, she would sit in bed with her husband and hold his hand. Wood shavings and sun perch surrounded them; old shingles and pieces of weathered boards found their way onto the bed and under the sheets. While watching the rain make patterns on the river, Bessie would sit there with Isaac. And she would say a prayer for her children's safety.

No matter how severe the storm, the Ruby-Jewels and Peter Faircloth always sat on their back porch until it was over. "We enjoy watching the river pitch a fit," they said. "But it's not something we recommend for just everyone."

On a gray October morning after five days of rain, Bessie stood on her porch and studied the swollen river. The cranes were in her arms, their heads buried in her hair. "You never liked storms either, did you?" she said to her pets. Isaac was sleeping soundly. He always did when it rained. Imaginary fish filled his bed as well as his dreams. Fish with wings and feet and feathers for scales were now being thrown into the Sabine. But Bessie wasn't thinking about her husband, and his dreams and his preoccupation with restocking the river. Nor was she thinking about Zeda Earl who had not been seen or heard from since the day she left home. She was watching the river and trying to estimate how many feet the water had risen.

The sun was trying to burn through the clouds, and that gave her some hope that the storm might be over. Here and there patches of sunlight fell upon the water, causing the foam to glisten like jewels in the bottom of a dark box. But the undercurrent had already eaten into the riverbanks, and, in spite of the sparkle upon the surface of the water, Bessie's worst fear was about to occur. "I sure hope they're out of there," she said.

They were all three sitting on the back porch and feeling

celebrated. They had popped popcorn, made punch and were discussing the crazy quilt they were about to enter in the fair.

"Something tells me we aren't going to win this year," said Peter.

"Sister, we can't let Brother entertain such a thought. It might happen."

"Sister, you're right," said her sister. "I'd rather die than not win the blue ribbon. Brother watch your tongue, especially in a storm like this one."

Their porch had floated to the level of their house. But they were confident that the water would rise no higher, so they continued eating popcorn, sipping strawberry punch and watching the clouds roll in. When a paper plate floated by, they all three jumped up at the same time to puzzle over it. Their feet pounded the floor. The walls began to creak. And the house swayed on its cypress poles. Then, in an instant, in a moment of time so brief it was almost as though it had not arrived, their house collapsed out from under them and washed away.

Bessie watched with steady eyes and a pounding heart. Some people said the noise of the house falling into the river sounded like a clap of thunder. Whatever it sounded like, everyone in Redd's store ran outside to witness a complete household washing away. Pots and pans and mattress and tubs of quilt tops, and colored scraps of material, and yarn, and pillows and crocheted curtains seemed as though they would never sink. And in the midst of it all were three bobbing heads. They were holding on to apron strings, shirttails and sleeves to keep from being separated. Lottie Faircloth went running to the edge of the water, but it was too late.

"They're the only children I ever had and ever wanted," she cried. "I loved them even when I didn't show it."

"They know you did, Lottie," said Bessie. She tried to keep her voice from quivering and her eyes from overflowing. But she couldn't hold back the tears.

When the Ruby-Jewels and Peter Faircloth went under for the third time, LeRoy Redd shouted, "They'll never come up again."

But Bessie said, "No, they'll come back up once more." When

they did, they looked straight toward her. They waved and blew kisses. She waved back. And then they were taken under for the last time.

"Did you see?" shouted Izzie Burrow. "They had smiles on their faces. I swear they did. I believe I heard some singing too."

"You heard and saw right," Bessie said, but only to her pets.

For a long time, she stood on the porch and waved to the foam, the raging currents and the whirlpools that had suddenly appeared where they had never been before. "That old river got mad today and took my children with him," she said. The cranes listened to every word. Perfectly still, they clung to her body with wings outspread. Heads and long necks rested on her arms, across her shoulders, on top of her head. "We all knew it would happen sooner or later." Bessie stroked her pets. "They knew it would happen, too. Sometimes, when you know something like this is bound to happen, it makes every day seem better somehow. Lottie can't see it that way, though."

Lottie Faircloth had to be carried home, put to bed and tended to all night. But Bessie refused to have company. "I just want to sit on my porch and be by myself," she said. The cranes sat with her. One on her lap, and the other two snuggled under her arms. While Isaac dreamed of fish flying through his house, Bessie, sitting on her porch, hardly moved at all for the rest of the day. When the sun went down, an owl came out of the woods and, for an hour or so, perched in the mimosa nearby. Neither Bessie nor the owl nor the three cranes made a sound. The night was completely still. Nothing moved, not even the air. But down on the water where the rambling house had been, Bessie heard, or thought she heard, the tambourine, and the spoons and happy feet pounding the floor. She closed her eyes for a few minutes and it all came back to her. Night after night she had sat on that porch and listened to them sing. She could still hear them and always would.

Oh how happy,
Oh how gay,
We have pitched
Our cares away.

Just us three.
Just us three.
When she opened her eyes, the owl had flown away. "I wish I could be going too," she said. "But I can't right now. Somebody's got to look after Isaac. Somebody's got to help him throw those fish in the river. And now we've got Lottie to contend with. How will we ever persuade her to go on?"

* * *

The next morning, Navasota's clocks woke her up. They were all striking at the same time. She dressed and hurried to the river. The sandbar had been washed away, but the currents were calm along the shore. Woodpeckers were flying back and forth across the water as though they had forgotten where they lived.
Navasota paddled her canoe downstream. Not far below Camp Ruby she found the three bodies. In their last effort to remain together, they had tied their apron strings to their sleeves and their sleeves to their belts. "I'm going to need some help here," said Navasota. She asked Billy Wiggins' Boy to assist her. They wrapped the bodies in sheets and carried them into the woods.
Soon they were standing before a live oak that was rotting from the inside. "This tree's about three times older than me," Navasota said, stepping over its roots and into the rotting cavern. "Everybody living inside here better leave now." Bats and owls obeyed her. She watched them flying off into the blinding light. "Here's where we'll put them," she said. "This old tree deserves a strong spirit."
"Ain't we got three spirits here?" asked Billy Wiggins' Boy.
"No," said Navasota. "Just one."
They placed the bodies inside the live oak and sealed the opening with rocks and mud. "There's only one person you can tell about this," Navasota said. "You'll know who that is when the time comes. If you tell the wrong person the tree will die, and that will cause you a whole lot of problems you don't need."
When Navasota returned to her house, the clocks were still striking. "Don't tell me I've put them in the wrong tree," she said. "That's not what I want to hear." She lit a bowl of sage and

sprinkled onto the fire a sweet white powder that ignited in the air. The clocks stopped striking.

Smoke Spirits visited Navasota that night, and in her sleep they told her that she was one hundred and fourteen years old. "That's enough living for anybody," she said as her spirit mingled with the smoke. "But I can't go yet. Tomorrow will be a better time."

The next morning she ripped the poster of the bareback rider off her wall and watched it burn. "People know as much about me as I want them to know," she said. "Anybody who knows more, better not be telling it." She threw her clocks into the river and watched them sink. Then she cast her magic scarves upon the water. "That old river needs these things in order to go on," she said. "I don't need them anymore."

She left her house with the door standing wide open and no fire burning inside. She knew the house would rot in no time. "Houses always do when nobody lives in them," she said to the ivory-billed woodpeckers. They were drumming away. "Pretty soon the world won't hear that sound anymore," she said. "Pretty soon there will be different sounds in the world."

She walked into the woods until she came to a pine sapling growing at an angle against a beech. The beech was hollow at the top. "That must be it," Navasota said. She balanced on the sapling. It felt like a swinging rope under her feet. "It's been a long time since I've walked something that had this much give to it," she said. Not far away Billy Wiggins' Boy was watching her. With her arms extended to either side she balanced her way up the sapling, one foot moving directly in front of the other, until she reached the point where the two trees met. Then she stepped from one to the other, but in doing so one of her beaded moccasins fell to the ground. Billy Wiggins Boy watched it fall, and when he looked up again, Navasota was no longer there. She had given her spirit to the tree.

PART SIX

A Place with Promise

For years Bessie had traveled upstream to clear the patch of ground that reminded Billy Wiggins who he was and where he came from. But the Thicket fought her every step of the way. Rattan vines and wild grape would spring up overnight, or so it would seem, and they'd cover everything in sight. Pine saplings grew with ease. Hickory, sweet gum and oak of many varieties were abundant. There was no stopping the growth. Bessie fought to keep Billy Wiggins's place alive, but in the end she lost the battle, not to the Thicket but to man. A pulp mill was built over Billy's special place. The mill was large and the tin roof reflected the sun with a blinding light that almost caused Billy Wiggins and his entire family to forget who they were.

Bessie told him to look for Ain't Nothing At All in other places. In desperation, he followed her advice. He looked for Ain't Nothing At All downriver. And there it was. He found it again. Then he looked for Ain't Nothing At All in the sky, and it was there. He looked for Ain't Nothing At All in the trees, and it was there too. It was also in the ripples the river left on the sandbar. Ain't Nothing At All was everywhere, and Billy Wiggins and his brood of children were part of it.

Bessie hated that pulp mill, not only for destroying Billy Wiggins's special place, but also for smoking up the air with the odor of glue. She hated it because its existence depended upon acres and acres of pine saplings that were cut each week and transported to the mill in logging trucks that groaned up the hills and could be heard, for miles and miles, ripping through the silence of her days. She said that the world was changing too fast, and there wasn't much she could do about it.

After Navasota had disappeared and left her house to the woodpeckers, the bats and the owls, it had seemed to Bessie that everything was different. Navasota's passing had marked the end of something. "From here on out, we're not going to be able to live like we used to live," Bessie said. "But that's not the worst part. We're not going to be able to believe like we used to either. Too much is happening."

Already on still nights she could lay in bed and hear cars passing on some unseen highway. She could hear sounds she had never heard before. And they were not the sounds of the world that she knew. The little sawmill down by the river was silent now. Bigger mills had taken over. And the air no longer smelled of pine and cedar like it once had. Bessie was sorry for that.

When the Ruby-Jewels and Peter Faircloth were washed away, half the Camp Ruby sawmill washed away too, and it was never rebuilt. Some of the workers moved on to other mills, but most of them stayed as long as they could with no income except what could be made off the river. Suddenly, Redd's business dropped off. If he had two customers a day he considered himself fortunate. And no one ever asked for a haircut anymore.

Isaac didn't know about any of this. Bessie didn't bother telling him anything that would upset the gentle rhythm of his last days. For all he knew, the Ruby-Jewels were still living. Bessie talked about them as though they were. She would tell her husband about the quilts they had made, and the fish they had caught and the new magic words they whispered over the water to persuade even the wise, old mudcats to leap out of the river. At times, Bessie found herself believing her words. At times, she found herself believing whatever she needed to in order to make it through another day. "I guess I've always been this way," she said. "I'm just now realizing it."

That year she especially looked forward to spring when the

lilies would bloom. On cold winter nights she would sit in bed with Isaac and tell him about her experiments. She would push aside the imaginary fish, and make a place for herself. She would take out her journals and charts and retrace her steps out loud. She had started out with an ordinary Lemon Lily, a Maroon Night and a Bright Dawn. And from there she had developed colors, shapes and sizes from single to double, and it had all been a total surprise. "You think you can control these lilies," she would say, "but they're single-minded and will do exactly what they want to do. It's best to accept that early on, if you can."

May was the month. "May will tell the tale," she would say on those cold nights when the wind blew hard against the house and spring would seem so far away. "That deep purple lily can't be far off this time. I can almost feel it blooming inside my bones."

When spring came, Bessie nervously awaited the appearance of the first buds. It seemed to her that the lilies were taking their time blooming that year. It seemed to her that everything had slowed down just to upset her. She didn't know what to do with herself and had trouble staying calm. While Isaac sat in bed dreaming and fishing and studying the clouds, Bessie paced back and forth inside the house and around the camp.

One afternoon, her feet took her automatically to the river, to the place where the ramshackled house had been. And upon arriving at that now empty spot on the Sabine she was again reminded of the truth: Her twins were no longer living. But there were days when she believed, or almost believed that they were. There were days when she could hear their voices in the wind that blew over the water.

She sighed and forced herself to notice the world around her. Up and down that stretch of the river changes were taking place. On the Louisiana side, several acres of trees had been logged out, and a new road had already been oiled and traveled on.

"When did that happen?" she asked herself. "One day when I wasn't watching, I guess. There must have been too many days like that."

The river was calm that afternoon. She waded into it and

looked down at her reflection. Her hair was gray. Her face was
wrinkled, and she was now slightly stooped. For the first time
she realized that she was not young anymore, and that she was
very tired. "Time has passed so rapidly," she reminded herself.
"It seems like this life of mine has only lasted a day."

To Bessie it was as though the world had grown old and worn
out right along with her. It seemed to her that the world, as she
knew it, was losing its need to go on. There were changes in the
air, changes in the softness of the breeze and in the smell of the
water. Rainbows of oil were floating on the face of the river, and
not far away the buzz of power saws shattered the stillness of the
day into more pieces than she could reassemble. A motorboat
sped by. "Why do they want to go so fast?" she asked herself.
"It's dangerous being on the river anymore. Didn't used to be."

She studied her hands and the network of purple veins leading to her fingers. At one time the veins had been small, but now
they were enlarged and some of them were broken. "When did
all this start happening?" she wanted to know. She dipped her
hands into the river and studied her palms. The lines in them,
all seeming to overlap at some point, reminded her of the network of logging roads, now there must be hundreds and hundreds of them, that crisscrossed the Thicket. Many of the roads
were traveled on by cars, and most of them were graded fairly
regularly; some were even covered with gravel and oil. "Soon,"
Bessie said, as she waded back to the shore, "there will be
telephones and electricity and new faces in the store." Part of
her looked forward to that.

Back home Isaac was calling her. His voice was like the howling of a dog. "He needs his medicine," Bessie said to Izzie
Burrow as she took a shortcut through his yard. "He always
sounds like that when he runs out."

Doc Broom was sitting on the porch when Bessie arrived at
his gate. "Isaac's run out again," she said, coming into his yard,
which was now enclosed with a wire fence. Broom's eyes were
closed, and his portable laboratory was at his feet. He wore no
shoes, no socks, only a hairnet that was crawling off his head and
a dingy white doctor's coat that fell above his bare knees. When
Bessie spoke he lifted one finger from an arm of his rocking

chair. Slowly, he opened his eyes, but he couldn't hold them wider than slits.

"I believe I swallowed the wrong medicine, Bessie," he said. "My eyes must be getting bad on me." A dark brown liquid dripped from the corners of his mouth. On the floor was the unlabeled bottle, its contents spilled, the floorboards stained.

Bessie realized that he was dying.

"I'm sorry for all the trouble I've put you through, Bessie," he said. She could barely grasp his words.

"I'm sorry for all the trouble you've put everybody else through," said Bessie. "I'm not sorry for me. And I'm not sorry for you."

Broom rocked to his feet. He steadied himself on the railing of his porch and then fell back into his chair. Bessie felt no remorse, no sadness, not even anger. Inside, she felt hollowed out. She took a breath, a long one, and her lungs rattled like a gourd drying on its vine. She wondered if her heart had grown so hard she could no longer feel, not even for the lowest creature that walked the earth. What she had trouble knowing, or at least admitting to herself, was the truth: She was trying not to feel, but she could not stop her heart from beating, even in Doc Broom's direction. In the end, no matter what she told herself, no matter how she protected herself from her own feelings: Bessie Overstreet cared.

That night Doc Broom was laid out in a coffin that his grandsons had made under his supervision. The coffin was padded with the feather mattress from Doc Broom's bed. It was his wish to be comfortable even in the grave and to have a coffin big enough to contain his portable laboratory. Mary Twitchell bought a new hairnet for his white mane, but she could not bring herself to put it on him. Elsa Mae did it without flinching, but she did not bury her father in his glasses. She needed them herself. She removed them from her father's nose and tried them on. They were far too loose, but she could see. "Oh," she said, looking around the room at her neighbors, "I didn't realize my eyes were so bad. Everybody looks so old now."

"We could have sat here all night without needing to hear that," said Lottie Faircloth. Although gray was snaking through her hair, she still plated ribbons into her braids and pinned them over her head.

"We *are* looking a little bit older," said Izzie Burrow, "but not that much."

"We're looking old enough to wonder which one of us will be the next to go," said Izella Wiggins. She was almost ninety and was praying for a hundred.

The next day Doc Broom was buried in Campground Cemetery where live oaks stood guard over the graves, and long fingers of moss fell like the hair of dark and forgotten angels over the wooden markers, some with no names carved on them. Bessie Overstreet placed a cedar wreath on the grave and then left with Lottie on her arm.

"I'm sure glad they didn't put Broom in that old coffin in the store," Bessie said to Lottie. "I'm thinking that Isaac might be needing it soon."

Bessie knew that Isaac would be the next to go. The moment Doc Broom died she knew that her husband's days were slowly running out along with the medicine he depended on. After he finished the last bottle, Virgil and Robert Douglas tried to match the ingredients, but it was useless. No substitute seemed to work. Isaac grew more restless by the hour, and one evening when he began howling and thrashing in bed, Bessie strapped him down. "I sure hate doing you this way," she said. "But I don't know what else to do."

Then she took the cranes in her arms and stood in the river while listening to Isaac howling with the dogs that had gathered outside the sleeping porch.

"If we stand here long enough, Pets, something good will happen," she said, as she watched the currents reflect the evening sun. The center of the river was lavender with streaks of red, but the sides were blue-gray, slow-moving and laced with foam. Bessie whistled a long, windy note, and the cranes, resting in her arms, straightened their necks. The day was slipping away, and the birds were almost ready to sleep. Their legs disappeared into the water, and their necks soon fell limp over Bessie's shoulders. They removed the pins from her gray hair and it fell to her waist. They burrowed themselves into it. Their bodies became her body, their wings her wings and their low whistling voices matched their keeper's.

As the sun disappeared behind the timber, and the last ray of light had left the river, Bessie prayed for Isaac's quick and painless departure. She also prayed that her time would soon come. The thought of living without Isaac was not living to her. The thought of being alone did not bother her. She cherished her solitude, but the thought of being alone without her husband, the man she had waited for in the river and loved so long, that was an unbearable thought, and she knew it would eventually become an unbearable reality. Above her Isaac was howling in perfect harmony with the dogs. It was hard, even for Bessie, to separate her husband's voice from all the baying, and the whining and the long throaty moans that seemed to originate from another time and place, another discontented and frightened creature that the world had forgotten.

The next morning she was still standing there, but by then, Isaac's howling had changed to constant laughter. The Ruby-Jewels had come back to dance through the sleeping porch and fish out the windows. Isaac watched them pulling in sun perch and mudcats, old bearded turtles and logs, tin cans and wagon wheels. "The magic fishing word today is *cucumber*," they said.

"Cucumbers," Isaac laughed. His voice carried all over the camp. "Cucumbers and more cucumbers."

Izella Wiggins woke up instantly and slid out of bed. "Who wants a cucumber?" she asked. "I don't believe there's a cucumber in the house."

Then she heard Isaac shout, "Collard greens!"

"Now collard greens I've got," Izella said, walking feebly toward her kitchen. "Collard greens I've always got. You can depend on me for that."

"Cornbread!" Isaac laughed. "The new word is cornbread."

"Who is laughing about cucumbers, collard greens and cornbread this early in the morning?" said LeRoy Redd.

"Isaac is," said Izzie Burrow. "That man must be starving to death."

Lottie ran down to the river. "Bessie," she shouted. "Get

your feet out of that nasty water and come home. Isaac's going to laugh himself to death if you don't."

"That's exactly what he's supposed to do," said Bessie. "We better be with him now."

Isaac's neighbors crowded into the sleeping porch or stood outside and stared through the windows. All around them fish were flying and magic words were materializing in the air. The Ruby-Jewels and Peter Faircloth, dressed in their uniforms of ticking, were fishing out the windows. They were catching coffee cups, tattered clothing and shoes of all sizes, with and without their laces. They were catching broken bottles, and baskets of flowers and bright colored birds with scales instead of feathers. They were catching the months and the seasons. October came flying through the window on a hook. Red leaves, like sun perch spawning in the shallows, filled the sleeping porch. Whirlwinds of December snow blew in and blew out again, and spring showers drenched the world with silver minnows that fell from the sky. Summer lilies blossomed on the heads of everyone standing there and waiting for all laughter to cease.

"People aren't supposed to die this way," said Brother Clovis Caldwell.

That made Isaac laugh even harder.

"We can die any way we want to," said Lottie Faircloth, "and that's a fact."

"I suppose you read that somewhere," said Mary Twitchell.

"No I didn't," said Lottie. "I didn't need to this time."

"This is the best way to go," said Bessie. From the corner of an eye she caught a glimpse of something. It could have been an old curtain flapping in the breeze, but it wasn't. She knew it wasn't. She had no curtains made of ticking.

Now I know what's so funny, she said to herself as she took her husband's hand in both of hers. Now I know who's here.

While fish of all sizes and colors were being pulled through the sleeping porch windows, Isaac laughed and his neighbors laughed with him. Suddenly, it seemed to Bessie that the house had levitated, that it was no longer sitting on houseblocks. It was in the air, and it stayed there until Isaac exhausted his lungs with laughter and drifted into an eternal sleep.

Izella Wiggins, holding a bowl of cornbread and collard greens, laughed at the foot of his bed until he drew his last breath. Then Bessie covered his face with a white sheet.

* * *

On the afternoon of Isaac's funeral Zeda Earl came home for the first time since she left Camp Ruby for another life. During her last year in school she had married the son of a banker. He was not the handsomest man in her senior class but he was the richest, and R. B. Goodridge had showered upon Zeda Earl all the things she ever wanted, all the things she had dreamed of and begged for; everything but a checkbook.

"You made a good choice," Zeda Earl had overheard her father-in-law tell her husband. "Your mother also grew up in a shack, only hers was on the Neches River. She's made the best wife a man could ask for because she came from nothing and wanted something a little better. A little bit better was a whole lot better to her, so she was easy to please. I gave her everything but a checkbook and she's never complained."

Without a checkbook in her purse, Zeda Earl returned to Camp Ruby. She now had two daughters, Daisy Irene, born the summer after her senior year in high school, and Iris Gail, who came into the world during the storm that swept the Ruby-Jewels and Peter Faircloth down the river.

Zeda did not bring her daughters with her, nor her husband. She returned alone, and had no second thoughts about coming back. She wanted everyone to see her.

Driving a black Buick with four doors and smoke-colored windows, she made new ruts around what was left of the sawmill, the sagging houses and several mattresses airing in the sun. Between the two mimosas in Bessie's front yard, Zeda hit the brakes. Dust flew everywhere. She waited for it to settle before getting out.

On the front porch of Bessie's house were six pots of begonias and Izzie Burrow drying up on the bone. He was rocking a baby—he couldn't remember whose—and watching the web worms working alive in the mimosas. Standing next to him was Peg Leg. His arms and bad leg were wrapped around a post. He was trying to roll a cigarette without losing his balance. Lottie Faircloth, grieving on the steps, was holding her head in both hands, and Mary Twitchell, her red hair brightly dyed, was standing behind the screen door and trying to see out. She had shredded two hairnets that day.

"Somebody come here a minute," Mary said to her neighbors inside the house. They were sitting around Isaac's open coffin. "Somebody come tell me who this is sitting in a fine-looking car. I ain't got no eyes n'more or I wouldn't have to ask."

Everyone except Bessie, who was resting in the back room, and Elsa Mae Broom, who was nursing her new baby, ran to the front porch at the same time: Lester Jenkins without his glasses; Bunyon Bostic without his shoes; and Clarence Pritchard without his wife. He still didn't have one. Two and three at a time they squeezed through the front door: Sally and Raymond Sticks and their eight-year-old daughter named Beauty. Gert and Bud McCormick plus three grandchildren, Carlis, Winnie and Bob, all fighting to be first. Next came Prissy Way Barlow, now a Brown and the mother of four boys, Matthew, Mark, Luke and John. "They're the ground that I stand on," Prissy always said. They followed her everywhere she went. Prissy Way's husband, Calvary, an evangelist since he was twelve, followed his four disciples out the door, and old Izella Wiggins followed Calvary. Using her cane as a weapon, Izella came pushing through the crowd to get a better view. She stood with her toes overhanging the steps and squinted hard at the car parked between the mimosas. The driver was just now getting out.

"I know who that is," said Peg Leg. He was still hugging the porch post. "But I'm not telling. The rest of you will have to guess."

Zeda Earl, dressed in black water-marked taffeta, and carrying a wreath of blue carnations, swished her way around the car. Long red ribbons dangled from the wreath—she had told the florist exactly how to make it—and written on each ribbon was the word *Papa.* She wore full makeup, high-heel shoes and a big-brimmed hat with a veil that touched her chin.

"I'm not sure any of you will remember who I am," she said, posed in front of her Buick. "So I'll just tell you and get it over with. My name is Zeda Earl Goodridge. I live in Splendora. I am the mother of two beautiful little girls, and I've come to say good-bye to Papa."

"Baby!" shouted Lottie Faircloth, now standing but still holding her head. "Bessie will be so proud."

"Lottie Faircloth, you have never called me 'Baby' before, so why start now? What's wrong with you anyway?"

"Zeda Earl!" Prissy Way Barlow now Brown, came running down the steps. The little disciples followed her. Prissy tapped Zeda Earl on a pleated sleeve and then whispered in her ear, "Dirty Ole Broom."

"I am no such thing, Prissy Way Barlow; don't you dare start that silly game today of all days; so help me I'm in no mood for it; and I never will be." Zeda Earl sucked in her veil with every breath. "Here I've gotten all dressed up to come pay my respects, and if you had the least bit of sense at all you'd follow my good example. That dress you're wearing looks like it's been hanging on a wire hanger for over six years. You better at least go home and press the shoulders out flat before you wear that thing to my daddy's funeral."

"Show your behind, Zeda Earl," said Mary Twitchell. "We're all just dying to see it."

Zeda Earl paid no attention to Mary Twitchell. Carrying the wreath like a shoulder bag, she stomped her way up the steps, across the porch and inside the house. The screen door slammed behind her, and the windowpanes rattled as she marched past tables of fried chicken and potato salad, cakes and pies and dumplings and sandwiches and iced tea already sweetened, all lining the way to Isaac's open coffin—the one Redd had never been able to sell. Bessie had bought it on time, but now Redd wasn't too happy with that arrangement.

Zeda Earl circled the coffin. "Papa don't look like himself." She stomped her feet.

"You're going to wake up Bessie," said Bunyon Bostic. "Better let the woman rest."

Bessie was already awake. "I'd recognize Zeda Earl's footsteps anywhere," she said, dreading the rest of the day.

"You've got Papa in the wrong place!" Zeda Earl didn't speak, she shouted. Bessie could hear her all the way to the back room. "Sweet Papa needs some sunshine on his face one last time. Now what we've got to do to rectify your terrible mistake is move him fast. It is my opinion, and I know you'll all agree with me, that the only place to put Papa's coffin is over there by the window. He won't look so sickly with some outside light hitting his face."

"That's where I wanted to put him in the first place," said Lottie Faircloth. "But nobody would let me." She was wearing navy blue, the darkest dress she owned, with a black scarf around her neck and black ribbons worked into her braids.

"Isaac can't go next to the window," argued Izella. "The flies can get to him too easy."

"They can get to him just as easy on the other side of the room," Lottie told her.

"Well, Lottie Faircloth! For once in your life you're right about something," said Zeda Earl. She shook Lottie's hand through the funeral wreath. "I congratulate you, and, I enlist your help."

Then Zeda turned to the neighbors standing behind her. "Will the pallbearers, whoever you are and wherever you are, please come forward and transport Papa to the place Lottie Faircloth has picked? He'll be more comfortable in direct sunlight, and he'll look more like himself too. Now, I'm going to go right now and stand on the very spot where his head ought to rest, and I know you'll think twice before you disagree with Lottie on this issue. We'll have no altercations among us today, not if I can help it. All of you know how much I just hate having a racket made over something like this."

She took the nickels off Isaac's eyes and jingled them in her fist. Then, swinging the wreath as though it were a tambourine, she sashayed over to the window and struck a pose. Six men including Peg Leg, picked up the dining room table with the coffin on it and carried it to the window where Zeda Earl stood impatiently rocking back and forth on her high heels.

When the sunlight fell upon Isaac's face, Zeda Earl clasped her hands under her veiled chin and shrieked, "Oh, he looks so

much happier now! Lottie Faircloth was right all along. Come
see, everybody. Come see what Lottie's done for Papa."

"Somehow this isn't turning out like I thought it would," said
Lottie. Her knees were weak and her head was swimming with
grief. She went back to the porch and sat down on the steps.

Everyone crowded around the coffin at once.

"I can't see a bit of difference," said Izella. "Isaac's still Isaac
to me."

"Well, you don't know how to see," said Zeda Earl.

"Well, my eyes are perfect," said Prissy Way adjusting her
glasses. "And I say we better bury him real soon."

"That's what I'm here for," said Zeda Earl. Shouldering the
wreath, she attempted to replace the nickels on Isaac's eyes. But
they were hard to balance. She had to work with them awhile
before they were in place. And, because of Redd, the coins
didn't stay there long. He had already decided that he should
have sold the coffin to the Broussard family. They lived only a
few miles away, had just lost a member of their family and had
the money to pay cash.

When Redd came to pay his respects, he took Zeda Earl off to
one side and told her she looked just like a movie star. "I do
wish more people felt that way," she replied. Then he asked her
to pay for the coffin in full, but Zeda Earl informed him that her
husband handled the money in the family and only gave her
what it took to buy the groceries. "I've got everything except a
checkbook," she said. "So I can't complain. Just wait until
Mama wakes up. I'm sure she has a little bit of money put away
for this occasion. If she doesn't have the exact amount now, you
can depend on her to come up with it in the not too distant
future. She's always been able to turn anything into a dollar."

Redd walked her back to the coffin. Over Isaac's body he
shook his head and made clicking sounds with his tongue.
"Something must be done about this," he announced to everyone in earshot. "This coffin is too short. Isaac's head's touching
the top. His feet's touching the bottom. And his knees are bent.
We'll never get the lid on tight. Our dear friend must be as
comfortable in death as he was in life, so I've scrounged around

and found another casket that's just about perfect. At least he'll have more room to stretch out in."

Redd had already hired some boys from across the river to make the swap. He motioned them inside. Before everyone's eyes, they lifted Isaac out of the casket. The nickels went rolling across the floor, and Zeda Earl ran after them. On the sleeping porch she finally stomped them down and put them in her purse. When she returned to the living room Isaac was lying in the cedar box the coffin had been shipped in, and the coffin was on its way to be sold for cash.

When Lottie Faircloth realized what had happened she screamed at Redd, "Nobody has any respect for life anymore!"

"I pray to God I outlive you," shouted Mary Twitchell as the coffin was being loaded in a pickup truck. "If I do, I promise to bury you in a pasteboard box."

Zeda Earl, embarrassed over not being able to pay for the coffin, decided it would be to her advantage to go along with Redd's decision. "Papa looks just like himself in his new box," she said. "When we get through settling him down, you'll all agree. Redd has done Papa a great big favor. I can see it. Why can't you?"

"Because we know better," said Izzie.

On the surface, Zeda Earl paid him no mind. She was determined to prove her point. "Will the pallbearers please come forward again?" She shouted as though the men had vanished to the other side of the camp, but they were only in the front yard. "Whoever you are and wherever you are, we need you now. Papa's beautiful new coffin is too deep, and we can't see his face from the other side of the room, so what I want you to do is lift him up and scoot him back, while I prop him up with a pillow or two. This is the best thing yet. Papa's going to look like he's sitting up in bed. That's the way he always slept anyway, and if his eyes fly wide open in the middle of the service that's not going to bother us one bit, now is it?"

After Isaac was propped up in the coffin crate, Lottie Faircloth said, "Let's get this funeral over with. It's very hard on everybody, you know."

"Lottie Faircloth, where are your priorities, anyway?" asked

Zeda Earl. "If you think all this is hard on you, just think about
what it's doing to me. I haven't visited Papa in years and years
and that makes me so ashamed of myself I could just about die
over it, so think about me for a little while, and you'll feel better
about yourself. Just be glad you're not in my shoes."

"Believe me, I am," said Lottie. "I always have been." She sat
down next to Bunyon. "Surely there's something else to life
than this, isn't there?"

"Yes, there is something else," said Zeda Earl. "But we've
forgotten what it is, and don't have time to think about it right
now. We've got Papa to take care of."

For once, Mary Twitchell said nothing.

Then Bessie, dreading every step, came into the room. She
had wanted a simple burial with no fuss, and no neighbors
gathering around, and no plates of food filling up the house and
no service. But no one knew how to bury anybody like that. No
one could accept such a thing, so Bessie had finally agreed to
her neighbors' wishes. She did not, however, allow them to
choose the grave site. That decision was hers, and she had
already selected the lily gardens. The new lilies would be
blooming any day now. They would mark the culmination of her
life's work, and something told her she would not be disappointed. She wanted Isaac to be buried where so much of her
energy had been spent. "I don't want him to forget me," Bessie
said, touching Lottie on the shoulder as she crossed the living
room. "That's why I chose to bury him with the lilies."

"Oh, Mama, Mama, Mama," Zeda Earl exclaimed, throwing
her arms around Bessie. "I know you thought I forgot all about
you, but I didn't. It's taken me all this time to make myself
presentable. And I didn't want you to see me any other way.
Come see what we've done for Papa. We've made him look so
comfortable."

"I've heard everything, Zeda Earl," said Bessie. "Redd's as
sorry as they come for doing what he did. But I'll make it up to
Isaac. He'll be buried in nothing before he'll be buried in that."

Then, Zeda Earl, who had just discovered the social value of
religion in Splendora, held her mother's shoulders and stared
obsessively into her eyes. "I've been worrying about something,

Mama. I know Papa was baptized, but I don't know if you have been or not. I was, just about a year ago, and my life changed for the better overnight!"

"I've been baptized," said Bessie. Her mind raced back to Sabinetown, to her mother, the wedding cakes and the yard filled with daylilies. She thought of her father working in his study and her two sisters sulking in the parlor. "In Sabinetown," Bessie said, "we were Methodists, all of us."

"I know all about Methodists, Mama." Zeda Earl lifted her veil so an expression of deep concern could clearly be seen on her face. "I know exactly how they baptize too. Sprinkling a few drops of water on somebody will not guarantee salvation. I am placed here to tell you this, and you are standing ready to receive it." She raised her voice to include everyone on the front porch as well as the living room. "Today we're going to baptize you, Mama. Yes, we are. We're going to do it the right way, and in the privacy of your own beautiful home. We're going to do it before Papa's cold in the ground too, because right now it's more important to save your soul than anything else in the world, and I truly mean that. I'm sure your galvanized tub is still hanging on the back porch. I'm going this very minute to fill it up with lukewarm water, hotter if you can stand it, and when the preacher arrives we'll get him to baptize you before he says a few kind words over Papa's body. You won't have to do a thing, Mama. We'll just lift you up and gently, gently, gently set you down in the waters of everlasting life. But first I'm going to put on a kettle of water, and then I'm going to choose something pretty for you to be baptized in because this is the most important day of your life, Mama, and in many ways it's the most important day of my life as well because I have helped you reach this decision."

Then she marched into the kitchen. "Somebody get in here and show me how to fire up this stove," she shouted. "Today Mama's accepted Christ as her savior. She's done so in a very personal and private way, and now we've got to heat up some water so we can baptize her comfortably before she changes her mind."

"Bessie don't need to be baptized any more than I do," said Mary Twitchell, following Zeda to the stove.

Zeda Earl attempted to set her straight. "Mama hasn't got the faintest idea what she needs, and while she knows a little bit about what she thinks she's supposed to need, it's up to us to help her go all the way."

"You don't need to be baptizing a person who's already good, through and through," said Izella, taking the kettle of water away from Zeda Earl.

"And you don't need to be upsetting everybody either," said Izzie Burrow.

"Don't any of you be standoffish with me," said Zeda Earl, pacing in front of the stove. "My dear sweet papa is dead. I never appreciated him during his lifetime, not like I should have, because then I didn't know the meaning of the name *Overstreet*, but now I do. My mother-in-law, Nelda Goodridge, who was raised on the Neches River, helped me to trace my name back, back, back, further back than any of you have ever thought about going, and on the Overstreet line, I'll have you know, we've found kings and queens. Yes. We've found knights and lords and ladies of all kinds. Yes. We've found dukes and earls and actors and architects, all sorts of important people. Yes. Yes. Yes. They are all there."

Bessie refused to listen any longer. "When you all get through doing whatever it is you seem like you need to do in order to bury my husband, bring him down to his grave. That's where I'll be."

After Bessie was gone, Mary Twitchell refused to hold her tongue another minute. "Overstreet's not your name," she said. A silence swept through the house. "Isaac changed it when he moved here. I don't know who else knows about this but me, but I sure am happy to be the one to break the disappointing news. Your daddy's name was Singleton."

"I always thought it was Broomstick," said Prissy Way.

"Shut up, Prissy," said Zeda Earl.

"Some of it probably was, and some of it probably wasn't," said Mary Twitchell. "But I can't go no further. It's something I'm not too sure of. Don't imagine anybody is."

"I can straighten all this out," Elsa Mae, still nursing her new baby, shouted from the living room. She rocked to her feet and sauntered into the kitchen. "Zeda Earl," she said, changing breasts on her baby, "you don't have one father, you have two. Not everybody does, but you do, and you should be thankful of that. My daddy was the father who brought you into this world, but he is not the father who will take you out of this world. Isaac will take you out. If you don't believe me, ask Billy Wiggins."

"I wouldn't ask Billy Wiggins the time of day, thank you," said Zeda Earl.

"Then you are a Broom," said Prissy Way. "I always suspected you were."

"What's all this about?" asked Lottie. "You must overcome your pitiful prejudice, once and for all."

Zeda Earl's head was swimming. A wasp was buzzing around her hat, and all the blood was draining from her face. Clovis Caldwell had just arrived to start the service, and Izella Wiggins singing "In the Sweet By and By . . ." was trying to move everyone back into the living room, but Zeda Earl wouldn't budge. "Where's my mama?" she said. "There's something I need to ask her, and it can't wait either."

"There will be plenty of time for that later on," said Lottie, trying to guide Zeda Earl to a seat, but Zeda Earl refused to be guided. She tore through the house looking for a door, just any door.

Bessie was in the lily gardens making last-minute preparations for the burial. The cranes were with her, and so was Billy-Wiggins'-Boy-By-Elsa-Mae-Broom. Bessie had asked him to make the grave a little wider, and he was doing just that when Zeda Earl came running down the riverbank toward her mother. The sand was deep. Her high heels tripped her. She got up. She tripped again. Finally, she slid the last stretch of the way. "For the last time," she asked Bessie, "who am I?"

"You ain't nothing at all," said Billy Wiggins' Boy, sticking his head out of the grave.

"I didn't ask you." Zeda Earl spoke with her teeth together.

"Be nice to my daughter," said Bessie. "For some reason or

other she's decided she needs to be here today, and I think she's right."

"Who am I?" Zeda Earl asked again. She was still sitting in the sand. "What is my real name?"

"People are given the names they are supposed to have for one reason or another," Bessie said. "Sometimes you're given a name that's not yours, and you have to go out and earn your real name. Isaac wasn't born an Overstreet. Navasota made him cross water. She made him plant two trees nobody had ever seen before, and she made him change his name. He thought of Overstreet. She didn't. It was his. She made him do all this to bring me into his life. He believed her too. But he didn't believe her enough. He had to build his house before he could really believe. That's when things started happening. If you believe in anything hard enough, and long enough, you can make all kinds of things happen. Isaac was a Singleton by birth. But he didn't die a Singleton. It came a time when that name didn't belong to him anymore. So you see all this tracing back didn't do you too much good in one way, but in another way it did you a whole lot of good because I believe, once and for all, you're about to place yourself."

"Who was my father?" asked Zeda Earl. For once she wasn't afraid of the truth. Bessie could see that in her eyes. They were steady and not filled with tears or anger.

"I'll tell you as much as I know," said Bessie. "Although I might be wrong, I believe you started out being Broom's baby. I was sick that afternoon. I collapsed, and he took advantage of that. I dreamed you were Broom's. But you did not end up being Broom's. Navasota took care of that. She saw to it that in my body you changed from Broom's baby to Isaac's baby."

"Can we believe Navasota?" asked Zeda Earl. Her face had turned white. Perhaps it was just the reflection of the sand she was sitting on, Bessie thought, but for a moment, for an instant and, for the very first time, she looked into her daughter's face and saw a flickering image of Elsa Mae.

"Can we believe Navasota?" Zeda Earl asked again.

"Sometimes I don't know. Sometimes it's better not to know some things. Sometimes we can find out what we need to know by not knowing what we think is the most important thing to know."

"You talk just like my daddy," said Billy Wiggins' Boy. His voice came from the bottom of the grave.

"I ought to by now," said Bessie. "I've listened to him enough."

"Mama, I want to tell you something I've been knowing for a long time," said Zeda Earl. "It's something I know with my head, but not with my heart. From way up there on the hill this ole Sabine River looks shiny and clean. But down here close it's dirty and muddy and smelly, just like everything else. Sometimes when I get real close to something I think I love, I find out I don't love it anymore, not the way I did. When I get up real, real close to something all the shine goes away and all the mystery and all the love. Sometimes I wish I had never gone to Splendora. I wish I had stayed right here and dreamed my life away."

"You don't wish that at all," said Bessie. "And I don't wish it for you. That's why I helped you leave. That's why I helped you get your clothes together and be on your way. As hard as that was, I knew I had to let you go."

"Then why didn't you let me know how hard it was?" said Zeda Earl. "Why didn't you ever tell me?"

"That's just one of many things I had trouble saying at the time," said Bessie. "I had trouble showing it too. I regret that now." Her mind raced through her life as she recalled her lost chances. There had been days when she had wanted to tell her own mother how much she loved her and didn't, knowing that her own mother had no time for sentiment and a display of affection, knowing that her own mother would have pushed her away and returned to her baking or gardening. Or, would she have? Bessie stared at Isaac's open grave.

"I wonder why I felt like I had to be so much like her, my mother I mean," Bessie said to Zeda Earl. "Why did I spend so much time doing the things she did? I didn't know what else to do, I suppose. I just never considered being another way. I wanted her to know, even after her death, especially after her death, that her life had meant something after all. That it had not ended. Every day it bloomed again. I wanted that for her. All these years, I've been keeping her alive and didn't know it. I think it's time to let go now."

"I believe this grave's wide enough," said Billy Wiggins' Boy.

"I believe you're right," said Bessie. Then she turned to her daughter. "You've come back when I need you the most. That means a lot to me. Even though I'm not good at showing it, just let yourself know that I'm trying to do my best. They're coming now. They're carrying Isaac to us. Nobody else around here, not even Lottie, will understand what I'm about to do. They'll all throw fits, but not as bad as the ones you can throw. That's one reason why you need to be here. I'm about to bury him in his last fishing boat. That's a fine idea, I think."

"Yes, it is, Mama," said Zeda Earl. "Papa will like that."

Billy Wiggins' Boy stood to one side as Bessie and Zeda Earl dragged Isaac's boat to the grave that was now much wider. They refused to have help. "This is something we've got to do ourselves," Bessie said. "It wouldn't be right to accept help from anybody else."

Zeda Earl understood.

When the neighbors arrived at the grave with Isaac's body, Bessie addressed them. "Somebody else needs that box worse than Isaac does," she said. "So I've decided to bury him in his boat. Zeda Earl agrees with me, and I know the rest of you will agree with her. You've already seen how she just hates having a racket made over something like this."

No one tried to stop her. The pallbearers came forward and lifted Isaac out of the crate and put him to rest on a patchwork quilt that was spread out on the bottom of the boat. Bessie made sure that he was still wearing his wire wedding ring. He was. And so was she. Then she tied a linen cloth around his face, and asked Lottie and Zeda Earl to help her wrap him up in the patchwork quilt. The Ruby-Jewels and Peter Faircloth had made it. "This was one of their craziest," said Lottie as she helped fold the quilt around Isaac's body.

"Mama," said Zeda Earl. "I want to put this wreath in Papa's boat." Bessie nodded her approval.

The wilted wreath was placed at Isaac's feet. Then Bessie took his last wooden fish out of a pillowcase. "These will go with him," she said. They were creatures with angel wings, with fins and tails, with human faces, human arms and legs, and yet, they were unmistakably fish: sun perch and alligator gar, shiners and old wrinkled mudcats with whiskers and fat stomachs. When Bessie was satisfied with their placement in the boat, it was lowered to the bottom of the grave.

"Zeda Earl and I will cover him up," said Bessie. "That's our job. We'd appreciate it if everybody went home now."

Isaac's friends dropped handfuls of dirt over his body and walked away. When they were completely alone, Bessie told Zeda Earl that she had something else to show her. After they had finished covering the grave, Zeda Earl stood up. She was in her stocking feet. Her black taffeta was covered with sand. She didn't know where her hat was, nor her gloves, nor her purse. She didn't care. "What else do you have to show me, Mama? I'm ready to see it now."

Bessie led her daughter to a corner of the lily gardens where the three small graves were surrounded by a fence of cypress knees. "There's no gate to this place," said Bessie. "We just have to step into it." They stepped into the enclosure where the cranes were bathing in the sand.

"Everybody thinks these are puppy graves," said Bessie. "But they're not. This is where I buried you. You tried three times before you were born. Three times you backed out on us, and the fourth time you got your nerve up. I hope we haven't made you too sorry of it."

"You haven't, Mama," said Zeda Earl. She had seen the graves, but she had never known about them. Bessie and Isaac had told no one, not even the Ruby-Jewels, of the significance of that place. Everyone had assumed it was set aside for the cranes.

"I feel like I'm looking at myself now," Zeda Earl said. "For the first time I think I'm seeing who I am. I'm not going to believe Navasota. I'm not going to believe Broom. I'm not even going to believe you or Papa. I'm going to try to believe Zeda Earl—and one of these days when I know a whole lot more about her, I'll really believe her. One of these days I'll make people's heads turn around because I'll believe her so much."

Bessie took her third daughter by the shoulders and stared into her eyes. "I believe you," she said. "I can't tell you how much I believe you, because I don't know how to say all that. But I do believe you, and I believe you will do what needs to be done. Now look here," she said, pointing to Isaac's grave. "I want to be buried right there with him. Nowhere else will do. Promise me you'll see to that. And promise me you'll take care of this place and not let anything bad happen to it. The world is changing so. See, you can smell smoke from that ole pulp mill today. They built it on top of Billy Wiggins' place, and they should never have done that. One day there will be so very few places left for people to be themselves in, and I'd like for this to be one of them. Even if they cut down every tree and every blade of grass for miles around, I want this place to stand as a re-minder of what a place is and what a place can do."

"I'll take care of it," Zeda Earl promised. And for the first time in their lives, they wrapped their arms around each other. "Oh, Mama, I always wanted to know what this would be like." Zeda Earl cried. "I always wanted to be one of your birds, because you seemed to love them more than anything else. They always got carried around and petted on. I hated those damn birds, Mama. I still hate them. I can't help it. I can't see one anywhere without thinking about you. And every time I see one, I want to kill it. I always wanted to kill those birds."

"Maybe I can help you not want to feel that way anymore," said Bessie. "After you got bigger I never knew what it would be like to hold you anymore. I didn't know what it would be like to hold the twins either. I always wanted to find out, but I wouldn't let myself. I couldn't then. I guess I was afraid of being pushed away. So I held the birds, and the Ruby-Jewels held each other and you didn't have anybody. Isaac was so sick by then." She took Zeda Earl by the hand and they walked back to the fresh grave. The three cranes did not follow them. "I need to be alone with Isaac," said Bessie. "It seems like a long time since I have been. This is the first night in so long that we won't be under the same roof."

"I'll return real soon, and bring my daughters to meet you," Zeda Earl said.

"Be sure," said Bessie.

They looked for her shoes, her hat, gloves and purse. Then, carrying these things in her arms, Zeda Earl walked up the steep slope. Bessie watched her. She'll forget and remember and forget and remember so many times before she'll really remember, Bessie said to herself. I know my daughter.

In a few minutes, she heard a car door open and slam. Zeda Earl was back in her Buick. On the hood, a little girl was painting her fingernails.

Oblivious to the child sitting on her car, Zeda Earl sat behind the wheel, and for a few minutes she watched the wind making tiny waves on the surface of the river. The water was silver, like tinfoil all crumpled up and flattened out again. It looked clear and clean, but she knew it wasn't. "I've learned so much today," she said. "Please, God, don't let me forget it."

Then she noticed the girl on her car. "Honey, get off my fender, it's just been washed!" Zeda Earl raised her voice. It was angry and harsh and carried all the way down to the river. For a moment Bessie felt as if she had been hurled backward in time. It was as though Zeda Earl had never left home.

Paying Zeda Earl no mind, the little girl just sat there painting her fingers and then her toes. "Young Lady!" Zeda Earl raised her voice louder this time. "Do you think you're sitting in a beauty parlor or what?" Bessie could hear every word. "Go find another place to paint your toenails, and go right now before I get out and slap you on both sides of your face."

The girl slid off the fender. "That's the ugliest child I've ever looked at," Zeda Earl whispered. Then, feeling ashamed of herself for having thought such a thing, she hung her head out the window and said sweetly, "What's your name, precious?"

Her sudden change in tone made Bessie smile and shake her head.

"My name is Beauty Sticks," said the girl.

"Beauty? Do you mean to tell me that's your name?" Zeda Earl was almost screaming. "You mean to stand right up and tell me that someone has slapped you in the face with a name you'll never live down for the rest of your life unless you change it. Now listen to me, precious Beauty, what I'm about to tell you is very, very important. Right now, before it's too late, you've got to decide what your real name is. *Beauty* simply will not do. It's liable to ruin your life. Take it from me, I know all about names."

"Who are you anyway?" asked Beauty.

"I'm someone who used to live here not too very long ago," said Zeda Earl. "But I left before your family moved in."

"What you ought to do is move back then."

For a moment Zeda Earl considered it. Then a look of horror came over her face. It was the meanest, ugliest, most frightened face Beauty Sticks had ever seen. She almost started to cry.

Without another word Zeda Earl rolled up the window. She backed up slowly. Then she took off like a bullet, like something had gotten after her, like she had nothing better to do than stir up the dust. She floorboarded the accelerator and created yet another road through the camp. She had to get back to Splendora fast, and nothing was going to stop her either.

Bessie smiled as she watched the dust rise up like a homeless cloud and slowly settle to earth again. "It's going to take Zeda Earl a long time to get used to herself," she said. "But she's on her way. One day she won't forget things so fast."

For a few minutes she stood in front of Isaac's grave. She had forgotten to bury his fishing pole with him. "I'll just stick it down in the dirt," she told him. "That will do until I can decide on the best way of marking your grave."

It was evening and the air was heavy. "Oh, Lord," she said, "sometimes I don't think I can go another step, and here I've still got a little bit more I need to take care of." She started up the steep slope to the house Isaac had built. The cranes followed her, but she wasn't thinking of them. Her thoughts had returned to Sabinetown and her sisters. "I wonder how long it's been," she said, "since they've mentioned my name."

* * *

That night Bessie slept without dreaming and without waking. The next morning she was filled with energy. She left the cranes in the house and walked to the river to check on Isaac's grave. Nothing had been disturbed in the night. The new lilies, growing next to the fresh mound of earth, were almost ready to bloom. "Two more days at the most," Bessie said. "Then we'll know for sure."

She got into her lily boat. It had been so long since she was alone on the river. "This is the last day I'll have the strength to do this," she said as she pushed her boat into the Sabine. Up the river she went, toward that old pulp mill she had grown to hate with all her heart, but she wasn't going to the mill, she didn't even turn her head as she paddled by.

"I know people have to make a living," she said, "but I sure wish they wouldn't smoke up the world while they're doing it."

Once she had passed the mill, she started looking for familiar sights. The river was different now. The trees she had once known so well didn't appear to be the same trees at all. They had fewer branches on them, or they just weren't there. Great patches of land had been cleared for houses, and new communities and new roads.

At Sabinetown she turned her boat toward the shore. She recognized the tree she had stood under while waiting for Isaac. Yellow cape jessamine still bloomed in its branches, but the branches seemed shorter. They no longer grew over the river. And the roots now extended from the earth like a dead man's ribs and disappeared into the water. She tied her boat to those roots and got out. She looked upon the tree as an old friend, but it made her sad to see it in its present state. "I always liked a tree that grew out over the water," she said. "I hate knowing that this one doesn't grow that way anymore."

Once on the high banks she could see the town. The first thing she noticed was that the church steeples were different; they were taller and thinner. And, from where she stood, Sabinetown did not appear to be as big as she remembered it. She wandered the streets looking for the block where the boardinghouse had been. She found a grocery store on that plot, and near it, a brick post office. Not far away was a variety store, a dry goods store and a café, all in buildings she could no longer recognize.

"That ole fire did more damage than I thought," she said.

"But if the fire hadn't come along, I suppose something else would have."

There were a few vaguely familiar faces on the streets, but she could not recall their names. Some of the older people she passed stared as though they were trying to place her, but in the end, they just walked by without a word. She could almost believe that she was in a different town, one she had never visited before. "If I can just find the spa," she told herself, "I think I can get my bearings."

When she asked directions, she was told that the mineral waters had long since dried up. "How do you people make a living anymore?" she asked. "The pulp mill down the way," the young man told her. "That's been a big help."

"Hadn't it, though?" Bessie said, and walked on.

She wandered until she found the place where the spa had been. A skating rink in a tent had replaced it. Then she followed the road to the two houses where Lettye and LaMerl had lived. The new occupants directed her to a Methodist home for the aged on the other side of town. She went there, looked for her sisters' names on the directory and asked to visit them.

"I used to know them long ago," Bessie told the day nurse.

"Too bad you didn't come last week," said the nurse. "Your friends were the stars of our annual fund-raising drive. LaMerl rocked in her rocking chair for five and a half hours in the middle of town. People dropped coins in her lap to keep her rocking. And Lettye, well, she rolled in her wheelchair up and down the streets and people made donations to keep her rolling. Between them, they brought in over a hundred dollars for our old folks home."

The nurse left Bessie at her sisters' room. Slowly she cracked the door. A strong fragrance of lilac wafted into the hall. She opened the door all the way to find Lettye and LaMerl sitting at the foot of their beds, a card table between them. Canasta had always been their favorite game. They were pink and fluffy in ruffled nightgowns, which Bessie was sure they wore all day long. Their fine gray hair was carefully waved. Bessie stood in the door looking at them. They were plump and spry and smaller than she remembered.

"It's about time you got here," said Lettye, putting away the cards.

"Yes, it is," said LaMerl, who was trying to color lips that were no longer there. "We've been waiting all day to have our sheets changed."

"The service you get around here these days is disgusting," said Lettye, arranging her butterfly sleeves. "You can't even get your bed made unless you beg."

"You do know how to make a bed?" asked LaMerl. "I'm only asking because you look like you're new."

"Every day there's somebody new, Sister," said Lettye. She was rubbing bright ovals of rouge on her cheeks. "What's this world coming to?"

"I don't know where the sheets are," Bessie said. "No one showed me. But I sure do know how to make a bed."

"The sheets are out there in the hall closet, even I know that," said LaMerl, pointing her finger and frowning with surprise. "Don't they tell you anything?"

"They never train new help, Sister. You know that."

Bessie went into the hall and returned with a stack of sheets. "I think you ladies will like the way I'm about to make your beds," she told them. "I think you'll sleep better tonight than you have in a long, long time. You might even dream things you've forgotten all about."

"I had a dream last night," said Lettye, "and forgot to tell it. I dreamed about our sister.

"Sister," said LaMerl. "How many times have I told you that we don't have a sister?"

"We most certainly do," said Lettye. "We just don't know where she is anymore."

"She was never our sister," said LaMerl, screwing on large pearl earrings. "She didn't act like our sister. I always wondered where she came from."

"She was different from us somehow," argued Lettye. "But she was still our sister, even if she did run off with some stranger. You took it personally and still do. I didn't. I don't take things like that personally."

"Yes, and that's your problem, Sister. That's why you've gotten old and mean and hateful."

"I am not hateful, Sister. Not to you, anyway."

"You most certainly are. You always have been."

"I am not. I swear I'm not. That's all there is to it. I'm not hateful."

While they argued, Bessie finished making the twin beds. "If I may say so," she said, "you ladies are very fortunate to have each other's company." She walked to the door to leave and Lettye and LaMerl watched her. There was something familiar about this new woman, but neither sister could say what it was.

"Sister, give me my glasses a minute," said LaMerl.

"Sister, you know I don't know where they are. Just squint if you can't see. That's what I do."

"Your sister was your sister," Bessie said. "I knew her. And she often remembered you."

"What do you mean, she often remembered us? Did she die or something?"

"She had a very good life," Bessie said. "But there were times when she missed you both. She told me so."

"Nobody could make up a bed like Bessie could," said Lettye. "After she made my bed I felt like I could sleep forever. I loved Bessie." She folded her little pink hands under her chin.

"Well, I didn't love her one bit," said LaMerl. "She was too much like Mother. But you're right. Nobody could beat her when it came to making up a bed."

"Can I have my bubble bath now?" asked Lettye.

Bessie slipped out of the room. She had heard all she had come to hear and was glad she had heard it. "Now I know where my twins got all their foolishness," she said. "I sure miss them."

More than ever before she was thankful for her life. Had she to do it all over again, she would still have gotten into Isaac's boat and left with him. "But there are many things I would have done a different way," she confessed, as she pushed her boat into the Sabine and looked back at her tree for the last time. "I would have gotten rid of Broom early on. I don't think I would have killed him. I can't say. But I wouldn't have just stood there and allowed so many things to happen. I would have taken better care of Isaac."

She turned her boat over to the river and floated downstream. "The air smells like poison now," she said, drifting past the pulp mill. "But I won't have to breathe it too much longer."

* * *

The next morning at dawn she waited in her lily gardens. Lottie Faircloth waited with her. The mature buds were ready to open. "They just need a little bit of sunlight," said Bessie. Patiently they waited. As the petals of the new lily slowly unfolded, Bessie felt her heart skip beat after beat. "Sometimes you can't tell what color they will be until they open all the way," she told Lottie.

But Lottie Faircloth already knew. "Oh, Bessie," she said after three lilies had opened completely, "please don't be disappointed."

The lilies were red. The most brilliant and vibrant red Lottie had ever seen. Their throats were streaked with lavender veins, and their petals were wide and delicately curled.

How did this happen? Bessie wondered. Years and years of work flashed before her. Years and years of cross-pollinating, and record keeping and planning and labeling and waiting and still the result was not what she had expected.

Bessie buried her face into her hands streaked with purple veins and twisted like the roots of a very old tree. She cried into those hands. But she was not crying for her lilies. She was crying for everything the lilies had given her and everything they had robbed from her life. She cried especially for Zeda Earl.

"Sometimes you have to accept things the way they come to you," said Lottie, repeating Bessie's advice of long ago. "Sometimes there's nothing else you can do. It's the hardest thing to learn, and there's no easy way around it."

Lottie Faircloth named the new lily the Ruby-Jewel.

* * *

That afternoon Bessie started carving Isaac's gravestone. She decided upon a thick cypress plank she had been saving for no known reason. She rounded the top with Isaac's carving knife, and sanded the surface smooth. She had never carved before, but she didn't consider that. Her hands moved automatically, and with more agility than they had known in twenty years. On the back of the marker she carved a bouquet of lilies and on the front a border of vines. Then she rested.

The next day she took a small crochet hook and carved three cranes on the sides of the plank. Their legs disappeared into water, and their heads extended beyond clouds and stars. Then she went back to the front. In an arc across the top she carved *Isaac Earl Overstreet.* Under it she was about to carve the year of his birth, but she couldn't remember it. Her head was filled with other things. Instead, she carved her complete name, *Anna Elizabeth Overstreet.*

She worked on the marker for an afternoon and a day. And on the evening it was completed she prepared to put it in place. After dark, when no lamps were burning in any of the houses, she carried the tombstone to the grave. Then she returned home, washed her hair, balled it up tightly behind her neck and dressed in her coat of feathers. It had been almost twenty-five years since she had worn it.

Into her arms she gathered her three sleeping birds. "I don't know what's kept you alive all this time," she said, leaving the house with her front door standing wide open. The moon was dark that night, but she didn't need light to see by. Her feet knew the way. At Isaac's grave she dug into the earth with her hands and placed the marker upright, anchoring it securely with rocks all the way around. Then she removed a short rope from her waist and tied it loosely around the necks of her pets. "Nobody will be willing to take care of you the way I have," she told them. "Not even Lottie." She tightened the knot around the birds' necks. Their beaks opened wide, but no sound came out. Their legs quivered. And when their necks relaxed, and hung limp, and their wings opened all the way, Bessie took them in her arms and lay on Isaac's grave.

The next morning Lottie Faircloth found her. The wings of the white cranes were spread over her body. Her face was pale and smiling. There was a heavy dew that morning. Fog was

rolling off the river and drifting through the camp. The trees
were dripping with moisture, and the Ruby-Jewels were leaning
against the tombstone Bessie had carved. Water was rolling off
their petals like tears.

EPILOGUE

Let It Be Known

N ot long after Bessie's death, electricity arrived in Camp Ruby. REA, Rural Electric Administration, had been around for years, but no one had wanted to string the cables through the Thicket. Finally they had to. But by then, nobody in Camp Ruby cared whether they had electricity or not. Nobody cared about telephones either. After Bessie's death all anyone talked about was leaving. Life just wasn't the same without her. "I never knew," said Izella, "just how much we depended on Bessie. Just what we depended on her for, I can't tell you, but we did. We must of. We wouldn't all feel so lost right now, if we hadn't."

A month after Bessie's funeral, Izella choked to death on a fish bone. A week later Redd suffered a heart attack while ringing up a sale and died holding on to a sausage sandwich. Mary Twitchell and Peg Leg took pleasure in burying Redd in a cardboard box, and then they packed up and moved to Hotel Dew, a thriving community with overnight lodging and the best used car lots in East Texas.

The McCormicks, the Prescotts and the Bostics moved across the river, just as far from water as they could get. The Sticks, the Stricklands and the McQuirters did the same. Robert Douglas and Virgil were sentenced to the state prison for robbing a liquor store, and Clarence Pritchard, who was getting on in years, advertised for a wife and married a beauty.

Izzie Burrow died of a sunstroke while collecting bottles along a new super highway, and Clovis Caldwell preached his funeral. All the trees had been cut in order to widen what had been a logging road. "And that," Brother Clovis said, "was the cause of Izzie's death. If the county had left well enough alone, we'd still have the dirt road, the shade trees, and Izzie Burrow."

Brother Clovis dedicated the rest of his life to saving the souls of Elsa Mae Broom, Billy Wiggins and their brood of white-skinned children. But the word of God didn't take on them. Their island in the middle of the river became known as Albino Island, and no one wanted to go near the place, especially at night when the inhabitants made music on tin can drums and sang to the moon.

Lottie Faircloth was the last to leave. She moved to Splendora and took a job as a substitute teacher, but she often returned to Camp Ruby to sweep out the houses and rake the yards.

"Let it be known that we loved our ole camp," Lottie would tell her students. "And even though nobody lives there any-more, Camp Ruby is still Camp Ruby, and it's still a *real* place."

Lottie's students worshipped her. They called her "Miss Let-It-Be-Known," and clung to her every word. She called them "little geniuses" and bragged on them constantly, with the exception of Zeda Earl's two girls. "It's not that they can't learn," she said, "they just don't want to. They act so much like Zeda Earl you can't stand being around them. It makes me feel like a failure to admit it."

Zeda Earl was now the trendsetter of Splendora. She had served on every committee from the Hospital Volunteers to the Ladies' Study Club. She founded the Splendora Little Theatre, and starred in most of their productions. She directed the annual Crepe Myrtle Pageant, and designed party clothes and parade floats. "As a society leader you are looked up to and gone along with," said Lottie Faircloth, "but, as a mother, you've got a lot to learn. I wish I knew how to help you."

Daisy Irene, Zeda Earl's firstborn, was fair in complexion and favored her father, but she still behaved like her mother. Iris Gail, the second-born, was dark. "Iris Gail is Zeda Earl made over," said Lottie Faircloth. "They could almost pass for twins."

Zeda Earl hated knowing that. She saw her own discontent breathing in another body too much like her own and that troubled her. So, she kept herself busy to keep from seeing too much.

From the very beginning the sisters were rebellious, especially Daisy Irene, the first to leave home. She fell in love with a man twice her age who lived near the city dump. He picked over the garbage and carried off everything he thought he could sell. His name was Clemmons, but after Daisy moved into his dirt-floor house everyone called him Lovie Dovie.

"Nothing could be worse than this," Zeda Earl said.

Then Iris Gail left home. On occasions she would return wearing diamonds and rubies in broad daylight. "At least Iris Gail has had the good grace to leave Splendora to live her life," said Lottie Faircloth. "Zeda Earl claims she can't imagine how the girl's supporting herself, but she knows all right. Sometimes I want to get down on my knees and say thank you Lord that Bessie's not living to see this."

One day Daisy Irene left town with her sister and for years Zeda Earl did not hear from them. During that time, just as so many people in Splendora had predicted, Zeda's husband, the president of the only bank in town, was convicted of embezzlement and sentenced to the state prison. After the trial, Zeda Earl, humiliated once again, went to bed for over a year and other than her servants she refused to see anyone except Lottie Faircloth.

Lottie kept a close eye on Zeda Earl. "I owe it to Bessie to do so," she said.

With Lottie at her bedside Zeda Earl relived her life, going over every detail, every minute, everything she could remember and many things that even Lottie had forgotten. Zeda would close her eyes and see herself as though watching a film. She would stuff her ears with cotton and still hear herself as though listening to a radio playing in another room. Day after day she listened to herself. Day after day she saw herself. And one day, after that year in bed, after she was so weak she could hardly walk across the room, she stopped hearing and stopped seeing. "I'm tired," she said to Lottie. "I'm tired of me. I've tried to be something finer than fine all my life, and I've been nothing. I never let myself feel like nothing before, but I feel like nothing now, and that nothing feeling is the best feeling of all. I always knew it was there, but I've been too busy feeling like something to get to it. Right now, all I want is my pride. My pride and my girls."

Hoping it would bring her daughters back, Zeda Earl started sleeping in their beds. She hung their pictures on all the walls and burned candles night and day. She started wearing long, loose-fitting dresses and balling up her hair. Makeup was now a thing of the past.

"You're looking more like Bessie every day," Lottie said. "Wonder what she would have done in a time like this?"

"I don't know what Mama would have done," said Zeda Earl. "But I do know what Papa would have done, and that's my next step." She sold her house, her furniture and all her jewelry. With the money, she bought Camp Ruby and the land surrounding it. She bought a used pickup truck and several loads of lumber. Hardly a penny was left.

"I have been the most forgetful person on earth," she said when she returned to the banks of the Sabine.

By then nothing was the same, and yet nothing had really changed either. Houses had rotted. The store had burned to ashes, and the tower had finally collapsed. No one lived there anymore. The cemetery was overgrown with weeds, and the wells were dry. Except for the lilies, the mimosas, and a few creosote poles leaning like staggering drunks, there was hardly any sign of a town left. But the spirit of the place was still there.

On the exact spot where Isaac had built his house, Zeda Earl built her own house. She built it with her two hands and without help. She knew nothing about carpentry, but she didn't think about that. She put on her gloves and worked. And at night she slept in her car.

Fishermen would stop and ask her what she thought she was doing, but she would give them no answer and refused their help. "This is something I've got to do all by myself. If I don't, it won't turn out right." That's all she would say.

For months she labored, and, when she had finished, she

stood back and admired her creation. Even though the house
was unpainted, and unleveled, and the seams showed and the
windows slanted, and nails stuck out on all sides, she liked it. It
was hers. She realized that some of the boards didn't meet, or
they overlapped where they weren't supposed to, but those
flaws didn't bother her one bit because she had done her best.
Her little house was a showplace, and she believed it would
bring her everything she wanted.

Most of all she wanted to see her daughters. She wanted them
to be proud of what she had achieved.

By then their lives were completely different. They had hus-
bands and families and lived far away, but Lottie Faircloth found
them. "Your mother has taken up a life of solitude," she wrote.
"Some people think she's lost her mind, but I know better. For
once she may have found it."

A few weeks later, on one of those clear afternoons when the
Sabine, reflecting a cloudless sky, seemed to forget that its
waters were muddy, Zeda Earl sat on her porch and watched two
tall, slim women step out of a rather small car.

At first she didn't recognize them, nor they her. Lottie Fair-
cloth sat in the backseat and watched their silent embrace. "Oh,
I feel like I can die now," Lottie said, crying with joy. "I'm tired.
My part is done."

Zeda Earl's daughters were now calling themselves Charlotte
and Christine, but Zeda Earl didn't care. "Sometimes," she said,
"the names we were given at birth stop belonging to us. Sometimes we have to go out and earn our names."

They were amazed to hear their mother speak this way.

"There's such promise here," Zeda Earl said, walking her
daughters down to the graves. "I didn't know that for a long
time, but I know it now. Just look at these lilies if you don't
believe me. It's a sight how they're blooming today." For a
moment they stopped and gazed at the flowers Bessie had
loved. "You know," Zeda Earl said, waving her arms in mock
exasperation, "there's no controlling what a lily is liable to do.
I've gotten out here and pollinated, and cross-pollinated and
repollinated, and still I can't get the colors to come out right. I

don't know why I thought I could. Now I just leave them alone and let them do whatever it is they need to do."

As they waded through the daylilies that were waist high, Lottie, too exhausted to leave the car, kept her eyes on them the entire time.

"You must promise me that you won't let anything bad happen to this place," Zeda Earl said. "There are so few places left in the world and this is one of them. I can see it."

"It takes special eyes, I guess."

Zeda Earl turned around. "Which one of you said that?" she asked.

"We didn't say anything, Mother," said Daisy who was now called Charlotte.

"No one said a thing," said Iris, now Christine.

"Oh yes," said Zeda Earl. "Someone said something." Her eyes filled with tears that gradually trickled over her swollen lids. "And I know who it was."

"Are you all right, Mother?" asked one of the daughters, Christine or Charlotte, Zeda Earl didn't know one from the other.

"I've really never been better," said Zeda. "Come, I want to show you where I'm to be buried."

It was going on late afternoon, and the tin can music from Albino Island could be heard drifting upriver. "Listen to that," said Zeda Earl, waving in some vague direction downstream. "Have I ever told you about Billy-Wiggins'-Boy-By-Elsa-Mae-Broom? Oh, what a devil he was. Still is too. He's convinced that we're kin. And who knows, he might be right. Just look at all these white spots all over my arms, that probably proves it. But that's not important anymore. He used to try to make me believe that I came from a place called Ain't Nothing At All. The more I wanted to be something the more Billy Wiggins' Boy wanted me to be nothing. You see, we were talking about two different things, but really we weren't."

"Mother are you sure you're all right way out here by yourself?" asked Christine.

"We're going to find you a place in town, Mother," said Charlotte.

Their concern pleased Zeda Earl. She embraced them as they waded through the lilies. "I know you think your mother has lost her mind, but she hasn't." Zeda Earl tilted her head to one side and listened. "Oh, hear that old tin can music. Girls, just listen to it. Those people can make a drum out of anything. They're happier than half the world, and they're not even dangerous either." Her eyes opened wide as she spoke. "I can still hear Billy Wiggins' Boy. That's another voice that won't ever leave me. 'You ain't nothing in this world, and never will be nothing in this world,' he used to tell me, 'not until you realize that your world ain't nothing to be something in.' I wonder if he would understand if I told him that I've made my world something after all."

"Mother," said Charlotte, "please tell us what's wrong."

"Nothing-is-wrong," said Zeda Earl, spacing out her words.

Then she drew a deep breath. "Oh," she said, squinching up her face. "Smell that ole pulp mill. Doesn't it just about make you sick?"

Then she pointed to her burial place. "Right over there where all those cypress knees are arranged like a fence," she said. "Part of me is already there, and that's where you can put the rest of me. That's where I want to be. Now, your grandparents are right over yonder. I take good care of their graves too, but don't put me there, because that's not my place."

"I'm going to write this down," said Christine.

"We don't want to interfere with what you want," said Charlotte.

"And we promise to visit you," said Christine.

"I'll believe it when I see it," said Zeda Earl. "You're just the way I used to be, both of you. You're not my daughters for nothing. You'll forget. You'll forget in five minutes but one day when you need to bad enough, you'll go to remembering."

A wind carried her voice up the banks of the Sabine and into the car where Lottie sat. Her eyes became cloudy with thoughts and images of long ago. Her trembling fingers inspected the braids that were carefully pinned over her head. She straightened her collar and checked all the buttons on her blue dress. Then she slipped off her shoes and closed her eyes.

Zeda Earl and her daughters attended the funeral in Splendora, but only a few people recognized them. They, along with many of Lottie's friends and former students, accompanied the casket to a shady cemetery that Lottie had already chosen. That being done, Zeda Earl returned to the river to wait for her daughters' next visit.

But when Zeda Earl's daughters were not with her, sitting on that ramshackled porch overlooking the Sabine, someone else usually was. She had loads of company, a fisherman or two, a few college students who wanted to talk to someone about long ago, an occasional reporter from a city paper, or some old hermit who wandered out of the Thicket to see what was going on. Bird-watchers also visited her, especially those in pursuit of the ivory-billed woodpecker. "Go home," Zeda Earl would tell them. "You won't find that bird anywhere on the face of this earth. The world's too noisy now. Its favorite trees have been replaced with the likes of that." She would point across the Sabine to a riverside estate of long, low, ranch style houses with backyard swimming pools and cement streets. "They could have built that someplace else," she would say, shaking her fists toward the subdivision.

For the rest of her life she was destined to sit on her porch and look at that cluster of what she called "fine, fine homes." There was a trace of bitterness in her voice when she talked about the new river communities, and yet she was sometimes grateful that they were there. "I hate to admit it," she told a visitor, "because there must be better ways of learning things, but those fine, fine houses over there remind me of what I have had, and could still have, and what I have gained."

She hated what was happening along the river, and that's why she tried to keep the past alive. And when she was very old, and her face heavily lined, her eyes still burned with the fire of memory and a spark of gratitude. Because she seemed to know so many things that other people didn't know, or had long forgotten, and because she remembered things that seemed to the modern world to be totally impossible, supernatural powers were attributed to her. There were many people who believed that she could solve problems by predicting the future before it turned into the present. But Zeda Earl knew better.

"Why that's the silliest thing I've ever heard in my life," she would say. "I can't solve things but I can remember things. And you have just now made me remember Navasota Blackburn. She could remember far, far back into this old world and she could also see the future, if she needed to. Navasota Blackburn could solve almost anything. They say, and I certainly believe it, that she could make babies change daddy's in their mama's womb."

Then Zeda Earl would show her visitors a beaded moccasin. "Billy Wiggins' Boy gave me this after I built my house," she would tell them. "It belonged to Navasota. I know where her body is buried too, but I can't take you there. All I can say is that she gave her spirit to a tree. I know which one, and I won't let anything bad happen to it. I promised Billy Wiggins' Boy that."

No visitor was ever turned away. Zeda Earl would talk incessantly, even after her audience had already said good-bye. She would tell about her mother's birds and how the eggs had been hatched, and she would explain how Isaac had restocked the Sabine with fish that no one had ever seen before. She would go on and on about Elsa Mae Broom, whose baby had been thrown into the river. And on many occasions she would get completely carried away talking about the Ruby-Jewels and Peter Faircloth. "They shared the same mind," she would say. "People find that hard to believe now, but they did. Back then all kinds of things happened that don't happen too often anymore."

But the story that Zeda Earl enjoyed telling the most was how her mother and father had met. It was her favorite story, and she told it over and over, even to people who had heard it dozens of times already. She saw to it that the story was remembered in the new households along the Sabine. And before many years had passed it became a tradition for a girl of a marriageable age to stand in the river and wait patiently for a young man to drift by and throw flowers into the water where she stood whistling, or humming, or gazing absentmindedly into the sky. Over the years, some good marriages were made that way, and some bad

ones were made that way too, but along that stretch of the river
the tradition was carried on for generations and generations—
even after Zeda Earl was buried near three small graves on the
banks of the Sabine.